Courtesy of the Rhode Island Historical Society

Gaspee

by: Alex Gabbard

Historical Fiction

Published by:

GPPress
P.O. Box 22261
Knoxville, TN 37933-0261

©2006 by Alex Gabbard
All Rights Reserved

Printed in USA

ISBN: 0-9755358-2-x
978-0-9755358-2-x
after 1 January 2007

No part of this work may be reproduced or transmitted in any form by any means, electronic or mechanical, including photocopying and recording, or by any information storage or retrieval system, without written permission from the author and publisher, except in the case of brief quotations embodied in critique articles or reviews.

This work is an accurate accounting of events as determined by the author from existing documents. Names of actual persons have been retained in the interest of historical accuracy, as have dates, locations, and conditions of the time. This work tells of the events in the actual setting of Narragansett Bay and is told in the vernacular some time shortly after the close of the King's Commission.

Cover and end leaf images courtesy of
Rhode Island Historical Society

Cover and text design, layout and art by Alex Gabbard

Prolog:

This book tells the *HMS Gaspee* story from the point of view of participants as drawn from surviving records. All the characters in this book were real people except Thomas Mayes, Capt. Brinley, and Molly Nichols. All settings are real, including Sabine's Tavern in Providence (that no longer exists), the White Horse Tavern (America's oldest operating tavern), Newport's Colony House, the John Wanton house and other structures that have survived throughout the Narragansett Bay. The primary locations are Newport, Bristol, Providence and Namquit Point (now Gaspee Point) near Pawtuxet, and the Bay itself.

Events of civilian violence leading to the American Revolution began with Rhode Islanders firing on the *HMS St. John* in Newport harbor in 1764. The same year, crewmen of the British frigate *HMS Maidstone* so angered Newporters that a throng of irate citizens seized longboats of the ship tied up at Long Wharf, dragged them onto the Commons and burned the boats in front of Newport's Colony House. The following year, 1765, the Stamp Act was imposed when read from the balcony of Colony House and incited the gathered citizenry to riot, burning effigies of the three prominent loyalists in Newport, smashing two of their homes and driving them from the town never to return. During 1769, the *HMS Liberty*, another revenue vessel with an over-zealous captain, was seized and set adrift, her timbers cut. The ship was scuttled, then burned by angry citizens of Newport. during a nighttime raid. The "Boston Massacre" of March 5, 1770 was another confrontation in the broadening conflict between British military forces and colonials that contributed to increasing opposition toward British rule.

The raid and destruction of the *Gaspee* on June 9-10, 1772 was carried out by Rhode Islanders largely from Providence as a clash of arms against British naval forces of the revenue service. An exchange of gunshots severely wounded *Gaspee*'s commander, Lt. William Dudingston, an action that brought Royal attention to the matter of "anarchy" in Rhode Island, a colony that had long enjoyed and benefitted from "free trade" that the Crown called piratical and attempted to control, and profit from, with a succession of Maritime Laws that taxed and further inflamed the colonists. The "Boston Tea Party" of December 16, 1773, eighteen months after the *Gaspee* incident, resulted the following year in the British closing and blockading the port of Boston, another of the "Intolerable Acts" leading to the American Revolution that blazed into open rebellion when land forces exchanged fire at Lexington Green and Concord Bridge in Massachusetts Colony on April 18, 1775, almost three years after the Gaspee incident.

In response to the destruction of the Gaspee, King George issued a Proclamation offering high rewards for apprehending the perpetrators of the raid. The Proclamation granted powers to prosecuting commissioners far beyond established law and was seen by the Rhode Islanders as setting the stage for British military occupation and suppression by rescinding their colony's charter as subservient to Royal prerogatives. Leaders throughout the colonies were so alarmed that they formed Committees of Correspondence, as a responsibility of colonial assembies, for timely exchange of accurate information, the first "common cause" among the colonies in America. Rhode Island Governor Joseph Wanton led the proceedings of the Proclamation with four principal judges of other colonies. He had authority to send many of his citizens, friends and enemies, to the gallows but he conducted the investigation to arrive at no convictions.

Three years later, the American Revolutionary War began, and Newport was occupied by British troops who destroyed much of the town, including its commerce and some of its homes that were taken down for firewood. After the British withdrew, French military forces came to the aid of the American cause, welcomed and housed in Newport during 1780-81. Polly Wanton, daughter of John Wanton, Governor Wanton's uncle, so entranced French officers that "charming Polly Wanton" was scratched into a window pane by a young officer. That pane of glass has survived and is in the collection of the Newport Historical Society.

Alex Gabbard

Spring 2006

Acknowledgments and Sources:

The Newport Historical Society
Newport Restoration Foundation
The Rhode Island Historical Society
The Warwick Historical Society
The Pawtuxet Historical Society
The Artillery Company of Newport
The Gaspee Day Committee
The Bucklin Society
The Rhode Island Publications Society
Providence Public Library
Brown University

Primary sources for this book:

1. *The Architectural Heritage of Newport, Rhode Island; 1640-1914*, 2nd Ed. Revised, Antoinette F. Downing and Vincent J. Scully, Jr., American Legacy Press, 1967.

2. *A History of the Destruction of His Britannic Majesty's Schooner Gaspee*, compiled by John Russell Bartlett, Rhode Island Sec. of State, Providence, 1861.

3. *Documentary History of the Destruction of the Gaspee*, William R. Staples, 1845.

4. *The Destruction of the Gaspee; Rhode Island Education Circulars*, Historical Series III, Horatio B. Knox, Dept. of Education, State of Rhode Island, 1908.

5. *The Influences of Physical Features Upon the History of Rhode Island*; Rhode Island Education Circulars, Historical Series IV, David W. Hoyt, Dept. of Education, State of Rhode Island, 1910.

6. *Pirates & Patriots of the Revolution: An Illustrated Encyclopedia of Colonial Seamanship*; Living History Series, C. Keith Wilbur, The Globe Pequot Press, Old Saybrook, CT, 1984.

7. *The Providence Gasette*, Saturday, December 26, 1772

Dedication

To the people of Rhode Island, past and present, for their uniqueness of spirit that so strongly shaped the colonial mind embodied in the Bill of Rights, and to all those past and present who have labored diligently to compile the history of the *Gaspee* incident toward raising awareness of the far-reaching importance of the raid and its aftermath in shaping the times that brought about the American Revolution.

Act 1

Chapter 1

    The cold morning mist reddened his cheeks and settled into droplets in his hair. Thomas Mayes waited for the Captain to repeat each morning's routine when ashore and remained carefully hidden on the opposite side of old Back Street across from the Captain's mansion. Thomas wiped his eyes to better see Captain Maudsley.
    As daybreak's first light illuminated the Captain's fine garden walkway to his doorstep, its misty presence came and went with the wafting fog. Then Thomas heard the unmistakable squeak and thud of the heavy front door opening and closing. A momentary break in the rolling mist revealed Captain Maudsley, tall and distinguished in his riding gear, standing silently on the stoop as he pulled on his gloves. The Captain's whale oil lantern sat at his feet as he gazed about the new day, unconcerned with the fog. He would soon be above the harbor mist on another vigorous ride. Thomas mimicked the Captain's tug at his waistcoat and deep breaths, practicing for the day that he would be a sea captain. As Capt. Maudsley stepped down the walkway and onto the newly re-laid cobblestones of the street, each step lighted by lantern light that swung by the Captain's tall black riding boots, Thomas quietly matched his steps.
    Silently moving to a new vantage point at the corner of the stable, Thomas listened as the Captain talked to Spartacus as he saddled him. The powerful chestnut made his impatience known; he was ready to leave the stable. Snuffing out his lantern, the rich merchantman soon sat astride his majestic white stockinged horse, and the two of them emerged from the stable. Proud Spartacus announced his presence upon the day with each hoofbeat onto wet cobblestones. Horse and rider vanished into the fog, and

Thomas listened as they set off straight up Griffin Street to Jew's Street and out to the cliffs once again.

Thomas sighed. He so wanted to ride into the wind on a fine steed, or just walk along the cliffs... anything instead of gathering more fire wood, more water, more trips to the mill, more tending the garden, more errands to the docks, more pan washing. With a heavy sigh, he moaned, "If I could go to sea again with Captain Maudsley.... If Aunt Nettie would just loosen her hold on me...."

He had made a fine cabin boy and dreamed of becoming a midshipman, then first mate; but now just turned fourteen, Aunt Nettie's stern regard for sailors allowed no talk of going to sea.

Thomas' soft bottom sailor's brogues did not echo with each step as did the heels of the Captain's fine leather knee boots, and he crossed Way-to-the-Neck silently and unnoticed as he slipped by gates and fences of houses leading down toward Thames Street and the wharfs. He strode like the Captain, walking proud and erect, practicing.

Then, realizing that he might be missing Captain Malbone, Thomas raced on toward the Bay, passing more fine homes of merchants facing their wharfs. He ran by building after building along mile long Thames Street's wharfside of merchant's warehouses, shops, and stores. Through them flowed the commerce that made Newport the pearl of the colonies, each warehouse stocked with goods soon to find their way into the market, including human cargo chained within some of them. At the corner of Brewer's Street, Thomas hid once again and waited. Breathing deeply to catch his breath, he anticipated Captain Malbone's entry into the morning.

More mist rolled in from the bay and masked the light of day so heavily in places that Thomas could see only a few paces, and he smiled to think that he had the perfect cover for watching the men he so admired.

To be a sea captain like them was his every wish. What glory that would be, sailing the high seas and laughing at the King's revenue ships that he would evade just as Newport's captains did. Wistfully, he recalled his cabin boy days while a lad of nine onboard Captain Maudsley's brig, *Echo*, back in the summer of '67 when they sailed to Barbados and the far-away islands. Thomas longed for new adventures. The wondrous sea had taken him to distant lands and filled his young mind with desires for more adventures to far away places, and he itched to see more.

The following year, on the Captain's recommendation, he sailed with Captain Malbone on the *Sea Nymph*, the newest three-masted ship in Newport at the time. They made port down the colonies on their trek to the Caribbean Isles where there were strange speaking peoples of all colors, each displaying their tawdry baubles. "Brummagems of poverty," the captain had called them. Those strange people took particular delight in finding everything about Thomas laughable, but he thought of himself as quite the real lad when faced with the smelly and unsavory lot who poked and prodded him to tell of the ship's goods, leaving little doubt of their intent. He stood his ground and told them nothing just as he had seen the Captain face down similar rabble. Thomas fancied himself an equal sea dog and parried their thrusts with similar thrusts, each bringing rolls of laughter as they feigned fright at the lad's haughty displays.

The Captain was firm with his demands from traders who always complained that he was a harsh tradesman. He had warned Thomas and all the crew that the Isles were infested with brigands and pirates at every turn, each trying their Cat's Paw buffoonery to steal away with a ship's goods, and the worst pirates among them were the merchants. They haggled all manner of manipulations using diversions of fine Italian hands to secure a ship's store for cheapest fare, lifted from the hold by night if they could.

"Learn the ways of trade without folly, lad," the Captain cautioned Thomas. "The buyer has a hundred eyes, the seller but his own. Therein lay their mischief whose mother is no bigger than a midge's wing, good advice to take to heart among life's learnings, young Thomas; we will be ruled by the rock if we fail to rule the rudder. Look about these isles and you see foul sorts all about. Let your rudder be a simple guide; what can be expected from a pig but a grunt? Good men are scarce." Thomas remembered.

With Captain Malbone's firm hand and good eye at the helm, the *Sea Nymph* delivered its cargo of Surinam horses belonging to Nicholas Brown, those hardy Narragansett Pacers highly prized by Caribbean plantation owners. He then traded ship's stores of cordage, cloth, lumber, tinware, leatherwork, furniture, and chandler goods for molasses, sugar and supplies for his rummery in Newport, then sailed back up the colonies where they traded in Charlestown for rice, indigo and cotton and on to Virginia for tobacco and Devil's root. The round trip took most of Newport's warm months, and Captain Malbone paid Thomas handsomely.

A tuppence a day was quite a tidy sum for a lad who turned ten on his second voyage. With some dealings of his own, Thomas' gatherings made enough to afford the purchase of a tattered leather bound book by the English writer DeFoe telling of the *Life and Strange Adventures of Robinson Crusoe*. During lulls in shipboard life and on cold winter days since, he read the story again and again, always being careful not to further damage the pages.

His earnings also afforded him a brass barrelled muskatoon with a broken stock that he had repaired with small cording bound tightly and varnished, a fine job he learned at the knee of Brinley, the John Damme aboard the *Sea Nymph* whose fine cut of the jib was always beset with the Gumpers. Thomas' haggling with a wily, one-eyed tar in a Barbados backstreet shop, who likely acquired the piece for its lifting, was a story told again and again among friends back in Newport and Providence Plantations, especially his best lad, Justin, who had adventures of his own sailing with his grandfather. And tucked in his blouse at his waist he carried a dirk and scabbard, said to have belonged to Cap'n Edward Teach himself. With it in hand, Thomas' imagination leaped into the throes of battle where the fearsome pirate rent its blade deeply into the body of some hapless sailor whose soul was separated in one swift stroke of the blade.

The door of Captain Malbone's mansion opened and out the captain stepped in quick stride. He crossed Thames street and vanished into his stables. Soon the clatter of hoof beats from one of his fine horses broke the morning silence. Thomas listened as the stallion pranced up Young Street and on to crest The Hill that rose behind Newport's stretch along the wharfs. From there, all up and down the island's interior were paths for riding amid gnarled giants whose limbs made great climbing for strapping boys. Trails led all the way out to the cliffs that crowned the wondrous sea, where breakers crashed far below with a beckoning lure that always enticed Thomas and the lads to test their courage by walking its ledges to the small beach far below at the base of the wall of rock.

Thomas imagined that, once again, Captain Malbone and Captain Maudsley would meet at The Point to plan their next voyages as they rode.

Every winter since he had sailed the Spanish Main with Captain Malbone, Thomas had set for himself another ride with the wind to that fair clime, but the fourth season was about to pass and his goal had not been met. He was no longer a cabin boy, now with few skills of the sea to offer a captain, and not yet the sailor he yearned to become. Aunt Nettie spoke strongly against going to sea, and she now had him apprenticed to Benjamin Nichols at the White Horse Tavern. But with every chance he got, Thomas watched the ships and talked endlessly with crewmen who came to the tavern. He longed to ship out, but Aunt Nettie cast no ear to that, insisting that he become a housewright.

"Bein' a cook first? Nay, an errand boy?" he moaned repeatedly. She sternly told of the crafts needed to build the houses going up all around the Bay, homes that would last the tests of time while ships come and go with heartache and grief, as she knew all too well, good ships and their crews dashed by the unforgiving sea never to return, lost into its depths. She permitted not a word of going to sea, and that was that.

After a stolen half-hour from his morning chores to watch his favorite captains, Thomas reluctantly turned to attend to those empty buckets he had left sitting by the town spring. Entranced by his imaginings of the islands that he was missing, he set off into the mist toward the Tavern and ran directly into the clutches of a burley seaman. His breath was captured so suddenly that he could not yell for help. Held firmly in a grasp that made him shudder with fright, Thomas gasped to breathe.

"Got yew!" the sailor snarled, his hold as tight as a metal choker. "Spyin' are ye? Such be the more reason to get the likes o' yew off the town's streets," the toothy tar grinned through his whiskers.

A second seaman emerged from the mist and grabbed his other arm. Then, Thomas' eyes grew with horror as the devil himself emerged from the fog.

"Captain Dudingston, sir!" one of the seamen stammered. "We got us a right good lit'le cook, we 'ave."

The young officer smirked. "Well done, well done," tapping his baton against the leg of his white trousers. "We are in need of a cook, lad. You will do for our needs. By order of the Crown and the command of Admiral Montagu, you are hereby pressed to serve duty to King George on His Majesty's Ship *Gaspee*."

Thomas turned pale with horror. The talk around Newport and Providence had not failed to reach his ears. Arrival of the HMS *Gaspee* and the HMS *Beaver* three months earlier had brought renewed anger with the King's revenue agents who had plagued the Bay's shipping in a contemptuous manner. The Royal Lieutenant's tactics of taking whatever he wanted, raiding farms and stores for goods seized for his purposes, always in the name of the King, left a trail of furious citizens who had repeatedly taken their concerns to the magistrates, ultimately the Governor, yet the man stood before Thomas free of the irons said to be the worth of his lot.

Thomas' thoughts raced through the stories he had heard of Dudingston's harsh administering of his post as the King's enforcer of revenue in the Bay, those hated Maritime Laws, using tactics said by the citizenry to be nothing but piracy. The fast schooners *Gaspee* and *Beaver* had so fanned the flames of defiance that they were the steady talk among patrons of the Tavern, especially among the whispering Sons of Liberty, and Thomas had often bent his ear to catch much of the news. Dudingston wasted no time at his post and had already confiscated the cargos of several ships entering and leaving Newport on no more than suspicion of carrying smuggled goods, whether or not papers of manifest were in order, and whether or not the cargo bore the brand of the King. To the ire of the colonists, he ruled the sea lanes as if the Bay was his dominion alone, doing so with actions that were hotly protested by growing numbers of merchant citizens. Patrons of the Tavern, the same that fueled a growing discontent against the heavy-handedness of British maritime actions, told of the boiling resentment growing within the colony.

Among Dudingston's first actions upon arriving in the Narragansett Bay was seizing a Nathaniel Greene cargo and taking it to Boston for disposition. Rather than resolving the matter in Rhode Island's own courts, as both the colony and British law required, he sent the craft to Boston where it was sold as confiscate. That incident alone fanned the flames of talk heard in Bristol to Newport, in Pawtuxet to Providence Plantations, Warren to Warwick, and every community throughout the colony. Dudingston was loudly talked of as a pirate in the King's uniform. No ship coming or going, not even oyster barks, slipped by the *Beaver* and *Gaspee*, and Dudingston displayed great delight in executing his station against any craft showing the slightest provocation to risk the run. No craft in the Bay was clear of his reach, and every merchant, excepting the Loyalists, were stung by his presence.

Circulating among the patrons of the Tavern and catching their talk gave Thomas ample opportunity to hear of the many plans, some spoken boldly, others under hushed breaths, to do in the ships and their captains. Until this foggy morning, the thought had never crossed his mind that *he* might become the subject of Dudingston's reach. And yet, staring into the face of the hated officer, caught in hand by his henchmen in the very mist relied upon to hide his own movements, Thomas would simply vanish. Aunt Nettie would never hear from him again and would fuss that he had run off to sea, not knowing that he was shackled to a hearth right there in the Bay. At this moment, he wished he were by the warm hearth of her kitchen or breathing fragrant bacon frying crisp on the hearth of the White Horse Tavern where he should be.

Thomas wriggled about and yanked repeatedly to free himself, but the seamen were much too strong for that.

"Bring him along," the Lieutenant of the Royal Navy commanded.

As the seamen pickup up their sail cloth bags of cabbaged goods, Thomas lurched with revolting suddenness. Being pressed to crew for the loathsome Lieutenant and the *Gaspee* crew caused him to wrench forward as his stomach heaved. The seaman on his right jumped back to avoid a drenching just as Thomas's footing slipped on the wet cobblestones. Regaining his balance, the heel of his shoe came down hard and square on the other seaman's big toe, its ingrown nail digging painfully inward resulting in a howl of pain. An instant's freedom was momentary good fortune, and Thomas ducked Dudingston's baton lash as he scampered quickly into the fog. He darted up Thames Street with the seamen, one hobbling, in close pursuit, both yelling repeated insults.

Turning toward a wharf in search of safety, Thomas slipped on the moist street stones; his feet flew from under him, and he slid to a halt certain that Dudingston and his men would soon be upon him. Springing to his feet just clear of their clutches, Thomas dashed around a warehouse with its familiar odor of unclean flesh mingled with stable sweepings and the pungent residue of rotting fish that floated in the wash under the wharfs. He dashed around rope coils and barrels and heaps of lobster pots heedless of Lt. Dudingston's order to halt. Running as fast as he could, he gained distance from them. Increasingly confined to their ships due to rising ill will among citizens, they did not know the docks as did Thomas. This morning was another of their foray's to cabbage, nay *STEAL* supplies, goods always said to belong to the King, therefore, the King's stores to be drawn upon at the Captain's will.

Racing up the waterfront, Thomas ducked in behind a stable to catch his breath, listening for sounds of his pursuers in the mist, hoping they would not emerge from the fog again. Then, there they were just a few yards away working their way toward him, looking around and under fish drying beds, netting strung up to dry between weather-beaten buildings, among barrels and kegs, crating and baskets. They stepped quietly through the mist in search of their prey, the occasional board squeaking or groaning under their weight as they neared. Having evaded the command of the crown and now a criminal, the Lieutenant's brass pistol struck fear in Thomas chest and his head pounded with each beat of his heart. Dark thoughts raced through his mind. Would he see the warming fire of the Tavern again? Would a lead ball in his back, a deserter of the King's service, be the end of him?

The thought of such a cowardly shot caused Thomas to grit his teeth and set his jaw. A new strength rose in him. Not Thomas Mayes! Not the lad whose namesake spoke of Newport's legendary pirates. He clinched his fists at the thought that he could rid Newport and all of Rhode Island of the Lieutenant for good, if he just had his muskatoon. But without it, he could only run. Grasping the ivory handle of his dirk, he envisioned its blade thrust between the Lieutenant's ribs. Life oozing from the officer's body as he lay dying on the wharf would be the talk of Newport. "Who could have done the deed?" everyone would ask, wanting secretly to congratulate the ripper.

But Thomas knew that a single thrust into Dudingston's chest would make him not only a deserter but a murderer and that he would have to kill each of them, then slip unseen into the mist keeping his silence ever after to escape the hangman. Stories of Black '23 when twenty-six men dangled from Newport gallows overwhelmed his every thought. Dudingston and his men had knives, too, and pistols, and he knew that they were much more friendly with their weapons. His thoughts of bravado quickly faded at the prospects of having their clutches on his small frame again. If discovered, he would be looking down the muzzle of the Lieutenant's pistol, then lashed to the mess deck where he would fry the crew's Devil's root and stir salt fish stew and make doughboys for the next seven years. He thought better of taking the offensive; escape into the fog was his only chance.

Slipping around a warehouse that greeted him with that all too familiar and sickening odor of flesh long overdue for bathing, amid clinks of shackling bilboes as their human captives moved about, Thomas grasped a stone and tossed it up Thames street, hoping its clatter would distract his pursuers with just enough diversion for him to vanish into a stable. But the whinnies of horses from within his chosen hideout gave his presence away, and he heard the sailor's footsteps and mutterings close on his location. Realizing that he would be caught if he remained in hiding, Thomas climbed the opposite gate and stepped silently onto Steven's Wharf. He would find all sorts of hiding places here, and if they cornered him, he could leap into the water to elude them. Not a pleasant thought on such a chilly morning, but better wet and cold than caught. He knew the subways leading underground from the wharfs would have to be a last resort, all kept secret from the British and the town's loyalists. He knew that care must be taken to avoid giving their existence away, a secret long protected by the town's merchants.

Making his way halfway down the weathered wharf, he crouched behind a mound of netting, ropes, barrels and lobster pots as the Lieutenant and his men methodically worked their way up Thames Street in his direction, poking into hiding places and shaking doors in search of open passages to interior hiding places, seizing further opportunity to take what they could along the way. Breathing heavily, Thomas prayed that they would continue along the warehouses rather than turn down the wharf toward him, and his heart beat raced in his temples when he saw them turn in his direction.

"Lad!" a raspy whisper came from behind. "Come aboard,

lad."

Thomas turned and recognized a grizzled old seaman standing on the bow of a schooner, motioning for him to hide aboard. Knowing his way around the craft, even if the Lieutenant and his men did come aboard, Thomas reasoned that he could stow below with a belaying pin or two that would crack a British head if need be. Whichever ladder they entered, he could climb out the opposite and dash back up the wharf to vanish in the fog. The lure of safety drew him to the old man and the haven of his cabin. Up the gangplank he scampered, then down a ladder inside. The old seaman pulled the gangplank back aboard and followed Thomas into the cabin. Both of them sat quietly and listened as the British sailors made their way closer.

"Wot's goin' on?" Justin asked, rubbing the morning from his eyes as he rose from his bunk.

"Quiet, lad," the old seaman ordered.

Thomas smiled to see his young friend again but held his breath. Shortly, the voice of the Lieutenant rang through the morning.

"Hail onboard! Hail there!"

After a long pause, the old man's gravely voice told of little interest and less patience. "Wot be yer need of this vessel?" he bellowed.

"A runaway crewman in service to the Crown; we shall come aboard and search."

The old man looked at Thomas, knowing that the boy was not a British sailor, merely a jack of the dust at the hearths and ovens of the White Horse Tavern. He stepped up the ladder to the deck, then scowled at the fleeting images of Dudingston and his men masked in the mist. He drew a pistol from deep within his salted coat and stepped to the gunnel.

"By order o' me flint in this 'ere pistol, I be captain of this vessel. Trespass 'ere and yew takes a musketball in the liver. Be a long misery in dyin', sir. Wot be your say now, mister?"

Unruffled, the Lieutenant stood erect and forceful, his uniform and polished boots displaying the fit of a British officer and a man who meant every word he uttered. He cocked the hammer of his pistol and aimed its polished brass barrel at the old man's head.

"By my authority as commander of these waters in service to his majesty the King, I shall board you, sir. I order you to stand aside."

The old seaman cocked his pistol and withdrew a second. Setting its hammer as well, he was another man who meant every word he said. His larger bores and longer barrels aimed at the

Lieutenant's chest spoke of equal determination.

"Be ye a bit young to die fer want o' glory, mister. Murder it be to lower a man on 'is own ship. Protectin' it be defendin' me rights, the law o' the sea wot we all sails under. Put yer webs aboard me boat without a whit of invite, and defendin' I be. Wot say you now?"

"I shall board and search under fire, sir," the Lieutenant commanded sternly. "Stand aside!" He ordered one of his men to pull the gangplank from the ship.

"Touch that gangplank an' terday'll be yer last, mister. Me thinks this be a cold morn fer dyin'," the old man growled.

The sailor cowered back.

"Fire upon my men, sir, and I shall take great pleasure in seeing you wither from a new hole in your head. Mister Cheever, you will set that gangplank immediately!"

"Aye, aye sir," seaman Cheever said as he lowered his head, not wanting to see the smoke from the old sailor's pistol as its musketball made a new hole in his head.

Dudingston had never lost a battle and relished the standoff, this one displaying to one and all, mostly himself, that he was the equal of Royal Navy officers rather than just the Revenue Service. Intent upon capturing Thomas at any cost, this encounter added sauce to the drama of his power.

"Ye thinks this old salt fell arf the lorry, dew ye?" the old seaman growled. "Wearin' piked colors o' the crown so's to take me ship is piratin', it be. Yer sailin' close to the wind an' soon to be knocked on yer beam ends, mister. Me thinks ye be no more'n a filthy sty-keeper what's out to cabbage yer way. Partin' yer body and soul be me right in defendin' wot's rightfully me own."

"My uniform, sir, and my commission in the King's service IS the law of the sea," Dudingston emphasized strongly, "and this port. Stand aside, I command you, or I shall deliver the wrath of no quarter!"

The old seaman set his jaw as he snarled, "Dutch reckoning be yer course, sir, makin' me a Dutchman if I yields."

That further insult inflamed Dudingston. "We are not Kilkenny cats, sir, your Roland for my Oliver is mere tittle. This matter is of grave concern for his Majesty's service. I shall board you. Stand aside! I command you!"

"Yers be skulduggery an' a spiggoty snab doin' the Gyp, says me dry powder in these 'ere pistols, sir. Flying Dutchman ye be, sir, agin the wind right soon to spill from these 'ere muzzles what push lead, and I means to use 'em on yer hang fire. Who ye be and wot be yer claim in papers lay beyond me knowin's. There'll be no settin' yer boots on this ship, so says me final words on yer

18

piratin'."

Thomas did not understand Dudingston's persistence, nor old Captain Jacobs' determination, having now led to the two of them with pistols aimed at each other, each no more than a trigger's pull from a grave. His thoughts raced over the tales told of Dudingston's rough handling of Rhode Islanders, claiming all of them to be no more than peasant vassals of the King. He and Captain Linzee of the *Beaver* continually trapped the colony's trade to bolster the King's till with revenue taken in applying the hated Maritime Laws seen by all colonists as purposed to rifle them of wealth for the benefit of the King and his minions. Taverners railed the harsh methods of Dudingston and Linzee, known well to Thomas, but this encounter held the life of Gramps Jacobs in the balance. Justin was horrified at the thought that his grandfather was an instant away from being felled by Dudingston.

"No more'n piratin' under the Union Jack," the tavern talk repeatedly proclaimed. "Kill the lot of 'em and be done with it," said the murmurs simmering throughout Newport and other towns. The White Horse Tavern was just one among many taverns of the colony where late night debates laced with rum laid plan after plan for dealing with the hated revenue ships and their crews. "Kill the rascal," they said of Dudingston. "Remember the *Liberty*!" some shouted. "Set upon that schooner in the cover of night and cut 'er riggin's, I say!"

Though just arrived on the *Sea Nymph*, Thomas remembered how Newport's men handled the infamous *HMS Liberty* and the ship's captain, the nefarious Lt. Reid, for unlawfully taking a brig and a sloop off Long Island. Even though the ships were out of Connecticut, Reid brought them to Newport for disposition. With boyish interest fanned by the heated goings-on, Thomas stood on Long Wharf back in the summer of '69 where he watched rising tempers among many citizens he had come to know. They took the issue in hand after the brig's captain tried to resolve the matter by going aboard the *Liberty*, only to receive hostile fire upon his quick departure. "Thar it be as plain as the day," taverners demanded. "What more proof need be showed; the injustice be on the 'ands o' Mister Reid, pirate, 'e is. An' wearin' the uniform o' the crown, claimin' commission! Where be justice in 'im takin' our free trade, leavin' a man empty-'anded fer 'is own work? Where be our fate lest we set to defendin' our right to our own property an' trade?"

Everyone knew that the brig's captain duly reported his cargo and showed his customs papers proving no attempt to evade revenue as claimed by Lt. Reid. And with no charges forthcoming after some days and no addressing complaints in the Vice-Admiralty Court against the Lieutenant, outraged men of Newport took to their own sense of right and cut her lines sending the *Liberty* adrift. When the tide sent the ship aground on Goat Island just beyond the harbor, they went aboard taking saws to her timbers, and right there in Newport harbor they felled her masts and tossed her armaments overboard. That done, they put her to the torch. Thomas remembered well the blaze and the temper of the town that sent it up in smoke; "Damned be the King an' 'is men for takin' leave o' the law from free tradesmen what earn their own keep," was heard over and over. Thomas heard them all, every brag and tale about what was done to the *Liberty*, and every plan to similarly do in the *Gaspee*, but never once did the slightest suspicion cross his mind that he would be the cause of a man dying at Lt. Dudingston's hand, particularly fine old Gramps Jacobs.

The gangplank settled with a thump on the wharf and Mr. Cheever crept back with his head down; the lump in Thomas's throat grew, his escape was less certain with each moment. Justin's eyes grew wide with fright and his mouth went dry. He could hardly speak. They knew Dudingston's reputation, and it left no doubt that the hated officer would fell the old captain in his tracks. Thomas' thoughts raced to having leg irons forged onto his ankles to keep him lashed to the *Gaspee*'s galley. He would never become a sea captain or see the Tavern or Aunt Nettie again. And Justin would never sail with his grandfather again, learning the ways of the sea for the day that he would become master of the *Annabelle*.

"Speak with the Lord, sir, or swear you soul to the damned, for I am coming aboard," the Lieutenant snarled as he took a step onto the gangplank.

"Yers be bandy words pullin' Alexander's beard, yew blaggard. Yew made yer gauche step, an' there hangs the sword of Damocles in balance o'er yer bad luck. Step across this 'ere gunnel bringin' sech onboard me own ship an' yew die with no benefit o' Clergy. Me colors be nailed to the mast, sir. So, speaks me last warnin'."

The lieutenant hesitated. He had stepped left foot first, rather than right foot. A moment of reconsideration came over him just as a stout voice bellowed from the opposite side of the wharf behind him.

"A spot of trouble, 'ave ye, Christian?"

Undeterred and untroubled by such superstition as right foot foremost on coming onboard all ships, Dudingston kept the bead of his pistol on the old sailor and took a slow, deliberate second step onto the gangplank.

"Be gone with you," Lt. Dudingston scowled over his shoulder toward the stout voice. "A matter of the King's service at hand here. None of your concern."

"Me thinks the matter is in hand, indeed," the stout voice returned.

"Aye, Captain," Cheever said. "We be lookin' down the throat of a musket."

Dudingston stopped in his tracks.

Through the wafting fog the stout voice bellowed again, "I know not o' yer business, sir, but 'avin' me sights betwixed yer shoulder blades be no more'n a fleetin' instant to dyin'."

In a cross-fire and beaten, Dudingston uncocked his pistol and disgustedly lowered it to his side. Stepping back off the gangplank, he snarled at Captain Jacobs, "I shall have my way, sir. Sail these waters, and I shall have my way," then added further insult, "Mark my words, Yan-Kee." Turning to the image on the opposite craft just visible in the mist, he snorted "And you sir. We shall meet under differing circumstances." He stomped off into the fog with his two companions close behind shouldering their takings.

Quiet settled over the wharf as each of the defenders considered the prospects of Dudingston using the fog to cover a shot at them, and eyes with pistols at the ready scanned the mist until a sense that the threat was clear won the day.

"Thanks be to ye, sir," Gramps Jacobs called into the fog, recognizing the stout voice that had come to his aid. Silence followed, each knowing that other ears were listening.

Without the slightest ruffle, while Thomas and Justin gathered their wits, the old seaman stuffed his pistols back under his coat, then pulled the gangplank back aboard and went below. He took a pinchneck from hiding in the cabin and put it to his lips, swallowing hard, then wiped them with his rough hand. "Ahhh. A fine marnin' fer splicin' the main brace with a bit o' grog. What say ye, lad, wot were the Lieutenant after ye fer?"

"To be 'is cook."

A scowl crossed wise old Gramps Jacobs' brow. "Aye, pressin' yew to 'is service, it were. Well now, yew keep yer distance from the likes o' that blaggard. The same fer yew, Justin. If'n the Lieutenant is in need o' a cook, any boy 'e can press will do. Yew boys mind me words kept close to yer chests."

"Yessir, grandfather," Justin replied, still numb from having waked into such tense moments.

Gramps Jacobs took time to enliven the temper of the morning's events by telling of more fishing and sailing to come, knowing that time so spent lessened the threat that might remain in the mist should Thomas try returning to the tavern.

Thomas liked the *Annabelle*, a fine schooner named for the old sailor's departed wife, and he sighed at the thought that Justin would become her master long before any such craft would come to him. Aunt Nettie would never permit such, having sent him to Newport to be beyond Gramps Jacobs' continual invitations for putting to sea with his grandson. He and Justin had spent many wondrous hours schooning the Bay and beyond on the *Annabelle*, and Justin never tired of Thomas' tellings of his adventures in the islands. The two of them seemed cut from the same cloth, and neither had any idea of what lay ahead.

In due course, Thomas parted from the *Annabelle*, with the old seaman's cautions not to breathe a word to anyone of what had happened. Carefully and quickly, he made his way back to the town spring and the empty buckets he had left there. Along the way he paid particular attention to voices, any voice, and any footsteps hidden in the cold June mist. He stepped lightly to the spring and filled each bucket, grasped the rope becket of each in hand, and turned toward the Tavern. Then, he froze in his tracks. An image caught his breath. There, just vanishing silently into the fog .... Was it? Yes, he was certain; in that fleeting moment a young woman in a white blouse and pantaloons, white stockings and buckled boots, her golden hair pigtailed to a white bow at her waist, a wooden bucket in each hand, vanished into the fog. Thomas' mouth went dry; a chill prickled his spine; he shuddered all over with a cold he had never felt before. He knew her.

Chapter 2

"Where is that boy?" scolded Molly, looking out the side door of the Tavern. "Can't see a thing in this fog. You reckon he's got himself lost in it, Benjamin?"

Benjamin and Molly Nichols, keepers of the White Horse Tavern, were third generation removed from Mary Mayes Nichols whose legacy still permeated the structure. Mary was the bonny sister of the pirate William Mayes the younger, and her kin in marriage to Robert Nichols were since then the keepers who maintained the Tavern in high stead since the rich days of her brother's return with great wealth "taken from them who can afford it." Tales of the capture of the Mogul's ship plying the Red Sea had long since become main fare told over and over in the tavern, as were the often repeated yarns about the winsome and true Mary who dressed in white and won the hearts of every patron with her smiles and cheer, while keeping herself in the memory of her husband following his untimely demise after just eighteen years of marriage. It was he who secured the Tavern from Mayes the younger, and Robert's ambition was to keep it in the Nichols family from father to son right on.

Once tongues were loosened by ale and rum, boastful galley packets from those who "remembered" the heist as a bold and daring member of the Mayes crew, though seventy-three years past, made colorful entertainment, only to be guffawed as double Dutch, mere flibbergib by others who proclaimed the reality of their own father or uncle or grandfather to have been among the crew. Never before had a ship had so many crewmen, and just who was or was not a party to the takings was less important now than the telling of another tale in fine manner. "Shoot us a line" was all anyone had to say, and the tales began, often keeping hours into the lee of the evening.

    Whoever was actually at the right hand of William Mayes the younger upon arrival in Newport back in 1699 was a matter of considerable prattle, and many so proclaimed their dear departed forbear, God rest his soul, to be the very one. Whatever the truth, the enormous wealth they brought with them produced a flurry of prosperity. Properties changed hands with regularity, and homes were built hither and thither. Merchants were made, and their ships kept commerce flowing handsomely, all envied by the British authorities. His was the second of the vast treasures to arrive in Newport, Thomas Tew bringing the first, followed by Mayes the younger's ventures five years later. Their combined riches gave a flourish to the town still talked about in story and rhyme, long since well honed lore of the Bay.

    Stories from their time, surely much embellished said Molly, gave the Tavern a warm remembrance among patrons who kept Mary's presence as well, many claiming to be witness in the wee hours of foggy morns of her silent walk to or from the spring. Mary and her brother were the talk of the Tavern, the dream of every Newport boy to have such adventures, and the wish of every girl to be so loved. They still lived in the White Horse Tavern, in every crack of its massive beams, in every flicker from its broad fireplaces, and in the late night candlelight said to wander its way through the confines well after emptied of patrons; just Mary making sure her hearths were warm and secure of sparks, so the tales go.

    Sagas often told of such great treasure still captured attention, the same that told of those with thirsts to get their royal hands on the prosperity it brought. Especially so the dastardly Lord Bellomont who set about to have Mayes strung from a yard arm, his contempt giving further rift between lordship and colonist, a rift that lay festering deep in the minds and hearts of true Rhode Islanders. Now almost four score years later, the stories of Lordly intent to abscond with the treasure in the name of the law, so naming the brave townsman a pirate worthy of no more than a noose, was a well spun block set in Newport's foundation, yet a stumbling block that British authorities and loyalists continually tripped upon in their quest to harness the colony's free trade so firmly fixed in the livelihoods of every seaman and merchant.

    Folk tale or fact, all was the same for the telling of another fine yarn, and many a boy living along Narragansett shores enlivened chores with pirate imaginings inspired by ol' "Long Ben" Tew and Mayes the younger. And those who sailed the bay dreamed of their own exploits to come and their bonny Mary to find. The firing of young imaginations grew upon the rift at the core of discontent with the British that set Rhode Islanders on their own course.

Among the Bay's flourishing mercantile establishments lay the wealth of many an unwary seamen who was easily separated from his cut of pirated takings by high living and envious merchants. All dealt in contraband, so echoed the proclamations of Cotton Mather, that stuffy Massachusetts minister and executioner of the last century who railed that Newport was a den of thieves. Each of the crew returned with more wealth than any seaman could hope to earn in a lifetime, said to exceed the worth of twelve hundred pounds sterling for each man, and therein lay Newport's future. Their takings changing hands over and over brought new goods aboard new ships whose profits built new homes and shops for merchants, and Newport grew. Said merchants received returns on their investments again and more with sales of new merchandise sold in every port bringing much profit to Newport and Providence and Bristol and other towns on the Bay.

Quickly was the lesson learned of just how hardmoney worked. Newport prospered mightily, bringing with it good lives for all, with peace among men of differing faiths given in law set by the written word of Rhode Island's own charter, the work of the Baptists. With high regard for their own governance, but not grown of those Massachusetts minds who claimed the ideal state to be an arm of the church, Rhode Islanders answered claiming the church of private lives and commerce of public lives to be set apart in law once and always with freedom of choosing a matter left to the individual. None other among the colonies could claim such recognized freedoms in its written law; such freedoms brought many new traders and Friends to the Narragansett Bay, and much contempt from the Crown's loyalists who set British law as the law of the land, not inventions by the colonists themselves who exercised governing council over themselves.

Even though common sailors knew little of such workings of money, mostly frittering away their takings in extravagance, crewing new ships built from earnings of all kinds showed itself to be the result of money changed from hand to hand, beginning with treasures taken proving to be a mighty fuel. Therein lay the spark that grew both Rhode Island's wealth, guided by the hands of its Quaker Grandees, and notions of independence born in unfettered commerce as a consequence of their pursuit of well-being, not a matter of family position but the product of one's own efforts. Newporters proudly proclaimed their shipbuilding and seamanship the rival of Boston with trade in all ports throughout the world, much to the dissatisfaction of home country regulators who sought trade only with themselves and effected such with those nefarious Maritime Laws that sent Customs Collectors and revenue ships of the Crown to collect taxes on all forms of trade.

Reverend Mather was just one of the voices from afar who condemned Rhode Islanders for thievery, but all who worked to better their lives spoke firmly that taxes for no benefit was nothing more than graft, nothing other than Royal freebootery. Work for profit was there for anyone, commoner or gentry, and anyone wanting to work for gain, seaman and lubber alike, were bolstered by tradesmen whose goods were in much demand among merchants who always sought re-supply at lowest cost and set value for profit. Newporters fashioned their town with polish because of such exchange, and fine homes steadily rose from such riches.

Captain Mayes the younger knew the value of his cut, ten times that of a crewman, and he took care to mete it out with prudence. It was he who secured the Tavern after his father made it such an establishment a score less six years after becoming a public house back in 1673, a century of years before the unfolding of this tale. Many a yarn spoke of bright eyed crewman thirsting for new adventure who spent their share from the Mogul in the Tavern trying to convince Mayes to put to sea again. He, with wisdom to savor deeds done rather than ruffle the Crown once more or prick fate again as did Thomas Tew, chose to maintain the warmth of his tavern with another round of good cheer hoisted among old compatriots. He was content with stories, and his tavern brought seekers from all corners to hear the tales, now contained in repeated legends told and retold. Many were the inquiries about the whereabouts of Long Ben's treasure, said to be buried about the Bay among other takings said to lay awaiting discovery.

Those characters of olde, so much a part of the tales of Narragansett Bay and Newport and so alive in the confines of taverns everywhere, gave much inspiration to cavalier tongues that fired young minds. Thomas Mayes was not alone among the Bay's youth who claimed descent from those cited in the Mayes chronicles set to word and rhyme by Bonny Mary and others since. Many were they who traced their lineage to a name recalled in recitation from distant times.

William Mayes the son was the great-grandfather of Thomas. Long since departed, he remained a lively post-mortem existence among various narratives, each elevating the bold buccaneer with embellished perpetuity, much to the proclaimed embarrassment of the loyalists who steadily cleared themselves of any pirating lineage.

Claims of staunch bindings to the home isles, the Crown and British law held no sway among the whispering Sons of Liberty, all said to be pirates by those who yielded to the Kingt. Yet, gold rounds bearing the Mogul's marks continued to quietly emanate from secret purses in exchange for desired goods. Among the Sons, not one gave claim to descendency from those "honest" citizens who gave aid to Bellomont's quest to catch his quarry, for there were no such men among those claiming to be true Rhode Islanders. And with the town council sitting regularly at the establishment just six years subsequent to Mayes the younger's renewal posting of the White Horse Tavern as an ale house back in '02, the structure, its keepers and Newporters alike, nay, the entire colony, gave substance in lasting memory for the value of citizen contribution to the protection of one and all as the common good expressed in written laws accepted by all, without need of the Mother Country.

Therein lay the long enduring legacy of William Mayes the younger, grown from Rhode Island's own answer to Massachusetts, Cotton Mather, and the King and his royal minions; a sense of independence long since established in the beginning of this fair colony by the much heralded Roger Williams, Ann Hutchinson and William Coddington, all expelled from Massachusetts for free thinking. They and their followers did purchase Rhode Island from the natives, from whence came the name of the Bay, lands once said to be unworthy of a passing glance, yet now the richest among its neighbors for its size.

The celebrated acts of Thomas Tew and William Mayes the younger and their crews continued to further Newport's livelihood far beyond their original doings as told in tavern tales. Though pirates known far and wide among others so bold, their spirits lay at the heart of the Bay, grown since into life and commerce sought to be conducted independent of Royal intentions. No better to see the difference with the home country than inheritance; no high born gentry of lords and ladies was to be found in Rhode Island, only those who worked for their own gain and bettered their lot through their own efforts. From finely crafted goods to purchase of dry stoes for shops and homes of high fashion to ship's chandlery of fittest effects, the colony's merchants grew their own wealth with their own hands.

The White Horse Tavern, now in the company of Benjamin and Molly Nichols, was the soul of Newport, where admonishments of Trinity Church took root. Here Thomas learned of lasting convictions imparted by Benjamin and Molly as their daily goal of quality offerings at fair prices, but always with a keen eye to profit and scorn of taxes. Within its stout walls he learned the Bay's commerce and politics the Newport way, and with the Tavern in a substantial state, its hearths warm and its pantries full, a coin or two once of the Mogul's treasury occasionally crossed the threshold to further grow the Tavern's own cache. Gold and silver, rare in coinage those days, long contributed to the Tavern's financial well-being. Passing mention of the Mogul's mark on another of those large rounds, or of doubloons from the Spanish Main, Spanish dollars, or hordes of pieces of eight in silver drew the adventuresome from afar, seekers with ideas of getting their hands on such riches said to flow freely in Newport.

Not so, in actual fact. Merchant and citizen alike knew well the value of hardmoney and kept it close to the chest, counting each copper to squeeze all its worth when exchanged. The bay ran with a general lack of hardmoney, gold and silver always being siphoned off in balance of payment to Britain's home industries at the expense of the colonies. That gave rise to promissory notes, and barter accounting for much doings at the Tavern's side door kept the establishment well equipped. Exchange for gold was uncommon, some silvers, but coppers mostly, or replacement of deeds done or goods exchanged for paper notes that made uneasy but dependable alliances if further trade was anticipated. Barter made goodly portions of the Tavern's needs in exchange for the day's meal and grog, overseen by Molly's keen eye and written on tick with exchange never put off for long. She cautioned Thomas repeatedly; a warm winter fire and hot toddies born of remembrance always exceeds the actual facts, so writing the exchange keeps the terms clear. Never was he to agree in words; business was always to be set in writing.

Molly was a firm keeper and an honest hostess, expecting and accepting no less from her suppliers and patrons, many of them being the town's officials who sat among the varied ship's company to learn of goings-on elsewhere. Secured by the doings of her pirating ancestor turned solid citizen of wealth, along with business maintained steady ever since, the Tavern nurtured the Bay's spirit of bold independence that grew entwined with notions of rights begotten of free trade and each individual's liberty, liberty to pursue life's work and well-being beyond one's born station. That seed now grown full in this time of rising conflict proclaimed the right of free men to earn as a result of labor spent. Such convictions were firmly rooted in Rhode Island-born minds.

Such legacies of the pirate came directly to Thomas Mayes, so named for both of Newport's famous buccaneers. With those legacies came that seasoned leather packet given him by his deathbed ridden father, elder brother of Aunt Nettie to whom Thomas' care was entrusted. The harsh gale of three years past took his strength, much to the sadness of Thomas and Aunt Nettie alike. Laid to rest in fine fashion in Trinity's yard, he joined the mother that Thomas never knew, having given her life for his in childbirth back in the late spring of '58. Family heritage changed from the hand of William Mayes the younger to his son, then on to his son, Thomas's father, whose oath upon the boy insured remembrance of those past, whereupon Aunt Nettie made certain Thomas kept his promise by relieving him of the packet before its contents became known. Always administering her duty firmly, she continually reminded Thomas that his life's mission was to secure a fine reputation by the efforts of his mind and hand, not the taking of others' wealth, unless earned.

Aunt Nettie never permitted talk of the packet. "Enough said about that," she scolded. "We shall see to it that yew learn a trade of worth, Thomas. A housewright," she ruled again and again. But never were the words said without further admonishment of the success she imagined him to achieve. "Now Thomas, be ye cautious that pride gained in success should never rise beyond good senses. Be wary of the path followed by that yob, Newport's own Judas, that Peter Harrison," she cautioned. "He may have been architect of the town's fine construction shown in the Redwood Library, the town's Brick Market and the Jewish Synagogue, excellent workmanship to be sure, but that man," she so thoroughly and often chastised, "was not to be imitated. Such a man of stature turned Customs Collector in New Haven, an EXCHECQUER!" she railed, "over his own people! 'Tis far easier to raise the devil than lay him, Thomas. See to it that you mark my words."

Her instructions were meant to insure that Thomas should never forsake his home and his family with such a turn. She insured that he always wore attire made of American hands, as did Providence's own magistrate and Governor-past Stephen Hopkins whom she so admired, and Henry Collins, housewright that she often spoke of Thomas imitating. Collins was Newport's newest architect and a worthy man of high esteem who remained true to his word and his people. Aunt Nettie often reaffirmed Thomas' future; in the coming years, at seventeen, after his years of apprenticeship with Mr. Collins, Thomas would then advance to Rhode Island College, recently established by the fine merchant Mister John Brown, to become an American man of letters, a gentleman of stature, the first Mayes to walk the podium of education. Aunt Nettie saw it all in her mind's eye, and with her stern guidance, Thomas had nothing to say about the course of his future but to stay on the road to success that she outlined.

Having such prospects before him was reassuring, though they strongly conflicted with the lure of the sea that drew him so. And Thomas often wondered what the packet contained. Meanwhile, Aunt Nettie placed him among relatives at the White Horse Tavern to mix in Newport's better prospects rather than home in much smaller Providence Plantations. Newport was much more exciting, to Thomas' liking, as it held many more wonders and opportunities, the sort that Aunt Nettie told would make for a firm foundation as a housewright.

Like Aunt Nettie, Molly set fair trade and wise handling of money among the most important things of each day. She kept Thomas thinking of expenses and profits, and neither Aunt Nettie nor Molly had kind things to say of those expressing loyalist sentiments. They had, however, learned the things to say that neither incited contempt nor revealed their own convictions to those customers who may be loyalists. All were paying patrons to be treated fairly. All were to be cultivated with welcomes, good food, warming fires in hopes of their return in the future, whatever the sentiments of proprietors.

These women in Thomas' life always spoke quietly and in private among like minds while men often spoke loudly and openly, especially those who frequented the Tavern's barrels of daring. There, under the influence of spirits, loose talk was said to be mere rumbustion, although many recognized that seeds of contempt were fertilized and grew to strength of conviction. There, the sermons of church became convictions, and proclamations of rising British tyranny were hotly railed. But all who knew the Rhode Island temperament knew that its display in armed resistance already demonstrated in Newport's harbor against the *St. John* and the *Liberty* was a growing denouncement of allegiance to the King, though rarely stated openly outside its taverns. Outspoken voices grew in numbers, first among voices from the whisperers whose use of the words "liberty" and "America" was frequent.

Thomas grew from such roots and remembered well the tongue wagging heard when he was just a boy, boasting even then of the right of citizens taking action in the burning of the *Liberty*. Though before his own experience, the flames of discontent had been fanned with the hated Stamp Act imposed on written transactions of all kinds. That Act inflicted a surcharge on everyone doing business on paper and spurred the sides of contempt into riots. No one accepted the British claim that writs and promissory notes, the sort that Molly believed was good for business, were subject to the purchase of a stamp to be legal. She carefully kept her writs among those she knew to trust, and when completed they were reduced to ashes in the fireplaces of the tavern.

Merchants cursed the Act and the stroke of the Royal pen that required the purchase of a tiny piece of paper bearing the King's seal. Without the stamp, the transaction remained null and void. That imposition on commerce irked traders who continually proclaimed the right of fair and free trade conducted among themselves at their own disposition, not the direction of the Crown that levied taxes to no benefit of those involved. Such was the rancor among citizens and merchants that their gathering on the Commons in front of Colony House grew to such anger that tempers flamed into action with the mob that lurched from there to the doorsteps of prominent Kingsmen, each one scurrying out back ways to hide on the Crown's ships in the harbor. "That," taverners continually railed with pounding fists, "be the way of 'andlin' the bloody British."

Parliament's Townshend Acts were immediately recognized by merchants as meant to further deplete the colonies of wealth. And there in the harbor lay, first, the *St. John* and the *Liberty* among other ships of the King's service, and now the *Beaver* and the *Gaspee* bearing more of the Crown's agents of revenue. Their captains, given to raids on sea and land, fueled growing wills to actions of retribution that put the entire Bay alight with feverish talk. And there at the head of Long Wharf sat the imposing focus of such ire, the Revenue House at Queens Hive. Everyone saw the fine building as a double edged sword both in purpose and function; it was both the long-needed trading place of the town, yet the gathering place of the King's agents whose eyes saw no further than revenue. The fire that burned within each ship's captain newly arriving in Newport, with manifest in hand upon entering the building, blazed into rancor from the burden of maritime tax that flowed from his pocket into the King's. Taxes, those hated duties paid simply for the privilege of doing business as subjects of the Crown, were the boils that festered.

Chapter 3

"Where 'ave you been?" Molly's welcoming voice greeted him as Thomas set the buckets on the floor, about to burst to tell of his looking Dudingston eye-to-eye and giving him the slip. "Off lookin' in on yer Captains again, 'ave yew?"

"Blimey! Wait 'til I...."

"Wastin' yer time again, yew 'ave," commanded Benjamin. "No need to go lookin' in on sea captains. Aunt Nettie'll have none of it."

"If she would just listen," Thomas lamented. "If I could go to sea with them, I'd make a fine midshipman. I'm strong and willin', but all I do is sit on shore and watch their ships sail by... and I just sit. Molly! You won't...."

"Lad, dreamin' 'bout larberin' around on the deck of a ship," Benjamin's stern voice scolded, "won't pay fer yer keep. Yew be keen to pay attention to Aunt Nettie; she wants yer thinkin' put to good use, yew bein' young with much opportunity ahead. Mean time, we got things to do 'ere. What's good fer yew, Thomas, is spendin' yer time thinkin' less on shantyin' about the sea and put yer mind to thinkin' on bein' a man o' letters. There be a good future in it, lad, a good livin'."

"I'm sure, Molly... out in the fog... I saw...."

"Do yerself good with spendin' less time dreamin' on ships and the sea and more time drawin' yer 'ousewrightin'," Benjamin continued.

"Bloody 'ouses again," Thomas mumbled. "That's all I 'ear. But Molly! It was...."

"And good advice it is, Thomas," Molly said warmly. "Newport has lost far too many of her best to the sea, your father as well, and those many who sailed away never to return. There's no future in temptin' the fates that ride the waves, Thomas. Just one tempest tossed and.... Well, we just don't want to lose yew in kind. Now, we got to get that water of yers on to boil, here's the pot. Got oysters and clams to shuck, fresh this marnin' from Captain Brinley. I'll 'elp. Got chowder to put on. Time gets by before we know it, and our friends will be along soon to taste our fare."

"And the wood box 'ere is a bit sparse," ordered Benjamin. "Need some splittin's, and don't forget to put up for the hearths. Need a day's worth to keep the chill pushed back. More would see us into the morrow, if yew be of a mind."

Thomas felt besieged. "I don't mean to be disputin' yer word, sir, but can yew make it clear to me 'ow cookin' and splittin' fire wood and makin' chowder and cleanin' pots 'elps me be a better 'ousewright?" Thomas asked.

Benjamin gave a long look at Thomas with a knowing nod, recalling his own dreams of youth held shackled to the Tavern. "I reckon it be part of what learnin' to work is all about, lad. Every day, startin' early, got things to do right on to night. Yew'll soon shed yer boy's notions and step into the man's world, and work is what awaits. Yer best efforts at workin' to get things done in a timely fashion so's to move on to the next is good fer whatever comes yer way, and makin' a name fer yerself buildin' good, solid structures is a fine trade. Make no mistake 'bout that. Better yew should think in sovereigns than farthings, lad. Yer youth lets pickin' yer life's work up to yer own choosin' now. So, me own advice is to step out onto the right path to start with, Thomas. Won't be so easy later."

"Will I be permitted to say...."

"No need. Aunt Nettie's already layin' yer foundation. The White Horse is just a stop along the way. Yew'll most likely be movin' on to apprenticin' yer 'ousewrightin' soon. After that, on to Providence Plantations and its new college of learnin' what Aunt Nettie has set her eye upon and is keenly proud o' boastin' about."

That statement took Thomas by surprise. He liked the Tavern and Molly and Benjamin and especially the patrons whose adventures he so admired, and even though his duties were a grind, he had not considered leaving. With excitement of the morning now given flight to ponderous thoughts of another apprenticeship, Thomas opened the door to go to the wood pile out back and mumbled, "It's work all day right up to dark, unless Lieutenant Dudingston makes a spot of bother."

"Thomas," Molly called out the door behind him, handing him a warm biscuit around a thick slice of savory bacon. "When yew are done with the wood, if yew'll trade fer mussels and shrimps, we'll have us a spot of bouillabaisse. I'll 'ave fresh bread bakin's, too."

"Yes ma'am," Thomas said, brightened by the thought. Molly's bouillabaisse put cheer in an always-hungry boy. Hers was the best on the island, and her request for ingredients from the Bay gave him another chance to get down to the docks even if only to look over the morning catch. He'd find somebody to tell about squirting out from Dudingston's clutches.

Soon, the morning turned bright with a warming sun that took the fog. Gentle breezes brought a welcomed day of warmth to the Bay. Without winter's cold whip and biting salt spray, oystermen and fishermen alike found their efforts filling their boats rewarded. Every captain had learned, though, to cast a wary eye to the sky and wind before taking on calm's invitation. To put out into Atlantic swells from the sheltered bay, from Newport's favored winter haven especially so, often proved foolhardy in the spring of the year. Staying at anchor to avoid the sea's quickly built lashings in springtime meant more business for the Tavern but less time for Thomas to go sailing or rambling with the lads. He yearned for summer.

"Top a'the marnin', Thomas." The familiar voice interrupted his wood splitting labors. Thomas turned to see bearded Captain Brinley at the fence along Farewell Street. "A fine lot of crabs, I 'ave , clean, mind yew. Yer mistress of the 'ouse be int'rested?"

"Yessir, Captain. I was just about to come to yer place. Knock there at the side door," Thomas said, then began excitedly. "Captain, I...."

"Scuttlebutt along the wharves this marnin' tells of Lieutenant Dudingston 'avin' 'is clutches close on to a lad what looks a lot like yew, Thomas, a jack o'the dust, so it be said. Recommendin' I be fer to stand clear o' that devil."

Thomas thought a moment. "What keeps 'im from sendin' 'is marines to manacle me to 'is duty?"

"Aye, so be it, lad, if 'e knowed fer certain it were yew what run'd from 'im. Mind yer best lookout, and keep a vigilant eye, Thomas. And stay off the boats, lad. Boardin' 'e does, and discoverin' yew crewin' at sea could likely put yerself right into 'is clutches with no say. Many a sailor's come pressed to the Crown's service in just such a manner. Step lively on shore and keep yer distance. Just so's yew know, keep rememberin' that not another soul saw yer presence on the dock, so's the lot of us can vouch fer yer presence elsewhere."

Thomas thought of Gramps Jacobs' gravely voice and started to speak.

"Keep rememberin' that," Captain Brinley continued. "Just 'is claim agin' yer'n that yew was elsewhere and not where 'e said is not likely enough to sway the Crown. Looks like a marnin's work of splittin's layin' there, to me."

Thomas got the message.

"Keep that under yer 'at, lad. Top a'the marnin," the captain said touching the bill of his cap.

As the captain stepped over to the Tavern's side door, Thomas grinned to think that he was the talk of docks, though he now knew his story had to remain untold, kept "under his 'at." Wanting to tell all the lads, to go yelling up and down the wharves that he gave Dudingston the slip, was now so tempered as if it never happened. Keeping it to himself was suddenly a heavy burden, one that he had to bear to keep clear of word getting back to Dudingston, or his marines might very well show up at the Tavern and manacle him.

Disgust giving him strength, Thomas slammed his ax deep into sections of tree trunk again and again. Pieces flew one after another. "An' supposin' Mary didn't 'appen, either," he groaned, "whispin' into the fog like that. Didn't get chill bumps and the shakes fer nothin', I did. I seen 'er, I did. Bonny Mary. I seen 'er. I did," he muttered with his strength fiercely driving his ax to split off another section in a single blow.

"Bonny Mary, yew say?" A voice startled Thomas. He turned to see the dodgy widow Coddington by the fence on her way to her morning delivery of her fresh butter, milk and cream to Molly, along with the sour widow Easton carrying a basket of eggs. "Oh, yes. Seen 'er I have as well, young man. I have. In the marnin' fog, I have. Yes indeed...."

"A fine marnin' to ye, Miss Coddington, Miss Easton" Thomas said. "Got to git on with me splittin's. Step on over to the door there," he motioned. Then swinging his ax again, he scolded the day, "Now it'll be all over Newport, me seein' things," he mumbled. "That dotty ol' moo will see to it fer sure. Blimey! Will I get the guffaws from the lads! Thomas Mayes, if yew makes one mention of Lieutenant Dudingston or bonny Mary, yew deserves to be a shackled dusty," he scolded himself. "Put such seein's out o'yer mind; t'weren't nothin' to it. Nothin'." His ax fell forcefully and cleaved off another section.

Chapter 4

While Thomas kept busy laying the sharp edge of his ax to splittings, the Tavern's suppliers made their morning deliveries to the side door. One after another they came, offering this or that, and Molly selected the day's fare in exchange for pence and silvers, tanners and bobs along with occasional pieces of eight that clinked into hand after hand, along with her ticks for those who accepted them. Thomas kept his ax flying; the sooner he got the hearths stocked, the sooner he would have hot johnnycakes and butter under his belt. The thought of hot molasses, maybe honey, made him hungrier, but what he really wanted to was to be off to the wharves. And soon enough, stuffed for the moment, Molly gave him her requests for delivered goods, as always, written in careful notation for each of her grossers;

Mr. Drury, deliver this morning, please
  For Queen's Pudding
      Dried currants or dried cranberries, 4 noggins
      Walnuts, shelled and chopped, 4 noggins
      Nutmeg, ground finely, 25 pennyweight
  For supplies,
      4 Coconuts or 1 quarten. Please do not shred
      Wheat flower, ground nicely, 4 quartens
      Sugar, ground roughly, packed tightly, 1 quarten
      Spanish saffron, 20 pennyweight
      Onions, large, 4 dozen
      Garlics, 20 bunches
      Olive oil, 1 pottle
      Salt, 2 packets
      Pepper, 2 packets

       Love apples, dried, 2 quarten
       Devil's roots, 1 bushel
       1 dozen hard pewter plates, I offer 1 shilling each
       1 dozen knives & forks, sets please, I offer 8 pence each set
       1 dozen pewter pints, I offer £8 for the lot
       and do you have new things from the islands?

Captain Malbone, deliver this morning, please
       Molasses, 1 firkin to exchange
       Good ale, 1 kilderkin to exchange
       Malted wheat beer, 1 kilderkin to exchange
       Your good Rumbullion, or from the islands,
             1 firkin to exchange
       Do you have new things from the islands?

Captain Brinley, thank you for your fine crabs and littlenecks of early this morning. I need further for bouillabaisse today, please deliver this morning
       shrimps, cleaned please, 1 pottle
       scallops, cleaned please, 1 pottle
       langostines or sea lobsters, cleaned please, 1 pottle
       cod fish, cleaned please, 1 pottle
       sea bass, cleaned, 1 pottle
       perch or snapper or flounder, cleaned, 1 pottle
       eel, skinned and cleaned and sectioned please, 1 pottle

Mr. Champlin, deliver this morning please,
       1 beefe side, cut lean please, aged 10-12 days.
       Salted beefe, 2 wrappings, 4 hands square
       Bacon, 1 wrapping, 4 hands square.
       I offer £5/10 for the lot.
       If you have fowl today, 4 plucked and cleaned for the spit.

    With Molly's lists for the week in hand, Thomas was out the door and heading for Thames Street before she finished her first scolding to go in a cantor, for the day was well in hand. Along the way he shouted over and over to those he passed, "Roast of Beefe, Molly's bouillabaise and Queen's Pudding at the White Horse today. Fannie daddies and macaroons!" making himself hungrier with each message.

    Quiet Mr. Drury, long a supplier to the Tavern, agreed to Molly's tick without contest, as did Captain Malbone's assistant, the Captain not yet having arrived at his rummery. But grumpy Mr. Champlin, always brassed off, complained bitterly at her offerings. Thomas left the tick in his hand with quick departure before the butcher made his usual complaint, "Tell yer mistress to send a cart along. Rob a man and 'ave 'im deliver, too...."

Dashing out the door, he almost collided with Governor Wanton making his morning walk. "Top o' the marnin', guv'na. Molly be layin' a fine spread today, roast of beefe and bouillabaisse fer the askin'."

"And a fine day to you, lad. Bouillabaisse you say. I may just have to partake of her spread."

Thomas, in a run, tipped his cap to the Governor and ran straight for Stephen's wharf to see Gramps Jacobs and Justin again, but the *Annabelle* had sailed, and across the wharf from where the stout voice had come sat no ship at all. No ships and no happening; their captains had put to sea with the last of the fog. Thomas recognized that Captain Brinley was right; staying clear of Lieutenant Dudingston was the thing to do, as these wise captains did. He chose as well and battled his desire to yell to everyone that he had given Lt. Dudingston the slip.

Thomas' last stop was Captain Brinley's house in the Cove. He ran through Queen's Hive on his way to Marlborough Dock, yelling his Tavern message over and over to the gathered, and nearly collided with tall Captain Lindsey of Providence Plantations, a master in the service of Nicholas Brown and Company.

"Ahoy, Thomas. Settle yer rambunctions," the captain cautioned with a grin.

"Apologies, Captain Lindsey," Thomas said, then took off in a run again, on to Captain Brinley's with no time to exchange pleasantries, not even a stop with the lads. Once there and out of breath, he told of Molly's needs.

"Full o'beans are yew lad?" Brinley said, looking at Molly's tick. "Aye, Miss Molly be in good fortune," and he began scooping her wishes into baskets, except for the eels. The captain flung his skinning knife to a thud in the dock by Thomas' shoe. "Yew be a good 'and with the knife, Thomas, but think not that yer dirk'll do a better job."

"Sailin' fer Bristol today?" Thomas asked as he flicked the knife point into the dock again.

"Aye."

"Mind if I sail along?"

"Lo, it's in yer eyes, lad; 'e's arf once more to dig up ol' Long Ben's treasure. Why not fetch a couple o' them chests o' doubloons an' silvers an' sparklin' gems what the hapless Cap'n Kidd stashed, too?" Captain Brinley chided with a pirate voice.

"Yew laugh, yew ol' tanky. Yew go on suckin' the monkey while I gather up a King's ransom, then we'll see who's turn it is to laugh."

Captain Brinley howled, hardly able to contain himself. "Thomas Mayes, if nothin' else, yew still be a fine laugh... Right good rum in them coconuts to suck upon, lad. Don't mind if I do," he said, stepping into his house for another tot of the morning, motioning Thomas in as well. "Yew 'ave changed not one whit, Thomas. Growed a little since we sailed the Spanish Main on the right fair *Sea Nymph* an' yer head still goes spinnin' fer pirate treasure." He growled his best pirate imitation, "Arrrr. Wot be yer mission in Bristol, lad?"

Thomas stepped back out into the day, grabbed the first eel by the head and stretched it out along a crack between two planks in the dock. Beginning at the throat, he sliced the length of the tender bellyside, then peeled entrails with a smooth rip. Slicing around the base of the head, then working the knife under the skin at the juncture of the slices, he separated enough skin to grasp, and while holding the head firmly in one hand, the skin firmly between thumb and forefinger of the other, he peeled the skin until it separated. Giving the skin a quick flick into the air, he said, "Aye, yew Mother Carey's chickens, 'ave a go at this." Gulls floating on the morning air snatched for it in a flurry of squawks and flapping wings that soon ended once the gulls took stock of their slippery findings and let it fall into the bay. Next came the head and backbone sailing through the air and another tussle, also discarded once recognized. Gutted and sliced, another after another soon added up to Molly's request, and with the last of the baskets on the cart, Thomas and Captain Brinley set their feet onto Marlborough Street toward the Tavern, tipping their hats and offering the morning's good will to passersby.

"So, keepin' yer silence, are yew?" Captain Brinley asked with a puff on his pipe.

"Lookin' in on Norseman's Rock an' Massasoit's chair," Thomas spouted. "Go ahead an' laugh."

"Well now, that be a fine mission," Captain Brinley confirmed. "An' no laughin' matter, what with some learnin' to be gathered." Looking into the sky for weather signs, he continued, "The goose hangs high on the marnin'. Be a good day fer explorin' the walk of the Norsemen. But ol' son o'Massasoit; that devil, Metacomet, be another matter." Brinley shook his head. "Quartered, the story says, parts spread whereabouts unknown, and fer me own sayin's, good riddance fer what troubles 'e brought this land. Set fahm and village alight all over...."

"Aye, from the lips of ol' tanky hisself," Thomas chided in return. "Told me that story ag'in and ag'in on the Main, yew did. So now am I to set upon seein' fer meself or must I be content with more o' yer tales?"

Brinley continued without the slightest notice of Thomas' comment. "...that 'e did; put flame to Bristol and Warren and Providence and Rehoboth and Dighton on that devil's rampage...."

"I've long 'eard yer words. Would yew show me of Massasoit?"

Captain Brinley paused for a moment. "Aye. Sat in 'is chair, I 'ave. Trekked the warrior's path, too, have I."

"Really!" Thomas said with the disrespect offered a braggart, having heard it all before. "Yew settin' in 'is chair an' such."

Brinley grinned knowingly. "Aye, indeed I did, lad. An' yew know well from me long tellings on the *Sea Nymph,* what fired yer eyes with adventure. Once a lad o' travels, meself, I was," Brinley said wistfully, blowing a long trail of tobacco smoke. "Right good times, them... back then... Growed on up to manhood and were since too busy sailorin', I was." He elbowed Thomas, "While yew was the captain's favored cabin boy, yew took in all them tales fer the truth and laid yer mind fer buried treasure while the wind took the ship o' treasure right along under yew...."

"Really!" Thomas blurted with surprise. "Captain Malbone was a-piratin', yew say? I think not, Brinley. A fine merchant 'e is, to be sure."

"Pirate in who speaks it, lad. Yew of all should know thet fact. Yew knows them tales of olde, them what lives in taverns all along the bay, where them what tells o' thet nefarious Earl o' Bellomont, Governor of Massachusetts an' New Hampshire an' New York, he who cast 'is greedy eye on wot was not 'is in Rhode Island, what armed 'isself with the law o' the Crown an' set fer yer own great-granddaddy, 'e did. An' Thomas Tew before 'im, eyein' one-third o' treasure taken in the name o' the Crown fer his own purse. Captured James Gillam, 'e did, an' William Simms, an' Joe Brodish an' ol' one eyed Tee Wetherly. An' what dew yew reckon went with their treasures? Dirtied 'is 'ands partnerin' with Cap'n Kidd, 'e did. Ship owner, 'e was. An' who did the swingin'? Hmm? Who dangled from the gallows? No need to set yer mind to wonderin'; it weren't the Earl. No Sir. It were the right good an' noble Cap'n what hung from Wapping Dock."

Thomas knew the story and nodded.

"Right yew are, lad. An' what be the learnin' in thet? After walkin' the Bridge of Sorrow, the Lord up above showed the good an' honorable Cap'n innocent, what with the rope separatin' on the first 'angin'. Well, now, a 'Hangman's Fair' the court aimed to 'ave, and a 'Hangman's Fair' they 'ad. Marched the innocent captain back up the gallows fer the second 'angin', they did. Proof be in the sign fer all what gathered to see, but dangle he did. Now, says me, who's to benefit with the Cap'n departin' this earth agin the will of the Almighty? An' what be yer s'posin's went with Kidd's treasures, two 'earty ship loads, so's they say? An' the Lady Bellomont's fine necklace worth ten thousand pounds; where'd yew suppose such a fine necklace come from? Where there's polished brass there be muck, be me own sayin'. An' thet be the learnin', Thomas. Keep a keen eye fer 'im who can be trusted in matters o' money and yew 'ave a trust fer yer life. A bird never flies with but one wing, a pair it takes. We be set on a new course in these times, what can't be done with one wing. Water past the mill does no grindin', so's we look to the future an' set the rudder lest we foul upon the rock."

"Gold hardens men's souls," Thomas recited. "Aye. Aunt Nettie teaches me well. 'The best o' men are men at best. Devil's children have devil's luck. A man 'ungry for wealth is an envious man. Idle 'ands be the devil's workshop. To be well served is to serve well. Out of debt, out of danger. Learning is better than 'ouse and land.' So say the proverbs... nay, admonishings. They fall from her tongue 'til I tire of them," grumbled Thomas. "Aunt Nettie an' her proverbs.... Heard them all have I."

"'Little thieves 'ang, great thieves escape,' so speaks the lives what we knows in more than tale, Thomas. 'Tis those great thieves what keep on thievin'."

"Enough of this drivel, Brinley! What became of Kidd's Moorish prizes, chests of gold and silver and fine jewels, they were? Where is thet treasure o' 'is? Still buried on Prudence Island, still there jes' fer the claimin', says me. Or Patience Island. Or Connanicut. Or Block Island...."

Brinley interrupted. "Or secreted away by the evil Bellomont and his kind what used the blood of other men to make their own gatherin's. If more remains, under what rock on what island or land dost said treasure lay in wait of yer findin', Thomas? In what cave by the sea lay remains to be discovered by lads such as yew? Sailed the coast with me own father, I did, an' 'im with 'is father before, an' lads from every port on back four score years lookin' where pirate treasure might lay hidden. An' found nothin'." Brinley took a long draw on his pipe. "Fer long hours spent, 'cept fishnets tended. An' be certain yew be well acquainted with the ways o' men what walk among us, them what use the law to their own advantage. What may yet lay from sight among these many islands and lands will surely be claimed by them what owns the land. If found, kept to themselves, if they knows what be the good in treasure. So, put yer thinkin' to this; what lay free fer yer diggin's now, nigh on to a hunderd years past?"

"Heard all the tales, 'ave I, Brinley. Me an' the lads...."

"Pirate treasures all 'round us, so say the tales what fires young imaginin', yet what hearin' do ye 'ave of the findin'?"

"What of the findin's in Jamestown, just a bit of Kidd's hidin's, they say? An' Point Judith? An' out on Sakonnet, an' on Cuttyhunk sands, yew tired ol' tar. What of them finds, an' more that lay among island an' land? An' what of Teach's own respite in Providence? Stash, I say. Where it lay 'idden is yet to be discovered, an' I aim to...."

"Aye, a good ear yew 'ave fer 'earin' the tales, Thomas. But ask yerself if luck o' findin's begats the devil's own revenge fer the trouble it brings. An' ask yerself if yer 'earin's be tavern talk or real findin's. Me thinks said tales be the work of blaggards what boast o' their knowin's what nobody gets to see but more blaggardry. Real findin's go untold, says me. There be yer learnin' in thet. Yer own Aunt Nettie what's come to be known as the sayer of Providence speaks well o' the 'earts of men. 'With treasure in hand, other eyes are tempted,' says she. So, lest those eyes relieve yer findin's, best a quiet mouth to keep."

"When I find a treasure, I shall be quite the lad, I shall...."

"When yew finds a treasure told to all, the King's men shall have recourse to descend upon yew as a pack of hounds. The fox hath no chance when driven by their law. 'Ave yew not tasted the wrath of Dudingston this very day? Dost yew want more of the same? Or dost yew choose to be free of envious eyes..." Brinley looked away, "as a poor man by keepin' yer own secrets?"

Astonished, Thomas blurted, "Brinley, are yew tellin' me of yer own findin's, long 'idden treasure in yer fisherman's house?"

The captain grinned, set his pipe and leaned into pushing the cart on up Marlborough Street and said nothing. Passing an outcropping of the season's first dente-de-lion along cobblestone edges, he stopped and picked among the taller of the golden yellow wildflowers and laid them on the baskets in his cart.

"Take care when yew looks down Thames Street there, Thomas, and yew'll see Newport's treasure. Look out in the harbor behind us at the forest o' masts and spars... there lay the treasure. Trade. If a simple folk livin' among Newport's 'igh and mighty 'elps build a merchant's fortunes and keeps me own days... I mean, keeps 'is own days comfortable, what need 'as 'e of blaggardry what brings much attention and trouble? Whether dug out o' the ground or found on the beach or earned in the market...."

Thomas could not contain himself. "Brinley! Yew be the one! Yew be 'e who walked upon a chest washed open in the sand at low tide. Yew ol' pirate, yew. Why not tell of such things?"

"Secreted away so's to belay treasure fever...."

"B-r-i-n-l-e-y," Thomas commanded. "Tell me more. Secreted away yew say."

"Aye, an' so's to keep greedy Tory 'ands from takin' what their laws claim to be rightful in the takin'. Piratin' is in the sayin', fer certain if it be the law sayin' so, lad. There be the learnin' in thet. 'E who seeks fortune gathers envious eyes, says yer own Aunt Nettie. An' 'e who reveals fortune gathers men of law, says Brinley. An' now thet yer knowin' includes me own fate, Thomas, yew swears by yer bleached bones to keep the confidence?"

Thomas stopped pushing and stood erect. He cupped his left hand around his throat, kissed the back of his right hand, spit in its palm, then slapped it over his heart. "I swears to yer keepin, 'From me own lips and 'eart what beats true, or me own neck to stretch an' bleached bones to rue,'" he recited, an old sailor's pact learned on his voyages.

Pushing the cart once more, Brinley continued, "A secret be a 'eavy burden, Thomas. So, keepin' yer oath be what separates the knowin' and the unknowin'. Therein lay yer keepin' in troubled times, these. 'Tis better to schoon smoothly through each day than chart fer troubled waters along rocky shores. So, me placin' in yer keep the knowin' swears to safe keepin' fer good and always."

"I swears it, I did," Thomas confirmed without further thought, still alight with the idea of Brinley's treasure horde.

"An' me keepin' yer own, an' yew keepin' me own, thet be our pact o' trust. Agreed?"

Thomas stopped in his tracks. The sudden recognition of what Brinley had said bore heavily on him. "Aye. Me eyes just flung open, Brinley. Secrets, those once of mere play hast become bondage to an oath that bears weighty consequences if revealed," he said. Thomas suddenly recognized that he had to maintain Brinley's secret while only trusting that Brinley kept his. What had long been his childish regard for pirating and treasure-seeking was now a pact in a world of severe trepidations. If he revealed even a hint of Brinley's secret, Brinley had right to reveal a hint of what he knew, and a dusty's life as a pressed British cook awaited Thomas. Fair in the revealing was the law of the sea.

Thomas shuddered with the thought. "Aye, the sword of Damocles 'angs near, Brinley."

"'Tis so, lad, an' there lay ministers of the Crown close at 'and who can sever the thread an' would gladly do so fer profit," Brinley said as he pointed at the British revenue ships, *Beaver* and *Gaspee* anchored in the harbor. "Free trade fer profit be piratin', so says the Crown whose ministers cower behind the guns o' yon ships lyin' under our noses, amid our own traders, spyin' on us all the while claimin' our trade be no more than wholesale piratin', the same made sanctified fer taxes paid. An' they, armed with powder and shot and the law, mean to take the King's cut for 'e who claims all within sight as 'is ownership, claimin' kingdom's right, sayin' the King is not possible to do wrong by divine right. An' their own takin's, a third measure, the consequences left unsaid in who makes the measures and who makes the takin'. Thet be where trouble burns deep. What greater piratin' can there be in takin' from them what earns it for them what claim only divine privilege and right of law writ in generous proportions by themselves for themselves?"

Thomas shivered as a chill ran up his spine.

"A good and just captain walked the Bridge of Sorrows to his 'angin', signed by the Almighty as innocent, yet 'anged 'e was by those who yearned to silence his voice. What justice be in such doin's?" Brinley asked. "Aye. Justice in the law, they always say! Humph! Justice lay only in Heaven. There be no justice betwixt Heaven and Hell what lay in the 'ands of them what make the law fer their own betterment. Justice be in staying clear of their 'ands and keepin' secrets in 'eart an' mind."

Stopped in a moment of realization at the front door of the Tavern, Thomas reflected on the new world that he had just come to know. Brinley filled in the moment.

"Blood what courses through yer body once walked these streets and lived in this here Tavern, Thomas. An' every day of it was to face the likes of Bellomont and his Tory eyes all around what could spring upon 'im without warnin'. Them who yearned to pad their own coffers with takin's won on the high seas by yer own great-granddaddy an' crew, they set their right in law, not in justice. Right of law said to remove the wicked, yet with coffers filled in the claimin', therein lay the 'eart of true wickedness protected by law. Were so, an' still so, showed many times. Mister Greene can tell yew, the takin' of 'is boat under tow to Boston fer disposition rather than within the colony as the law we sails under 'as long said. All o' Newport knows well that pirated takin's from afar feeds the lifeblood o' our colony, the same lifeblood that the Crown siphons away with its Maritime Laws an' those infernal stamps what cost 'ard coinage. Therein lay kinship, ministers and money, gathered by law to bolster their own holdin's. Yer own forebear's freedom, an' yers an' mine and this whole land, lay at the will o' law an' the makers thereof who take from them what build the riches of this colony. The knowin' and the unknowin' stands apart, Thomas. The knowin' be the Sons of Liberty whose 'ands steer a new course. Yer own 'ands can 'elp steer that course, by bein' a man o' letters."

Thomas could hardly contain his response. "Sons of Liberty!" he blurted. "Oh no! I am not to be counted among those scallywags what bring discord with them."

Brinley motioned Thomas to quiet his voice. "Careful, lad.

Tory ears listen. Lest yew forget, Thomas, yer own birth is from this land, Rhode Island, America. Yer roots lay in this soil an' the ways of this land. Whether reckoned or not because of young years, yew be American in a land what can be made into its own only with the strength of mind to do so."

This new realization smacked Thomas from his imagined treasure hunting, and he nearly lost his footing on the cobblestones at the sudden recognition of being recruited into the whispering Sons of Liberty with a binding of secrets, his and Brinley's.

Chapter 5

Molly picked up the dente-de-lion and twirled its stem between finger and thumb, distant for the moment. "A fine gentleman yew are, Captain Brinley," she said with a smile. Then turning her attention to his cart, she said admiringly, "A fine set of makin's. I offer six bob, six fer the lot".

Brinley grinned at Molly's paltry offer. "Now Molly, we been knowin' each other a long time now, an' yew knows yer offerin' be low, what fer the goods an' the cleanin'. Tegious be the hullin' o'me shrimps, extra effort fer the veinin', too, what yer patrons say be the good merit of Molly's bouillabaisse. I says me shrimps be good fer two bob alone."

"CAPTAIN BRINLEY!" Molly scolded. "Two bob fer a pottle be a piker's price! I shant pay it."

"Aye. Be on me way. Back door of yon Pitt's Head Tavern offer better welcome. Got me other customers waitin'."

"Brinley!" Molly blustered. "Always the difficult quibbler. Yer shrimps be no use beyond the marnin'. I offer a bob, six. That be me best offerin'."

"Yew be offerin'? Nay, Molly, I be offerin', you be takin'. Me price be two bob, six and writs fer twice yer fine fares an' a couple o' pints o' ale at me own choosin's."

"Now Brinley," Molly scolded. "Yew takes me profits. One fare and one pint an' no more be me best offer."

"Two bob, six as well?" Brinley asked, pushing his cap back on his head.

Molly sighed, having lost her negotiation. "Aye." She turned to Thomas, "Bring a crock, Thomas, lest our highwayman seek a ransom fer 'is baskets."

Upon Thomas's return, Brinley was smiling and Molly was

writing her ticks.

"Yer dusty 'ere be a fine 'and with the skinnin' knife," Brinley said. "These 'ere eel be the testimony. Finest makin's fer bouillabaisse, what cannot be the same without."

Sensing financial relief, Molly looked closely at the eel. "An' fine cuttin's they are, Thomas. So, Brinley, you wish to make good on Thomas' handiwork, do ye?"

Anticipating such a response, the Captain moved to quick wit. "Nay, nay. Me thinkin' be clear; the work in eel lay in the skinnin'. So, what say, a bob, six alone?"

"Ten pence, alone," Molly countered.

"Aye, ten pence it be. Though, Molly, I be needin' a good 'and at the tiller fer the day. Me boat lay full from the bay what be destined fer Bristol. Thomas be a good 'and...."

Molly stomped her foot. "Yew scoundrel, Brinley. Yew bargain fer me profit and conspire to make off with me 'elp to boot."

"Lo, Molly, we both knows what work be yers in the kitchen or me work in the bay be work all the same, an' a long day of it, fer what me back painin's say." Brinley straightened with both hands pressing his back. "I makes a right fair price and delivers goods what benefits yer till in fine fashion. Be needin' a 'elpin' 'and fer the day. Returnin' with eventide."

Thomas kept his urge to plead to himself and gave a reasoned request. "Splittin's are in, Molly, hearths, too. Delivered yer ticks. Told of the Tavern's fare all around..." then realizing he should not have said that, he hastened to add, "And me eel skinnin's be yer's fer the takin'."

"Beset with conspirators, one an' all," Molly proclaimed in a huff. "An' when 'ungry patrons come callin', what am I to do without me 'elp?"

"What better a gesture to 'elp gain yer till but to offer me finest eel and Thomas' work fer nothin'? 'Ow be thet bargain, Molly?" Brinley rubbed his whiskers, taking a draw on his pipe. "Lest I reckon me eel at a bob, six."

Exasperated, Molly saw that she was in trouble. "Yer terms be met with 'ard money, I s'pose?"

"Aye, thet be the case, with yer writs as well."

Molly scowled, knowing she was beaten. Bouillabaisse without eel wasn't bouillabaisse at all, and even though she could decline, with harbor patrons arriving, expecting her bouillabaisse as already announced along the wharves by Thomas, she had to have eel. Molly waggled her finger at Thomas. "Aunt Nettie'll be sure to learn of this treachery, Thomas. Yew know 'er feelin's on the matter of sailin'. Yew stands alone on answerin' to 'er, mind yew."

"Aye," Thomas said, unable to hide his smile.

"An' I shant save fer yer likin' a spot of bouillabaisse or macaroons beyond me patrons."

"Aye. Me an' ol' Brinley'll spoon up a red flannel hash or pine-bark stew fer our keep, if time permits from all the work." He and Brinley exchanged glances, Thomas grinning broadly now.

"All the work, indeed," Molly scoffed. "Flibberdejib. Yew two are conspirin', that's what yew be doin'. Well, the marnin's wearin' on, an' more preparations are now lay before me. Set me makin's in the side door, Thomas, an' yew scoundrels be gone with yew."

As Thomas turned to hauling basket after basket of the Bay's treasure to the Tavern's side door, Molly slid the dente-de-lion into her hair. Captain Brinley's out-stretched hand, calloused and rough compared to Molly's delicate hands that she kept soft with oils from the island, received her counting of pence and shillings, along with her writ. He stuffed the lot in a pocket of his peacoat.

"A fine day fer doin' business, Molly. 'Spect to have snapper and lobster on the morrow, fine littlenecks as well. Be droppin' by yer door come marnin'."

Brinley was fair, always adding enticements to his offerings to sweeten the bargain for her, and Molly rather liked their spirited exchanges.

"Won't be needin' eel fer boiled pot or chowder for mad hare dumplin's, Captain. Got Devil's root comin'. See that yew look after Thomas."

"Well blow me down, mad hare dumplin's, yew say?" the captain quizzed. "Really!"

"Aye. Set me hunters out to gather fine hares fer the morrow. More than fish in the sea comes to me tables, Captain. Might yew consider me other suppliers."

Brinley smiled. "Aye, Molly. Be keepin' them dumplin's in mind fer me writ. A fine day to ye," he said, touching the bill of his cap. "I shant trouble yew on the morrow, lest I come along in the eve for them dumplin's."

"Now, now, Captain. Littlenecks fer chowder in the marnin'. Don't be so hasty in yer ways. An' bring oysters fer pan fryin'."

That fare further raised the captain's eyebrows. "Well now, fannie daddies be better fare than me own red flannel hash any day." Stroking his whiskers, he continued, "Might jes' 'ave to use me writ, come the morrow's supper 'ere in yer tavern. Dumplin's and fannie daddies, too. Um-um. Jes' might be wanderin' on back this way, come the morrow's eve."

"An' a warm welcome shall be yers, Captain," Molly said, glancing into his soft grey eyes. "A fine day to ye as well, Captain."

Thomas noticed Molly's glance, her smile, and Brinley's unusual willingness with her. As she stepped up the steps into the Tavern, Brinley could not remove his eyes from her every movement.

Thomas could not resist; "Brinley? Yew be showin' yer eye fer Molly?"

Captain Brinley stumbled for words, and re-set his cap. "Aye," he sighed. "Me and Molly it was, once. Each the apple of the other's eye when not more'n sprigs. Missed 'er, I did, an' a longin' I earned ever since, never to find another like 'er. A fine spirit not to be tampered with now."

"Yew and Molly?" Thomas laughed. "When yew were sprigs?"

Captain Brinley slowly turned the cart around. "Aye, growed up together right 'ere on Marlborough Street, we did, and a fine up-bringing it were, too. Never noticed, did I, that other eyes cast upon 'er when venturin' took me to sea in 'er prime, what stole me away... me own.... Rightly worth sayin' now; me own true love."

"What!?" Thomas gasped with a chuckle.

"Aye, sailed away, I did. Never thinkin' 'er wavin' after me was 'idin' her warm but broken 'eart beatin' fer me. Gone, I was, too long fer a young maiden's needs."

Thomas thought about Molly's comments in agreement with Aunt Nettie's, and what had once been unconnected, disparate pieces suddenly fell into place. In that moment he understood more of their guiding him away from the sea. But the revelation of Molly in Brinley's past intrigued him.

"Really! What say yew... a story of love! Brinley, a burley ol' whiskered tanky, a salt o' the sea, a yeoman in the belly o' yer ships; yew and Molly?" Thomas could not resist a laugh.

"'Tis the makin's o' life, Thomas, the pairin' o' every boy and girl seen in most every 'ouse there is, 'cept me own yearnin's was too much boy fer 'er waitin'. Benjamin, me own best lad, and a good lad 'e be fer certain, what with our times a'rompin' the Bay. 'E made a better 'usband than me own wanderlust offered. Always arf on another venture, hither and yon, leavin' Molly to 'er lonesomes. Not a fair life fer a young and pretty thing what 'as feelin's, too." Brinley looked back at the Tavern with a sigh. "Molly and this ol' tavern be a sight better'n Molly in me own kitchen, what with no children of 'er own. Sech be the case set me thinkin' and wonderin', yet Benjamin, what carries on the legacy of this 'ere tavern, yer past, I might add, in 'is an' Molly's 'ands... 'er 'ands what hath not coddled her own what bore from her own womb. There be good merit in sech keepin's, Thomas, good keepin's but sad fer one whose notions of motherin' lay unfulfilled. An' good it be of Molly to turn 'er 'ands and 'eart to it, keepin' this 'ere ol' tavern the bay's best, what with ghosts and pirates and treasure the talk what fills its timbers. An' takin' account o' them spirits what wander this haunt will pass from 'er, too, askin' who's to be the next keeper?" Brinley asked as he knocked the ashes from his pipe.

"Brinley," Thomas quizzed, missing the last point. "Keepin' treasures hid, and keepin' yer own 'eart to yerself... yew be a man of many secrets."

"Aye, all be the same, each with 'is own secrets. Yet who's to be master of time? None, I say. The feet of Molly's own children are yet to be 'eard upon this structure, the time for bearing near past. Who better than yew to carry on the Tavern's legacy?"

Thomas was thunderstruck. Suddenly his thoughts came together. Aunt Nettie's determination that he become a housewright; Molly's teachings of business and getting to know Newport's merchants; Benjamin's pushing him to get more work done; all saying that learning to be a man of letters was his destiny. It all fell into place for the first time; he was in training to become the next master of the White Horse Tavern.

"Me!" Thomas blurted. "Tavern-keeper!" As he mulled this revelation, the two of them strolled back down Marlborough Street to the Captain's home on the cove, tipping their caps and offering the day's welcome to those they met. Thomas was noticeably quiet as Brinley began another recitation, this one told on their long voyages but with roots unknown to Thomas at the time, now revealed.

"An Old Sailor's Lament," Brinley began.

> All ye young seamen, come hear what's told;
>   Of roving bachelors and mariners bold;
> We tame high seas, gallant sailors to the core;
>   And pirate hearts of fair maidens there on shore.
>
> Now don't let her die, a lonely old maid;
>   Pretty miss of fair keel and tempting gaze;
> Tell that bonny lass, we'll a-merrying go;
>   With song and dance 'neath starlight aglow.
>
> Court winsome girl, your days to merry be;
>   Dash all bewares and loose sails to the breeze;
> Give her your heart, a home for your roost;
>   A warm cottage hearth and soft hand to boot;
>
> A mariner's sigh, as shore sinks from sight;
>   Warm thoughts of her, help splice the blight;

In tender arms, silver and gold won't compare;
    For memories of olde waft long on salt air.

Lest the morrow brings return to the sea;
    Where bold rover's tales be all to achieve;
Riding waves long, gives ponder to thought;
    What distant ventures behind might have wrought.

'Tis a mariner's lot, sailing port to port;
    Long crossings with need in each a cohort;
Better than we, however gallant we plot;
    They better than we for knowing our lot.

'Tis jollies we seek, mere barmaids our best;
    In every port they've seen our old quest;
A strumpet to larboard, a trollop in kind;
    'Tis all that we shall ever hope to find.

With cheer yet knowing, she plays cat 'n' mouse;
    Fetching eyes wanting to get in your blouse;
Sayin' "come roving sailor, come be my own;
    "Lay rest fears of another night alone."

Good memories all, none left untold;
    On long voyages when days are slow;
Beware your young heart, for she steals your soul;
    And cleans your pockets of silver and gold.

When "My saucy sailor," whispers she,
    "Come hither Jack and fear not to make three;
"Frolic with good lilt, bravo your cause be";
    Just another choice for her night's short spree.

A mariner's sigh, as shore sinks from sight;
    Thoughts of fair maiden seeps into the night;
In tender arms, you'd give silver and gold;
    Traded for tossed seas so wet and so cold.

Remember well lads, fair hearts that beckon;
    Yours gets torn 'twixt sea or young maiden;
To cast away one, and yield to the other;
    Leaves the heart knotted in long disorder.

Go down to the sea, then leave all behind;
    Sail fair wind and pray sun to shine;

Yet storm tossed be, sailor's pact with the sea;
   In tempest lost leaves her to lonesome grieve.

Go up from the sea, turn back to siren;
   Where old mariner's souls lay there in;
Gales once fought, 'tis young sailor's delight,
   Another and more makes a withered life.

Young dreams of ventures, the sea's restless call;
   'Tis yours to decide when standing tall;
Listen well young tar, before all is rent;
   'Tis better young lives with warm maiden spent.

This time, Thomas heard new things in Brinley's rhyme, and his thoughts drifted to past adventures, wonderful adventures in the islands. He knew the siren call of the sea from the first port he made and yearned to sail again, but now with concerns far greater than as a young cabin boy.

"More than anything, Brinley, I want to sail with Captain Malbone or Captain Maudsley again. I cannot tell yew 'ow strongly so I wish to be at sea."

"Nay, young Thomas. 'Tis not the sea yew wish to ride; 'tis the ports-o'-call and ventures therein yew seek. Good captains they be, good captains Malbone and Maudsley, and fine ships they sail, the *Sea Nymph* and *Echo*, yet each a merchantman what makes port often in fair climes without sailin' the deep sea. Less fortune sails with a slaver amid each day rank with stench, the stank of foul human filth where yew sails with no glory an' low wages. There be many what sails such, others on the seas with the Royal Navy where yew'll find the sailor's lot be long days and low pay as well, always at the baton o' the officers what rule the day every day."

"A merchantman, Brinley," Thomas interrupted. "To be a sea captain one day with a fine ship, too. There be my 'eart, a true man o' the sea."

"Yew be foolin' yerself, Thomas, rememberin' through a cabin boy's eyes said adventures when sailin' the best there is to sail. Most 'tis not the best; most be old ships what creak an' strain to stay together fer makin' port one more time. Look out in the Bay there, an' tell me what you see, lad. Masts o' ships makin' a forest o' timbers risin' from their anchors, thet be what yew see; wharfs filled with commerce come from far distant ports to Newport, old and new ship alike. Lonesome days at sea be sparked with a few days in port fer unloadin' and loadin' goods, fer trade, fer commerce an' frolic, then back to sea. Beware the spark, Thomas, what leads yer eyes to the sea and missin' the smile of Mr. Drury's young daughter."

"What?" Thomas blurted.

"Yer not seein' what need be seein', Thomas. Walked right by the young miss, what was tryin' to catch yer eye, and didn't see what needed seein' fer castin' yer longin's to sea ventures what's seen in yer mind's eye alone. Look behind as you go, lad."

"Mr. Drury's daughter. Sarah?" Thomas blurted again. He whirled about to see that he had, indeed, not even noticed. The girl and her father were walking in the opposite direction.

Brinley recited again:

Young dreams of ventures, the sea's restless call;
   'Tis yours to decide when standing tall;
Listen well young tar, before all is rent;
   'Tis better young lives with warm maiden spent.

"Weren't jes' sayin's fer long sea days and lonesome nights, Thomas. 'Tis a way o' life yet fer yer own choosin', an' courtin' fer a lady to be yer Molly... a Molly of yer choosin' to take to yer own home be a far better life than cold sea spray and crackers with stale beer and tanky's rum to warm yer innards. Heed me own words and what yew knows to be the sailor's lot, Thomas. There be learnin' in usin' yer eyes fer seein' what need be seein' this day and those soon to come."

Chapter 6

With their sail billowed and Bristol in sight, Thomas masterfully handled the tiller of the *Molly B* while pondering Brinley's continual asking what was the learning in something. The morning's learnings had already been revelations, and sailing with a fair wind from Newport past Hog Island into the shallows of Bristol Bay gave him time to think. Cool sea breezes in his face, the surface of the bay in no more than modest wavelets, helped put his thoughts together into a future with direction that he now recognized more clearly would be guided by Aunt Nettie, the Tavern, Benjamin and Molly rather than his own wanderlust to see the world. His thoughts settled into one fact; Brinley was right, sailing to see exciting ports of call was long lonesome days at sea for a few days in port loading and unloading cargo, then back to sea. He had been on adventure when a cabin boy, a boy living in a small world then, now in a world suddenly bigger and threatening. The breeze helped clear the muddling in his mind into newly recognized facets of his life that had gone unnoticed before, each requiring attention beyond a vivid imagination and yearnings for adventure.

"Brinley?" Thomas asked, disturbing his companion's slumber. "Yew fared well on the *Sea Nymph*, John Damme, tanky, a man of strong arm and will. Yew've got a good 'ouse on the Cove and this fine sloop for fishin' and sailin'. Yew've got netting and cages fer haulin' the catch o' the Bay. And I learnt this day o' yer stash o' findin's in treasure. Why is it that yew never took a wife after missin' Molly?"

Brinley tamped the cold stock in his pipe with his finger, methodically packed another stock into it, and re-lit his pipe with several puffs. "Jes' the way things turned out," he mused. "A plot o' land and fahmin' said plot of ground gave no appeal to me own interests, what bein' a sailor. Drawn to the sea, I was.

"Now near to bein' broken down and lookin' back, John Damme, tanky, Master-at-Arms... all sech sea duties as yew speak means bein' a crusher, and yew knows well, a crusher's duty makes no friends. Yew take notice, Thomas. To this day not a soul from them days past can I say is friend. Not a friend in the world 'ave I from voyages past. Yew knows well, I yet live alone, nary a visitor most o' me days." He paused to take another long draw of his pipe.

"But I does well enough fer an' ol' salt, what with the attention from me neighborly womenfolk who wish me well and gift me from their kitchens fer me own gifts of the bay's bounty, scrimshaw and such, and stories o' places seen." Brinley paused, looked out over the morning. "Lonesome in the evenin's, though. Gone so long, was I, followin' that itch that could not be soothed, never ashore long enough to fancy more than a wench. An' time jes' got by me. After a time early on, I weren't a lad no more. And, fer me, none could measure to Molly. After that, after Benjamin and Molly tied their knot, all me time I kept lookin' for another, but weren't none fer the likes o' me, a salt o' the sea. Truth be known, Thomas, with Benjamin and the Tavern, Molly be far the better than with me, says I. A sailor's life takes a kind...." His voice trailed off. He hung his hand overboard, fingertips slicing through the water as if caressing a mistress. "A sailor I be an' a sailor I'll die. Me own fancy care not no more, but longin' I knows well, lad."

Brinley settled back with nothing more to say and closed his eyes in a doze, the morning sun basking his face with warmth. The gentle wind pushed their craft along as Thomas kept fitting the pieces together. He now knew why Brinley was beset with the gumpers; never a smile on his face, never an inkling of adventure in his outlook; he had nothing to look forward to but an empty house and a cold hearth. Those images crept into Thomas' thoughts; an empty house was uninviting. A cold crept up his spine. He had never known such a feeling, what with Aunt Nettie and Molly making their presence in warmth.

Bristol lay in the distance ahead, and Thomas steered for Merchant's Wharf where a brig lay tied and sundry other boats plied in and out. In those quiet moments gliding toward his destination, he saw the mainland climb from the sea in works of construction that rose from the soil, ships, wharfs, homes and businesses alike. Brinley was right, shore was where seamen took delight.

Then, Brinley sat up with a start. "Hard a-starboard!" he yelled just as a seahorn blared from behind Thomas. "Hard a-starboard!" Brinley yelled again as he lurched over to the starboard gunnel and laid his body weight well overboard, aiding in the craft's sudden change of course. Thomas pushed the tiller to lock and looked over his shoulder to see a brig bearing down on them.

"Ahoy there! Make way!" came a voice through the seahorn.

The *Molly B* laid over to starboard just as the wash of the brig's bow wave arrived and set her to rocking. Her bow dug into the Bay, then rose just to slam back into the surf with each passing wave. Brinley and Thomas held on to keep from being thrown overboard as distance between the *Molly B* and the giant of the sea gradually increased. The dark hull of a water-logged slaver passed near, towering far above. Out of danger. Brinley settled back, his jaw set from the fright. "An' what be the learnin' in thet, Thomas?" he said with a stern face.

For not keeping proper watch while at the helm, lost in his own wanderings and paying no mind to the hazards of the sea lanes, Thomas was speechless with mortification. Without Brinley's quick action, they would be swimming in the splinters of the *Molly B*, his fault, and Thomas knew the learning without doubt. He watched the brig glide on toward Bristol docks ahead and mused, "A better lubber I'd make?"

"Aye," Brinley nodded.

The quiet moments that followed settled the affair, and when passing other fishermen to tie up at the dock, Brinley raised his voice to tell of selling off his catch well under its worth. A strong voice answered, "Yew ol' sea monkey! Ahoy mate!" and Brinley looked up the wharf just as a bearded seaman waved his cap as he strode along its planking, with a companion matching every step. The two exchanged sailor's verbal barbs as Brinley climbed up a nearby wharf ladder. Thomas tied off the *Molly B* and scrambled up behind him to witness the threesome toss the morning.

"Whatever yew've got for the sellin', consider it off yer 'ands now, if it be the marnin's catch," the bearded sailor assured Brinley.

"So it is, fresh as daybreak's dew," Brinley said. Coins and notes changed hands, but his companions seemed to have other business with Brinley.

"Got yer catch by the *Gaspee*, did ye? T'aint easy these days, what with the devil's own eyes of Dudingston and that first mate of 'is, Dundas, they call him, castin' to the horizon fer collectin' dues from our pockets."

"The *Beaver* as well," his companion said with a scowl. "Be it far from me to give quarter to CAPTAIN Linzee, 'e calls 'isself, or to that foul Dudingston. Pirates one an' all, if yew asks me, takin' from skiff and merchantman alike in the SERVICE of the King. Robbin' the sea lanes, I says, one an' all."

"What be the news from Newport?" asked the bearded sailor.

"Same..." Brinley extended an arm to Thomas and drew

him to the threesome. "We 'ave a brave new spirit in our midst. Captain Potter, Captain Swan, meet my fellow Newporter new to our...."

Thomas awkwardly extended his hand for shakes, feeling suddenly a part of more than he knew about.

"Thomas be the dusty of the fine White Horse Tavern."

"Aye," exclaimed the bearded sailor in a moment of revelation. "So it is, the one who lingers and casts an ear to what's said in private."

Thomas suddenly recognized him, an infrequent patron who always sat among the whisperers near the fireplace.

"Sons o' Liberty…" he remarked before thinking. The threesome cautioned Thomas to quiet his voice.

"Aye, now," the bearded sailor whispered. "Some things need be kept close to the chest, young dusty. Tory ears abound."

With a quick exchange of words for a future meeting and the boat emptied, Thomas and Brinley put out into the bay again with the *Molly B* slicing smoothly through the calm water. With Brinley's experienced hand on the tiller, they soon angled onto a stretch of stone strewn shore and crunched to a stop near shore as the water thinned. Climbing out, Brinley motioned for Thomas to follow. There, just beyond the lapping surf lay a masive flat, black rock larger than a skiff.

"There's long been sayin's that this 'ere be Bristol's own Norseman's Rock," he said, pointing to inscriptions on it. He bent closer to the flat side to see the strange markings better. "These markin's still keep their secrets, none 'ciphered so far. Many a good man tried, even sendin' off rubbin's and tracin's to Oxford, but not a soul knows what they mean. Viking markin's o' long times past, most folks say."

Thomas fired a question back. "Tell me Brinley, 'as anybody looked under this rock? It's so big that many men would be required to move it. Just the place to hide pirate treasure."

Brinley shook his head. "Yew be 'opeless, Thomas. We stands on the trail of them Vikings of yore, an' yer mind is arf searchin' out diggin's fer Long Ben's treasure. What runs through your 'ead all the time, lad, nothin' but ventures and pirate treasure?"

"But this be a good place, a good place to 'ide such takin's."

"Back to yon boat, knave." Brinley pointed, shaking his head. "Got much to see, we 'ave, to be back in Newport by eventide."

Sailing along the coastline and by the point, carefully schooning just off the shoals to starboard, Brinley pointed at them saying, "Old writin's say that them Spring Shoals was what Lief of Brattahlid, son o' Erik the Red, wrote about as the mouth of a fair lake." He motioned off to port beyond the shoals into Mount Cove.

"First steps in the New World, they was; thirty-five companions and 'e put ashore 'ere. They set foot first on the Land of Flat Stones they called Hellaland up in New-Found-Land. Seen that land with me own eyes, right inhospitable, that. Unwelcome, too, good reason alone fer 'eadin' to the southward looking fer safe passage from the rocky coast. When comin' to woodland up Nova Scotia way, naming it Markland, they did, Lief and his Vikings landed again, so's the tales say, only to sail on, bearin' close to land to starboard. Sailed their shallow draft long boat, they did, into our Narragansett Bay. Some say the date were of seven hunderd seventy-two years past if datin' from this year. That would be the year of our Lord one thousand. Named one island that pleased him Rhodt Island, meaning Red Island. Claims say this Viking island to be the beginnin's of our own fair colony's name, Rhode Island. Viking it was. Here rose tall forests with much game as far as the eye could see. A rich land o' wonders what the Viking adventurers was first o' Europe's kind to sample. Sailed on, they did, say the chronicles, to a place where a fresh water river flowed out from a lake across shoals, these very shoals as does this Sakonnet River flow from this very cove. They could see further, as we can now, but could go no further until high tide permitted their craft into the Cove they named Hop. Here, the flow ran laden with salmon in lengths and abundance as never seen before, all riches of the sea like none among them ever imagined."

Brinley steered the *Molly B* northeasterly into the cove and pointed out flat-topped Mount Hope. "By learnin' the markin's o' the land, sech as Mount Hope there, takin' its name from Hop, meaning a sheltered inlet from the sea in their tongue, they took note of the lay of the shore and gave descriptions o' their findin's for others to follow. And follow they did, four expeditions, I'm told, come to this cove.

"Being a favored locale where land meets sea, I reckon that Lief an' crew put ashore directly ahead there, and made winter camp in the lee of yon mount. Large shelters they built, dwellin's fer their base fer explorin' further. An' what did they find? Writin's of olde say they found game aplenty in forests thick, with glens of grasses tall, and goodness all about. Fresh water in every direction filled with fishes, too. An' grapes by the cluster. 'Twas 'ere, back then, a land of wonderments what they come to call Vinland, right 'ere it was." Brinley pointed up the Sakonnet. "All up through this land to the neck, they wandered over their winter's venturing, livin' off this land that was as fair a place on this earth as ever seen before or since, a land so fair as nowhere to be found in their icy vastness to the Northward from whence they came."

Thomas was enthralled. Even though he had heard the tales before, and he and the lads had sailed the Bay often enough that he knew every inlet and nook, Brinley's tellings made the stories come to life.

"Storied lot, they be, Thomas," Brinley continued. "What wrapped in furs and hides, with axes and broad swords in hand, accustomed to livin' on the thin edge of survivin' amid the frozen harshness of the North. To them, this was like discoverin' Heaven, to set foot on the promised land of lore, with a steady 'and on the tiller guidin' to this very spot," he emphasized, a point that Thomas understood completely. "And they set their findin's in tales told, some among them hence puttin' the tales to word, what we tell o' yore lo these many a year after them. Me thinks fer certain, this land is nary a look like they saw it back then, what with fahms all about now, their livestock on pastured land that once lay thick with tall timber, long since cut fer building 'ouses, bahns, towns an' such. Wondrous land they saw, rich an' plentiful so that cattle needed no 'ouse feedin' in winter." Brinley patted the gunnel of the *Molly B*. "And timber for buildin' boats and ships of all craft what's sailed the Bay an' beyond on to this day."

Brinley drew an arc of his hand across the horizon at the boats all around, fishermen, merchantmen, ferrymen with sails aloft, billowing in the breeze. "All this is civilizin' the land an' the sea fer high profit, say the bankers in England, them whose richness benefit from steady flows from this wealth around us from our pockets into their pockets, robbin' both the seaman an' the sea. Me own thinkin' be thet them what saw such wonderments and tol' in their venturin' tales would muse about 'ow the land come to ruin in our time. Forests gone, schoolin' of salmon long since put in our feedin' pots so's they come no more, grapes by the cluster, rich and purple from the fine soil and the wahmin' sun growed high into trees on vines all about, now in fahmyards fer tables an' wine-makin', mostly, gone from the wild. Game so well fed on Nature's bounty that their eatin' was better'n the King's own table, now pushed back into the far hinterland where huntsmen go. That's what me thinkin' sees in the old ways, lo so many a year ago. Yet, 'ere it remains in wonderment to this day, people all about a-tamin' the wild what once was. 'Spect that's the will o' our own mankind, changin' the earth. What be the learnin' in thet, Thomas."

"Huh? What?" stumbled Thomas to regain his thoughts.

"You been driftin' off on pirate treasure again, lad? Didn't 'ear a word…"

"Oh! I did, sir. Heard every word, I did. Jes' thinkin' with yer words, me own thinkin' on yer words what made the picture o' them days in my thinkin'. Wonderments o' me own. 'Reckon,

Brinley? Reckon their shelters still lay about?"

"Nay, long since departed. Stones what once rose by their 'ands into structures long since been stacked into foundations of our own buildin'. If they could jus' tell us their stories, them stones. Three winters they stayed with dwellings to account fer their doin's. Liefbooths, they called them, named fer their leader what steered their passage to this fine place. Nothin' left now but the tales."

"The Indians, Brinley. You forgot the part about the Indians," Thomas reminded him, having heard the tales before.

"Ah, the Skraelings. Right you are, lad. Some what come down the lineage to me own grand-daddy's time was only protectin' what was once their own, from generation to generation passed on down, the land worth fightin' to keep but lost. Thorwald, the stories say, met 'is end long about Cape Cod, an arrow shot felled 'im. Then came another of the Viking expeditions to Vinland, this one led by Thorfinn Karlsefne who followed the recollections of Lief an' the tales told. They come to Monthaup, our own Mount Hope here, and settled in long enough for some to trade with the natives an' to take Skraeling wives; took them into their dwellings built up among those left by Lief of his expedition past. Skraeling women, said to be tall like their men, with sallow skin and dark hair long down their backs, their large eyes and broad cheeks said to be of a beauty that the lean Vikings of blond hair and blue eyes saw to their likin's. Their Skareling wives brought many a skill of the wild an' proved to be worthy companions.

"Lo, the moons waxed and waned into the next year when a great numbering of Skraelings grew in hostility and came about to war. Upon their weapons came the first hostility of record between them from the Old World and the New, and from it a lasting memory of Freydisa, Erik the Red's own daughter. 'Aving made the voyage an' wishin' to keep 'er new 'ome in this worthy land, 'er Viking valor rose to the need o' the occasion, an' needy it were. There on the battlefield lay her compatriot, 'is sword rendered from 'is hand to lay idle in a time of grave danger. She, being of 'er father's darin' blood, Freydisa sprang upon the field, 'er mass o' red hair aflow in the air, to grasp the sword in 'and an' strike 'erself across 'er bare bosom, screaming 'er last act in this world a challenge to die in the 'eat o' battle. Such a shrill apparition swinging broadsword with dispatch struck fear in the 'earts o' them Skraelings an' terrified them, an' they left the field. Freydisa saved the day, but with further counsel, she an' 'er fellow Vikings saw their numbers too few to hold against repeated attacks. Thereupon, they left this country to the Skraelings an' returned Northward.

"An' lo, many more the moon has waxed an' waned to this day when their colony, long since forgotten but fer lore, and their blood cleansed from but a drop Skraeling blood, is but tales an' no more.

"Is it all just tales with no memory? Wonder do I of thet memory, however faint an' hinting, that long forgotten facts still reside in lore o' tales told, a drop of truth 'eld by long faded memory in tellin's from peoples to their young an' so on to us. There lay Bristol Rock what we've seen this very day. There be its carvin's clear as the day, and that of Dighton Rock further inland with markin's that baffle still. Each makin' its hint 'tis likely, me thinks, to be their story. Likely so, but mystery long since bears upon their existence; still me wonderin's turn an' say, 'if their inscriptions could be read, what wonders might they tell?' Some say thet the largeness an' flatness of Bristol's rock was their gatherin' place, a shoreline landmark convenient fer seein', whereupon they gathered an' feasted, there to leave markin's fer others to follow. An' follow they did, Lief an' Eric an' Thorwald an' Freydisa an' the others came to this land, for we see the charting o' seas, shores an' land as told in lore still with us."

Brinley took a deep draw on his pipe and gazed about the shoreline. "An' they were beaten away, remainin' only in legend to make no difference. What will our time tell in times hence, Thomas? What difference will we make? Are these difficult times we live now to become the makin's of a new world of our own? Will we succeed, or will we fail as did the Vikings? If we succeed, 'ow will that destiny be manifest? Will we be masters of our own land or no more than the puppets of stranglers from afar who take from us an' from this land fer their own gain?" Brinley looked straight at Thomas, "We face times o' partin' with them what must be beat away. We are the new Skraelings; this is our land now. Will we fight for it?"

As the *Molly B* scraped lightly on the bottom, Brinley continued. "We 'ave before us the shore of Vinland, a place of more than seven hundred years past where peoples o' different ambitions sought new beginnings, yet left no more'n markin's in stone. Will we stand and fight fer liberty from oppression that we of Rhode Island colony know as our own work, or...?"

Brinley recognized that Thomas did not grasp the question. The boy was lost in his own visions of Skraelings and Vikings in battle with images of the screaming Freydisa flailing a broadsword alongside her desperate defenders, her flaming red hair flying in the wind.

Chapter 7

The sun lay gently to the west as Brinley manned the tiller and Thomas raised the sail to schoon back to Bristol. "What be yer learnin' in the day's explorin', Thomas?" he asked.

Thomas, holding onto the mainmast, shrugged and squeezed his stomach. "Me midlins speaks loud fer a spot o' red flannel stew what we boasted about this marnin'." He pulled another nibby from his pocket and gnawed its hard crust into crumbs, then scooped a handful of fresh water from the river to his mouth to softened the crumbs making them easier to swallow. "What do I see? Rocks an' trees an' fahms an' fences… T'ain't no learnin' 'cept in me own thinkin's."

"Aye, so it is," agreed Brinley. "Stories and tales what pricks young imaginin's; therein lay the tellin's what we remembers throughout our livin'. An' just as all before us 'ave done, we looks at the rocks, the land, the sea, an' we walks away into our own times. Only our imaginin's speaks of what hath transpired in past times, an' our tellin's passed on in stories an' writin's to others is all thet history tells us."

Brinley knocked the ashes from his pipe to prolong the moment. "Yet, each day we all contributes our efforts at our own survivin' while keepin' the ship containin' us in order an' on the right course. Each of us doin' 'is part, but some don't see the course. Them what do charts it. A partin' o' ways means settin' a new course, Thomas. Mind yew heed the coming crossroad, an' plot yer own course, lad."

Thomas stood erect, steadied by a hand on the mainmast as he strained to look to the shore all around, and did not answer.

Brinley sighed, his efforts to no avail. "Aye, lost in another world."

The *Molly B* rounded Bristol Point barely schooning the shoals on a falling tide, and Brinley set the tiller for Bristol. Once tied to the wharf, he asked the whereabouts of Captains Potter and Swan, then headed for the Golden Rose, only to learn that they had last been seen at the Boar's Head. Walking Hope Street amid the wafting fragrances of hearths alight with suppertime simmerings gave Thomas' stomach another twist. "Me midlins are in a snit. Reckon we can get a spot o' actin' rabbit with a clagger toppin' at the Boar's Head?"

"Chowder, most likely," countered Brinley.

Thomas' mouth watered at the thought. He could eat just about anything by now.

The heavy door of the Boar's Head swung open to a gathering of sailors among heavy wood tables and chairs, the fragrance of wood smoke and tobacco in the air.

"No Devil Dodgers in this hole," Captain Brinley said to no one in particular.

Immediately recognized, Captain Swan hailed Brinley. "Ahoy, mates. We 'ave in our company the fine an' worthy teller of rhymes, Captain Brinley of Newport. No finer cut o' the jib will ye see in sailorin'. Step to the fire an' shoot us a line, Brinley, another right fair tellin' what yew does so well."

Thomas recognized that Brinley was in welcoming company that knew of his talents. After inquiring of the tavernkeeper about supper, he settled into an out-of-the-way chair and sat back for the show.

"Accepin' no ackers," the keeper said gruffly.

"Aye. Coppers and shillings 'ave I," Thomas said.

The keeper nodded acceptance. "Chowder an' loaf or bangers in the snow? Figgy duff fer afters."

"Chowder, heapin' with Devil's root," Thomas replied, distracted by the welcome that Brinley received. The keeper left and returned quickly with a bowl filled with clam chowder heaped with chunks of potatoes, a small bread loaf laid in it and a tankard of lad's ale to wash it down. Next came a bowl of steamed suet pudding with figs. He handed Thomas a gibby that the boy instantly sank into the chowder for that first mouthful to quench his cravings.

"Now yer bob," the keeper said holding out his hand.

Thomas paid as Brinley stepped to the mantel of the huge fireplace and propped his foot on a log on the hearth.

"'Tis the *Rhyme of the Mariner's Three*," he said. Gazing into space and with a slow crossing of the audience with an extended left hand, he began;

'Twas the bleak fall of '55, when the *Sister Anne* lay splintered/ Dashed on Sankoty sands off Nantucket, first winds of winter.

Mariners three, blown ashore they were by kind Providence hand/ With stout cask of rum nearby, full to the brim and tight of band.

He of massive beard all ashiver, grew warm when that keg to see/ "Ahoy mates," merrily says he, "to the cooper lifted spirits be."

Spake he of the quaint pigtail, cold and shaking now warmed as well/"Belay me hearties, to the ship what bore yon cask o'er fierce sea swell."

Quoth he of the beaked nose and piercing eye, chilled, beaten and sore/"Avast! To the sea what hath borne ship and sound cask to this fair shore."

With head sealed tight, the three rolled leeward on to Nantucket town/Seeking shelter from tempest, grown apace in winter's cold frown.

Humble towncryer, brass bell in hand, spake scant news out so late/"'Tis Tuesday's night," says he. "God willing, morrow will be a new Wends'day."

From atop Seven-Foot Hill, he faintly spied a shadowy three/ Dancing with whoops 'round strange cask, minds drawn from the heavenly.

With bell gripped firm in hand, his hasty retreat to town with tidings to tell/"'Tis Tuesday, the third day. Beware! Comes a sinful three to quell."

At town's edge on Moor's End, did pause once more the mariners three/To broach their cask another, before yielding to new company.

"Heave ho, me hearties," strongly said he of the massive beard/ "To the cooper of good eye and hand, what did fashion our cask here."

"Steady ho, me messmates," loudly spoke he of the quaint pigtail/ "To the ship what safely bore fine cask through pitched storm and gale."

"Stay the course me tars," quoth he of the beaked nose and piercing eye/"To the fickle sea what hath brought ship and cask to this fair isle."

Cried they with boist'rous whoops and cheers, deep thirsts they did slake/Amid howling wind and snow blown athwart, in sheet and cold flake.

On town square with riotous glee, joyous mariners circled their cask/Another round and more for thirsts of three knotty souls their task.

Friends of tranquil isle 'round them came, from warm repose rudely shorn/By rash sounds of whoops and cheers amid brisk wind of chilly morn.

Read town Selectman of thick spectacles, worker of righteousness/ By lanthorn light to mariners three, their town code and behest.

"Banished!" said he, "All strong drink from our fair Isle Nantucket"/ "Waters confiscated and those moved by Devil's voice to gaol lock it."

Much scuffling with sundry craniums cracked, those of mariners three/Low in numbers and libation reduced hauled off to gaol so bleak.

Into gaol on moor's edge, tho of disrepair for long lack of need/ Last held rambling minister of odd faith, a vagrant not to heed.

Towncryer, gaoler, ringer of curfew, keeper of all confiscates/Behind came he rolling cask of Devil's soul into gaol to gate.

Bare boards alone for miscreants, welcomed repose for buffeted three/Soon were buried deep in restful slumber, tempest left in the lee.

Turbulent night and scant pasture, shelter sought of Nantucket sheep/Through open door they came, to crowded repose with the snoring three.

Through wee hours into new morn deep, sea winds blew with piercing blasts/He of massive beard came roused to lanthorn on cask there flickering sat.

"Avast and belay me!" he shouted, and then with raucous vigor once more/Sat towncryer ag'in said cask, his face of fond figure and warm report.

A heavy boot sent gaoler down, arms with affection to surround/Said cask there he caressed tenderly, its base he lay around.

"Well, shiver me timbers!" spat he of massive beard, mates now roused/There gaoler and cask sat, with town's sheep slumbering all about.

"Heave ho and avast!" scornfully cried he of the quaint pigtail/"Blow me down!" he of the beaked nose and piercing eye loudly railed.

Out they ran from windy moor to town square, there to roar lustily/"Ahoy, ahoy and ahoy yet again!" called they to come and see.

Lights in tranquil abode windows appeared, then burgesses did follow/With muskets and lanthorns, out they came into cold morn so hollow.

With no word, mariners three led Selectman and kind to yon gaol/Snarled he of the massive beard. "Snoreth yer gaoler athwart our barrol."

"And sheeps! We mariners three, what logged many gaols in far climes/O'er distant sea swells nor buffeted main, never one such as this kind."

Selectman in faltering tone, spoke well of their gaol and keep/But gaoler fallen from grace wrapped in dark arms lay fast asleep.

Nodding of heads among friends of that isle, "Agreed," they all said/Towncryer and keeper of confiscates had sinned, there lost his head.

A buzz of sympathy passed among them, said bearded friends one and all/For gaol key lay pocket bound with he, subject of the fall.

He who cherished said cask, opened a slit of one eye there to see/Smiling with content, he uttered a most languid and faint "whoopee!"

A mighty oath from he of massive beard, tore through the windy night/The key sought from pocket here and there, with haste then brought to light.

Into Selectman hand the key he placed, "Out with sheep, lock the door!"/There into repose mariners three, turned again from tempest moor.

Yet they of the tranquil isle tarried, for friend with pity and scorn/ "Tho," spoke Selectman with wise thought, bold sight beyond the storm.

"Appearances are thou has erred in drunkenness, with shame has brought/Yet perhaps not of rum, perhaps drained with zeal for duty sought."

"Brothers," spake he. "Concern have I of content if this be rum/ "That has so vainly maligned our dear brother, here lay overcome."

Among those circled, none gave word of dissent, and there relieved/ From gaoler's feeble grasp, a pannikin then dipped in cask to retrieve.

Selectman of heavy spectacles spoke thus, "It hath the taste of rum/"Tho' I of imperfect knowledge ask brothers, dost rum give such hum?"

Each tasted in agony's doubt, then passed to next who so gave doubt/Such was their innocence, all left unsure what rum was about.

As grey dawn grew from distant horizon, bringing moor's new light/ He of the massive beard rubbed eyes and roused amazed at the sight.

There encircling said cask, they of the tranquil isle lay all about/ On barren floor in sundry poses, slumbering as winds blew stout.

"Well furl me mainsail," whispered he of massive beard with broad grin/Beholding said gaol, the brothers and sheep and cask that lay therein.

"Avast ye lubbers," with laughing eyes spake he of the quaint pigtail/"Ahoy," said he of the beaked nose and piercing eye, seeing same tale.

He of massive beard crept to Selectman's hand, the key to retrieve/ And mariners three removed their cask, no brethren roused from his sleep.

"'Tis a Christian act we do," whispered he of the massive beard/ "Undisturbed slumber a deed of charity, locked behind this door here."

Well-hooped cask rolled to harbor shore, soon aboard boat with fair wind/Sailed they from Nantucket isle, whose son's in gaol lay still on moor's end.

"To the cooper who fashioned sound cask," said he of the massive beard/A fond slap he gave their treasure, "to his hand heartily I cheer."

Said he of the quaint pigtail, "Me hearties, belay and stand by!"/ "Heave ho lads!" boldly quoth he of the beaked nose and piercing eye.

Upending their cask tilted and tossed, side to side with great lust/ They came to hearty rage, empty it was! Not a drop issued thus.

    With the last sentence, Captain Brinley bowed as the hushed crowd broke into cheers, one among them hustling a mug of ale into his hand. Back slaps and compliments followed, a tale well told, and for the first time, Thomas saw Brinley smile.
    "With fine thanks to one an' all, I call upons me mate, Captain Potter to follow."
    Further cheers erupted for everyone knew Captain Potter's skill at rhymes. As Brinley planted an elbow on the bar across from the fireplace, Captain Potter took the place where Brinley had stood and said boldly, "Now, ye crusty ol' tars, I shall tell of 'ow a real man of the sea 'andled a wife." He began, "*Blackbeard's Wives.*"

    Legends tell of his fourteen wives,
      Their demands, no poorer could a man be.
    So, pirating he went with Brethren of the Coast,
      High buccaneering on the sea.

    The ghost of one, a fair lass of sixteen,
      Is said to wail "T-e-e-e-a-ch" mournfully.
    Her spirit stirs on a full May moon,
      Hung, she was, from a twisted tree.

Behind his house in Beaufort Town,
   Her tears begged mean Cap'n Teach.
But shadows frolicked in fire's raw flicker,
   They danced Devil's Due, and all did see.

That fury cast her moans on night's wind,
   Her spirit to wander restlessly.
Just another tale, sea dog of them all?
   For storied old Pirate's Lair this be.

"Har!" yelled a patron at the closing line. "Wedlock be the dreaded padlock! Damn the lashin' o' thet infernal ring! To the high seas, I say. An' let thet Dutchman's anchor set!"

"Hear! Hear!" confirmed another voice amid the uproar. "Be well served, lads. Serve first yerself."

Brinley glanced at Thomas with another grin, each of them thinking of his earlier "*Sailor's Lament*" about the loss of Molly.

Another sailor stepped to the fireplace and rendered.

Come me brave lads, let's drink old England dry;
Let's hoist each tankard an' give 'er a try.
'Ere's to 'is 'ealth, that knave King George,
A fine toast in 'opes 'e falls off 'is 'orse.
What does I care if me thought's are but farce,
Nay, just me hopin' 'is fall breaks 'is royal arse.

Rolls of laughter filled the Boar's Head, and tankards were lifted high in cheers. As the frivolity simmered into mumblings of discord with the Crown, another patron stood, swinging his tankard, his cap flat aback. He slapped his companion on the back, and recited;

Bonny young milkmaid, so buxom an' gay;
Now our knave Jack 'ere's lookin' for play.
Best stand clear, Jack, there's trouble I say;
'Tis bailiff's daughter out from 'is reach this day.

"Oh ho!" chuckled another sailor, thet be a galley packet what'll get the scuttlebutt a flowin'. Mark me own words, lads. T'ain't a finer filly in Bristol, but t'ain't a meaner bailiff what watches o'er her."

An unidentified voice rose saying;

When I was young, many troubles I got;
One day in May, I even lost me pot.

> In childhood played, together we did;
> Lost 'er to another, sadly I did.

More chuckles followed as Thomas looked at Brinley again, knowing what was on his mind. Brinley rubbed his whiskers just as another voice buried from within the crowd sang out;

> Now let us be jolly, drive off all melancholy.
> 'Tis a fair glory hole here, fer an eve o' folly.
> A spot o' ale or a dash o' rum;
> Lift yer fists mates, make yer bellies hum.

"Hear! Hear!" confirmation rang out, and many lips were parted. Inspired by the moment, a scruffy old sailor of diminutive size stood to ask;

> Aye, lads, drink up an' drown all sorrow.
> Ahoy, mate, a bob might I borrow?

"Hmmm?" he pleaded, not a copper in his pocket.

"Tis but ol' Jack Strop we 'ave 'ere, lads," a sailor nearby said, pulling the old man down into his chair. "Ol' Jack, what's not worth a dash of Lots Salt on deck, even with a mop, but what can drink any one o' us under the table when another man pays."

While everyone laughed, Thomas noticed Brinley handing a coin to the keeper and whispering to him. A tankard of ale quickly wound up in front of the old man. Brinley's voice sounded over all, "Farewell mates. Eventide approaches an' Newport calls."

Laying foot to State Street, the pair was soon into Bristol Bay with the dipping of the sun. Under sail toward Hog Island and Newport with a soft breeze filling her sails, the sun glistened off Bristol Bay's ripplets. Brinley steered into open waters of the Narragansett, then noticed, in the distance, a sleek two-masted schooner that lay hard with the wind. He scowled, "*Gaspee.*"

"What?" Thomas asked, breaking his mental flights of fancy while looking back at Bristol.

"There, off to port ahead," Brinley pointed.

Thomas sprang to a new position for a better view and shielded his eyes from the sun's reflections off the water. Seeing a packet further up the Bay also under full sail, Thomas assessed the moment with surprise, "'E's givin' chase!"

Brinley clambered up on a thwart to see better, and the two of them watched as the *Gaspee* closed on the craft well ahead.

"Is thet the *Hannah*?" Thomas mused out loud. "Yes, I'm sure of it. Thet's Captain Lindsey's boat, the *Hannah*... I've seen it often in Providence waters... an' this mornin', when the captain was comin' in to the Hive, I almost knocked 'im on 'is beam ends. Ran right into 'im, I did. Sailin' fer Mister Brown, 'e is."

Everyone near and far knew of the company of Nicholas, Joseph, and John Brown, whose family and their commerce had become a cornerstone of Narragansett trade. Brinley squinted and shielded his eyes as well. Taking his looking stick from his pocket he stretched it to one eye and scowled, "Thet scoundrel Dudingston! What business hast 'e for chasin' a merchantman?"

A large white cloud emerged from the forward gun port of the *Gaspee* and a huge spray of water erupted well astern of the *Hannah*. Brinley could not believe his eyes. "The bloke is firin' on 'im! What in blazes is 'e doin?"

Thomas was enthralled. He had only heard of sea battles and had never seen a cannon fired in anger. A resounding BOOM! reached the *Molly B.* Awestruck, the pair in the small craft stared in disbelief as the report echoed again and again across the bay. As the *Hannah* disappeared northward beyond Pappasquash Point, the *Gaspee* closing, Brinley pulled the tiller of the *Molly B* hard a-port. The sudden change of course nearly tossed Thomas into the drink, but grasping the mainmast tightly, he hardly noticed as he watched the *Gaspee* sail up the Bay after the *Hannah* toward Pawtuxet and further on to Providence.

Brinley steamed, "Firin' on a merchantman! Thet John Bull... damned be 'is 'ide. There'll be no dodgin' Pompey on this one, bearin' 'is guns on a merchantman."

Steering straight back to Bristol and a hasty tie up, the pair was soon on the wharf spreading news of Dudingston's deadly turn. Townsmen had heard echos from the cannon but did not know their origin, and once told, the *Gaspee* laying chase to a well known and respected commercial packet flamed into the talk of the town. Captain Brinley headed straight for the Boar's Head where he knew he would find Captains Potter and Swan still downing ale and stuffing more bangers dipped in ketsiap, that new and tasty paste of love apples and spices that had recently become the rage. Up the wharf he went for Pike's Alley across from DeWolf's slave warehouse just off State Street with Thomas in tow, and just able to keep pace with each of Brinley's determined steps. Along the way, not a word was exchanged as Brinley huffed his anger. They marched by the warehouse, its foul odor well known to them, and turned down the alley, then through the door of the Boar's Head.

After a quick exchange, Captain Swan, the best horseman of the three, was off to Providence to tell of the sightings, to ride forthwith carrying the contempt of Bristol's Sons of Liberty for Dudingston and the *Gaspee*.

Chapter 8

Onboard the *Gaspee*, Lt. Dudingston boasted proudly, "I shall have the scoundrel, Mr. Dickinson. Keep to the chase!" He yelled down the deck, "Chief Gunner, charge your guns. We shall fire a last warning. Damn these Yan-Kee Rhode Island scum, Mr. Dickinson. Damn them! Damn them all! Pirates to the last. Not a decent man among them." He snarled. "Another 'captain' shall cower before me. He'll heave to or I shall make splinters of his freeboard."

Midshipman Dickinson observed, "She has the wind, sir."

"Curse the wind, Mr. Dickinson! We have greater sail, and I shall set upon her with the vengeance that is mine." Yelling across the deck, he commanded, "Bo'sun, arm the crew. We shall board the rogue. Fire the brand as well."

With all eyes upon the *Hannah* ahead, being reeled in by the faster *Gaspee*, the crew readied with arms to grapple and board. The sails of the British revenue schooner bloused full, as did Dudingston's chest.

The crew of six on the *Hannah* watched the *Gaspee* close with increasing concern. At the rudder, Captain Benjamin Lindsey grew increasingly alarmed at the prospects of chancing the run. Knowing that the ship's manifest had been cleared of revenue in Newport just hours earlier that day, he saw no need to heave to for the *Gaspee*. "Make all the sail she can, lads," Lindsey commanded, "or Dudingston will have us. Damn his pirating hide."

A deeply distressed young crewman ran to Lindsey saying, "Captain, sir. The Lieutenant will likely press me to 'is service, sir. I shant be want to do 'is bidding."

"Nor I, lad," Lindsey confirmed. "Fetch me musket. If the blaggard boards me, I shall fight his thieving to the last."

The nervous seaman was not convinced. "A musket be a small arm agin 'is cannon, sir."

"Right you are. Yet, our day is not done." Captain Lindsey felt the wind and took stock of the lowering tide. "Belay me last. Let me musket be. I want no part of Dudingston's evil. We shall stay to the lee and put in at Pawtuxet." Noting the shallows that he knew well, he reconsidered. "Nay. We shall stay off the bow so's to keep from her guns an' lead her onto the sand at Namquit. Are ye with me, lads?"

Cheers erupted from the small crew as they leaped to their duties and ran up a topsail, knowing that their low-draft packet was sure to gain the advantage as the Bay shallowed.

Onboard the *Gaspee*, Lt. Dudingston, shook his fist furiously. "She's putting on sail. Damn the heathens," he cursed as he turned to the sailor at the tiller. "Steersman, come about to port. We shall put the devil to starboard." Yelling across the deck, he commanded his crew to ready for battle. "Gunners, bring your guns to bear. Fire to stern a warning."

The boom of the cannon horrified Captain Lindsey and his crew, horror that was further amplified when the shot erupted into a tall plume of exploding water behind them. "My God!" Captain Lindsey exclaimed. "The rogue is firing on us! Damn 'is wretched soul. The man is daft as a loon, firing on a merchantman."

One of the crew shouted, "I 'ave great fear that 'e shall have us, sir. Wot shall we do?"

"We are not yet in his clutches, lads. We need only lead 'er to Namquit, then I shall leave the scoundrel high on the Point." At that, Lindsey assessed the water's depth as land slowly approached ahead. He steered a line to remain in front of the British schooner, avoiding the hazard of a broadside from her swiveling culverins. Looking back at the *Gaspee* and shaking his fist in plain view, he mumbled, "Hold to the chase, yew bastard."

Lindsey's display infuriated Lt. Dudingston. "Curse the shipwright who built this ship without a bow-chaser. Mister Dickinson, let that be a lesson to you. The value of a forward gun is shown in just such a case as this. The scoundrel simply plies to your bow and you have no offense. Damn the shipwright and this heathen as well!"

Escape of the *Hannah* looked increasingly doughtful, and Dudingston sensed that he had the ship in his grasp. Flush with the feeling of conquest, he observed, "She's laying in for Pawtuxet. I have her, Dickinson. By God, I have her! Bo'sun! Set to the branding iron. I shall mark every cask and keg of this pirate, and its 'captain' as well, if I were not a gentleman. Steersman! Ply to her port. We shall heave her to before she can make Pawtuxet."

Dickinson was not so sure. "Not to question, sir. The draft, sir. The tide be thin."

Dudingston grasped a line and leaned into the wind, urging his craft on. "Damn the draft, Mister Dickinson. By my King's commission, I shall have the rogue. This one shall not escape me. Bo'sun! Prepare to grapple. Heave her to off the starboard bow."

Captain Lindsey smiled to see his plan working. With the first sound of the *Hannah's* hull scraping sand, he pulled the tiller hard to port as crewmen laid their weight along the starboard gunnel making the course change more abrupt.

Now near to hearing range, Lt. Dudingston called out through his seahorn, "Damn you, Yan-Kee. Heave to or risk your goods, your ship, and your crew." Receiving no response further enraged him and brought another admonishment to Dickinson. "Once again these impudent colonists defy the law of the sea. I should hang them all, if it were my will."

Satisfyingly, Captain Lindsey scowled back at his adversary, "We shall see who is the better man, Dudingston." As the *Hannah* turned out into the Bay, he yelled back to the British vessel, "I shall leave yew, sir."

The larger *Gaspee* could not maneuver as quickly and slowly heaved over to starboard to continue pursuit just as a sudden shudder shook the ship. Its keel ground hard into the sandy bottom on Namquit Point, just where Captain Lindsey planned. All onboard were thrown off their feet, and loose ship's wares flew about the deck.

Lt. Dudingston sprang to his feet and ran forward, shaking his fist at Lindsey, yelling, "I shall see you hang, you bastard! Hang, from the highest yard arm. You hear me? I am in the King's service. You'll hang if it's the last thing I do in these waters, Yan-Kee."

Captain Lindsey tipped his cap as cheers erupted from the *Hannah's* crew, followed by a hearty laugh as they sailed on, soon out of sight.

Several miles up river, *Hannah* crewmen tossed the boat's fenders to tie up at Town Wharf in Providence while the crew wildly exclaimed of snaring the *Gaspee*. People flocked to the wharf to catch the news, and John Brown, a stout man short in stature, followed by two other men employed by the Brown family merchants worked their way through the crowd to meet with Captain Lindsey.

"Is it true Benjamin," he asked excitedly, "what is being said of the *Gaspee*. Grounded?"

Captain Lindsey was apprehensive with his reply. "All true, I am afraid, Mr. Brown, sir. Though, I shall hang for it, if Dudingston gets 'is way, the devil's own way, I fear, what with 'is claimin' King's service. We saved yer ship and cargo from 'im, all legal stamped at

Queen's Hive, but I fear I shall hang for riskin' the run."

Brown recoiled. "Surely you must be mistaken, Benjamin. Hang you say. Surely not!"

With a discouraged tone, Lindsey further voiced his concern. "'E 'as seen me, sir. Come the morning tide, 'e will be off the Point, an' I fear that 'e will set upon me. Certain of it, I am, sir."

Another man, Abraham Whipple, a sea captain, worked his way through the crowd to join them. Behind everyone, a line of slaves in chains newly arrived from Africa trudged into a warehouse, the door closed behind them. Whipple scolded abrasively, "What in God's name have you done Lindsey? The King's wrath be upon us for this. It is not enough that the Crown taxes us into slavery and steals our commerce, now the King's loathsome inquisitors will try us as pirates and sea-rovers."

Brown intervened. "Nay, Abraham. Dudingston has Benjamin. He has seen him."

Shocked, Whippled grasped Lindsey's arm, "Praise be to heaven, no, Benjamin. Tell me it is not true."

"Alas, 'tis true, my friend, every word of it."

Whipple turned to Brown, "We cannot allow the scoundrel the satisfaction, John. What shall we do?"

Brown, thinking out loud, agreed. "Aye. A bit of a sticky wicket we have here. Dudingston will claim a King's commission, we can be certain of that, if he has it. If not, he won't set foot off his ship for fear of arrest. Even the Governor knows not of his commission, I am told. However, Admiral Montagu has assured the Colony House that Dudingston is within his right. If that be the case.... Sadly, I am afraid Dudingston will likely come for you, Benjamin. Perhaps you should consider retiring to the interior for a bit."

"Me missus, John. She cannot travel, and how will a sea captain survive behind a plow?"

"Aye. Right you are. We shall think upon it." Reconsidering, the five of them chatted among themselves as a plan materialized. Brown confirmed their decision. "You have done well, Benjamin, well, indeed. Snaring this rogue is just the opportunity we need." He turned to one of the men who had arrived with him, Ezek Hopkins, saying, "Secure the use of the best longboats, Mr. Hopkins. Captain Whipple will secure the town's drummer. We shall collect ourselves at... at, Sabin's Tavern just up from Fenner's Wharf at six bells, seven o'clock. Quickly now. We have tasks to attend to forthwith. Captain Whipple will send a rider to Warwick for Nathaniel Greene, Jacob and Rufus, or their appointed. As you well know, they have dealings with Dudingston in the courts with his taking of their ship and its goods to Boston in violation of the law. We shall discourse upon the matter in their company."

As Whipple hastened away through the crowd, a thin, frail old man who had heard the commotion and wondered what was underway followed some distance behind. Clear of the dock, Whipple came upon Dr. John Mawney, a young but learned man of stature, on his way to the wharf to inquire as well. The thin man ducked into an alley to listen as the two talked.

Whipple, excitedly, waved Dr. Mawney to the lee of a nearby building. "Great good fortune has come to us. Dudingston's stupidity has left him aground on Namquit Point. Our good *head sheriff*," he winked, "has a plan to seize him for the claims in the courts for the pirating of Mr. Greene's craft and its cargo among other claims of graft we know all too well."

In the alley, the thin man listened intently.

Dr. Mawney was appalled. "Seize him? An armed ship of the line? Come now, Captain. Surely you are not suggesting that merchantmen are the better of Dudingston and his crew?"

"I am, indeed."

Dr. Mawney recoiled with alarm. "My God, man! A hail of gunfire will be your reward. If not a musket ball, then the noose. You can be sure of that in these difficult times with the Crown."

Whipple pounded his fist into his palm. "So be it, then. Or the hell he brings to our commerce will be ours in greater proportions. We have now a rare opportunity to strike a blow in the name of law or bend at the knee to continued whipping of injustices the Crown heaps upon us with the likes of Dudingston and his dastardly ways. We haven't a moment to lose."

Dr. Mawney, impressed with Whipple's conviction, smiled. "This will be quite an undertaking, sir."

"Good. I was certain that we could count on you," surprising Dr. Mawney.

"Count on me? What on earth for?"

"We are in need of a rider of your stature to take the message quickly to the brothers Greene in Warwick who have proceedings in the court against Dudingston. We shall meet at Sabin's Tavern at six bells to discourse on the matter."

Not yet convinced, Dr. Mawney wondered, "Is this another of your Tory hunts, Captain? I shall be cursed to be drawn into it."

"Cursed you are, my friend, as all of us will remain if we do not shake the King's yoke from our necks. The die is cast. We shall be freed by fire alone. We must act and act now while the opportunity beckons."

Thinking quickly, Dr. Mawney complied, "Curses of the witch Cutty Sark pale beside my thoughts of the dangers we enter. Nevertheless, sir, I shall ride to Warwick forthwith and return."

The thin man in the alley smiled to learn of the plot and fondled his coin purse, thinking about the riches soon to be gained. He snickered, "I shall soon fill thee with the King's gold."

Dr. Mawney turned to his horse tied nearby as the thin man slipped from hiding and almost collided with Captain Whipple on his way back to the wharf. Whipple grabbed him by the collar, "Inquiring of another man's business from the shadows, are ye?"

The thin man became fearful. "Nay, good captain. Just a cobbler plying me trade."

"Do I not know you? You are the Massachusetts shoemaker newly arrived from Mendon, with your son apprenticed. Ramsdale, are you not?"

"Aye, I be the same, Captain. A fine set of boots I make for ye, sir. Suitable for the good Captain. Hmm?"

Whipple was suspicious of the man's motives. "I shall expect to see you among us, sir."

The thin man shuddered with fear. "Nay, kind sir. I am but a frail man. I cause you no harm. Only a simple cobbler am I. You know of my shop. You know of me. Please, sir. I beg of you. I am but...."

"Yes, yes. I know of you indeed, and where to find you, should the need arise," he emphasized. "Be gone with you."

The thin man scampered off as the captain marched briskly toward the wharf, then reconsidered. With an about face, he stepped quickly along to the home of one-eyed Crooch and knocked on the door. Old Crooch, hump-shouldered in his tattered French and Indian war overcoat, opened the door slightly to peer out. From his unshaven and unshorn countenance, a mouth of only a few teeth, he scowled, "Wot be yer need of this 'ome?"

"Peter," Captain Whipple said, "We are in need of your services forthwith, sir. We must have your drumming about the Commons and the Square." The old man flung open the door, brightened with his call to arms, especially so when a shilling passed into his hand.

"Aye, sir. Wot be the nature of me drummin's?"

"Around the town center... we must be called to Sabin's Tavern at six bells. With urgency, Peter. The evening nears, and shops are closing upon a matter of grave concern. You must go about with drummings of Training Day. An' do not be quick to return home. We must be certain that the word is spread widely."

Soon out the door with his old tri-cornered army hat a-cock on his head and already drumming, Crooch set off toward the Commons while beating out a cadence that quickly drew the attention of nearby boys and passersby. The boys fell in tow as Crooch passed the home of Deputy Governor Sessions who looked out a window to see what was going on. Seeing the boys, he concluded it was just more of their play.

"Hear ye! Hear ye! All hail! Training Day and town meetin'! Sabin's Tavern! Six bells!" Crooch repeated over and over, emphasizing each phrase with a drum roll. As he made his rounds people gathered, with the *Gaspee's* grounding the first exchange of news and each teller with his own ideas about what should be done. With the Town Crier drumming out Training Day in the setting sun, the town took on an excited air. Passing Sabin's Tavern, glances from patrons within made for passing conversation, presuming that the boys were up to high times before suppertime.

A rider arrived at the Commons just as Whipple passed and hailed him. "Captain Whipple, sir," he yelled to get the captain's attention. "A word with ye, sir."

"Aye, in good time, to be sure, Captain Swan. Your arrival is most fortunate. We have the *Gaspee* aground on Namquit Point."

"Aground!" Captain Swan exclaimed. "Well now, thet be fitting retribution. I 'ave arrived to tell of Dudingston firing on a merchantman."

"Right you are, sir, Captain Lindsey's *Hannah* it were. The tale began with his arrival within the hour, an' our town is in a flurry over it. Come, we shall discourse on the matter."

A distant bell rang in pairs of two beats. "Four bells, Captain Swan," Whipple said. "We have but an hour to come to terms with the day."

In quick conference, Captain Swan was back on his horse setting a rapid gait back to Bristol. Along the wharfs among gatherings of men here and there, the topic on their lips was the *Gaspee*, but as Training Day always did, citizens of Providence turned out, some with muskets and powder horns, each man ready to do his duty. Main Street along the wharfs rapidly became a beehive of activity as the dinner hour drew patrons to Sabin's and other public houses, as usual for the time of day. Gentlemen of the area, travelers seeking overnights, and businessmen on travel made their way up the steps of his tavern making no particular note of the evening. Old Crooch continued his drumming around the town center, the Commons, along the wharfs, among boys marching about and excitedly drilling in militia fashion.

A half-hour passed and as five bells rang out, a group of men collected at the head of Fenner's Wharf across from the tavern heatedly exchanged debate of Dudingston's actions.

"Dudingston is a common thief, I say," said one man forcefully. "He bade 'is crew steal me best sow for their table, 'e did. Stole me firewood chopped meself, said to belong to the King, 'e did. Where be yer English law to thet, I say? A rascal 'e is. Takes in the name of the Crown offerin' no pay. Outright piratin', thet!"

"And what of our own Rhode Island law?" another man added. "Dudingston claims a King's commission, above our law 'e sees 'isself. The pirate stops every ship, even oyster boats, and seizes our commerce. Rufus Greene can tell you that; 'is schooner, the *Fortune*, and cargo taken. Crewed on it, I did. Twelve hogsheads of rum, stolen an' branded, I tell you, an' sent to Boston instead of Newport for disposition, contrary to law. Took the *Fortune* for sale, too. Outright thievery, that. The rascal showed no authority but 'is uniform an' a saber, come aboard an' knocked our good Captain to the deck, saber drawn agin 'im, an' confined 'im to quarters while we was taken under tow. I 'ears that even the guv'ner is set to bring the tyrant to justice."

Another in the gathering proclaimed, "Aye! 'E's but a stinkin' sea rover among us preyin' on our commerce, 'e is. We oughts to 'ang the rascal, 'ang the thieving rover, I say."

"Don't listen to this old sailor and his tales," another argued. "Beware the ground ye tread, good friends. We be talking treason now, and hangin' be our fate. The Crown done stationed his revenue ships to afflict our commerce. Do ye wants troops takin' over the town, too?"

That thought quieted the crowd. What to do about Lt. Dudingston was not so clear beyond boasting. Yet, everyone felt the temper of the day growing to do something to show their long festering discontent.

The first man returned to his view. "Me thinks 'im a scoundrel unfit for the company of Thomas Tew or William Mayes the younger, or ol' Long Ben 'isself. Gentlemen pirates they was, with riches taken from them what could afford it, the Grand Mogul in the Red Seas. Me own granddad, God rest 'is soul, sailed with Mayes, 'e did. This rascal is but a common rogue, a thievin' common rogue, says me."

"Aye, all true," his adversary continued. "Lest we forget, good citizens, Cap'n Kidd had a commission. Hanged he did, no different than a common rogue danglin' at the end of a rope, even with the Lord's pardon. These men o' law what the King surrounds hisself and sends into our midst, they brings verdicts what puts nooses around the necks of fine citizens, all said by law courts to be rogues. Take heed, friends; never forget Black '23 down the Bay there in Newport, I say. Hanged me own uncle, they did. Seen 'im die, I did. Just a wee lad, I was then. Hanged 'im, they did."

The first man ignored the warning. "Take the no good rover, I say, an' see for ourselves if 'e 'as a King's commission! Me thinks the matter be resolved by the Guv'ner 'isself. Doing our duty, thet be, fine citizens one and all. Present the both of them to Joseph

Wanton, the 'ighest law. Who's with me?"

Cheers erupt just as John Brown, Abraham Whipple, Captains Lindsey, Hopkins and other men of Providence walked quietly through the crowd and up the steps of the Tavern to the large southeast room. While some citizens remained outside and continued arguing, others followed inside, some with their muskets and powder horns. Once inside the room, John Brown stoked embers in its fireplace until they glowed with heat. When the door closed behind the gathering, he and Abraham Whipple quieted everyone.

"Gentlemen," Mister Brown began. "We have a most serious problem to attend to. We all have heard from Captain Lindsey that the *Gaspee* rests aground within striking distance from where we stand. However, we know that Lieutenant Dudingston has seen our good captain, and if I am any judge of his character, I am certain that he will seek his revenge."

The crowd offered its disapproval.

"Gentlemen, gentlemen, please. We must prepare for action with little time. I have received word from Jacob and Nathaniel Greene. As you know, they have complaints in the courts against Dudingston who eludes process of law, to the great loss of their goods, and, I suspect, greater losses to all of us that will transpire when the *Gaspee* floats free in the morning tide and Dudingston begins his vengeance."

Someone in the crowd yelled, "Arrest the scoundrel. That's wot I say."

Another among them offered, "Burn the blasted schooner. That'll stop 'im."

A chant erupted, "Remember the *Liberty*. Remember the *Liberty*. Remember the *Liberty*."

Loudly, Mister Brown cautioned, "Gentlemen, if you please!"

A voice in the crowd rang out, "Cut 'er masts an' set 'er adrift. Sent 'er crew packin', we did. An' wot did the bloody King give us? Nothin', 'cause 'e couldn't find us. Burned the *Liberty* right there in Newport harbor under the cover of night, we did."

A different voice joined in, "Dudingston's been a pain in the arse for too long now. This is our chance to snare 'im, thanks to Cap'n. Lindsey. Three cheers for Cap'n Lindsey."

As cheers erupted, Captain Whipple worked his way to the door to answer a knock. Several more men came in. He responded to the cheers in a firm voice to quiet the crowd. "We believe that the law is with us. You have, no doubt, read the remarks of Chief Justice Stephen Hopkins, the brother of Ezek here; Lt. Dudingston has failed to uphold his sworn duty of an officer of the Crown by not presenting his warrant to the Governor. Nay, he has yet to present his papers of commission he claims to have to any governing body of this colony. If he has no commission, many among us think his actions that of piracy."

A voice yelled, "We should get the scoundrel's papers an' see fer ourselves, cap'n!" The crowd agreed.

Captain Whipple motioned for quiet. "Governor Wanton has repeatedly expressed his discontent with Dudingston's actions to no avail. Yet, it is said, Admiral Montagu is in full accord with Dudingston. Thus, there is much confusion on point of law in this matter. What is contested is a simple question; Are we ruled by the King's military or courts of law? Furthermore, which courts of law, our own or those of the Crown? That is the issue, gentlemen. With no state of martial law declared, we believe our own courts of law must prevail. However, since affairs of the *Gaspee* remain without doubt to us all that her crew exercise themselves lawlessly, we conclude that Dudingston operates outside the dominion of any commission. We may, however, be quite incorrect about the matter, certainly in the eyes of Admiral Montagu."

Another voice asked, "Wot would yew 'ave us do then, Captain? Let 'im loose when 'e is near to our grasp?"

Murmers of discontent and calls for action swept the assembly.

"Beware, gentlemen. The Admiral claims superior authority to law, claimed to be the highest authority in the land, authority exercised on his own accord as administered by his crews who answer only to him, quite independently of our colonial law."

A voice blurted, "Wot be the need o' law, then? We agrees to abide by wot we knows to be the good for us all, written law o' the land. Thet be the real law, I say!"

"Hear! Hear!" the crowd agreed.

Captain Whipple motioned everyone to calm their voices and said with firm conviction, "However, we conclude that we are in the right to snare the scoundrel for due process of law."

Everyone agreed as a voice called out, "Well then, Cap'n. Let's haul 'is 'ide before the court fer the law to decide," and was confirmed by the combined voices of the other men.

John Brown agreed, "Action it is, then."

The crowd cheered the decision as Brown quieted them to hear the plan.

"This being Training Day," he said, "our actions must remain collected and usual. We shall mold bullets and similar matters of drill. Our purpose is as follows: we seek volunteers for an expedition. We shall lead a raid upon the *Gaspee* for the purpose of capturing Dudingston to present him to the court of Rhode Island."

The crowd erupted with approval, but Captain Whipple cautioned everyone to remain quiet. "We need not loudly tell of our mission, and neither can we fail, for if we do fail, rest assured that we will be hunted down and tried as traitors to the Crown. We speak of what the Admiral has warned against, treasonous acts, my friends, and if captured we shall be executed at the will of the King and his court. The Tories among us have eyes and ears for the Crown. We must succeed, and we must keep our senses and go about our task forthrightly. Tell not of your enterprise, but perform your chosen task with haste as honest men of integrity. Who is with us?"

Slender, nineteen year old Ephraim Bowen stood forward, "I shall be proud to accompany your expedition, sir." He grasped the lapel of his friend next to him and pulled him forward as well. "And be it known that Joseph Bucklin will man the attack as well." Bucklin was in the midst of pulling on his knit cap and was taken by surprise.

The crowd laughed as each man, one by one volunteered in an expression of unity. It was a proud moment. Unnoticed, a thin man at the rear of the room slipped out the door.

"Captains in my employ know the waters well. We shall have six long boats, one or two additional boats will join us down river. Assign yourselves to the boat of your choosing along Fenner's Wharf. Once on the river, Captain Whipple will guide the line on the right, Captain Hopkins the line on the left. They shall guide us to the shallows of Namquit Point and lead us to success. I give you the Captain."

The crowd offered confirming approvals.

"You have, no doubt, heard Admiral Montagu's threats," Captain Whipple said. "He has sent a warning to the Colony House in Newport upon hearing news of outfitting a vessel to fend off the *Gaspee* and the *Beaver*. Steel yourself against his threats to hang anyone so doing as traitors to the Crown, rogues one and all to hang as common criminals. I caution you again, do not take our actions lightly. We venture into life and death, first at the hand of Dudingston and his crew in defense of their vessel, and secondly from condemnation by the King's ranking commander in the colonies. Reassess your involvement for the last time, gentlemen, for we have little time to prepare. None among you will be thought less of a man should you walk beyond that door."

No one in the crowd moved.

"The rascal needs 'is whippin'," a voice declared. Another joined in. "We stands with you, Cap'n."

Captain Whipple surveyed the gathering, "Succeed in our mission we must do. And afterwards, each of us must fade back into our normal duties of days following without braggings, knowing nothing but hearsay, or such will bring the King's men upon us."

Each man knew clearly what was expected of him, and each stood firm, knowing that the men beside him now held measures of their fate in common. "Aye, Cap'n," someone said. "'Tis time for action." Everyone agreed.

"So be it then," Captain Whipple said. "We shall cast off well after nightfall and be joined by boats from Warwick and Bristol on our approach. Each boat captain shall have a guise. I, the Sheriff of County Kent. We shall approach the Gaspee from the bow to avoid her side-mounted guns and her aft swivel guns. Upon survey of our assembly at the ship, I shall speak first as Sheriff, engaging to arrest Lieutenant Dudingston. That will be your signal to board. Do so rapidly. Move to capture the crew, but take care not to cause injury, for that is not our purpose. We shall exercise our chosen path with determination but without ravage. We shall take the crew, bind them and transport them to the cellar of the gambrel-roofed house off Still-house wharf in Pawtuxet village, adjacent to Benjamin Smith's shipyard. The cellar is to be their quarters for further disposition. The clouds give us a moonless night, much to our advantage. The tide is low 'til the morn. Our good *high sheriff*," he motioned to John Brown, "having once been grounded on that very spit of land, knows the shallows well. Thus, gentlemen, we have but a few hours to do our bidding. Surprise shall be our foremost weapon. Muffle your oars and locks carefully, make not a sound. Each boat captain will take his boat to within grappling distance, or upon the sand of the Point if the tide is sufficiently low. I fear that we shall engage their fire, perhaps not of cannon but musket and sidearm. Thus, we shall have a surgeon among us. Pray his services will not be needed. God speed, gentlemen."

With the plan in place, each man settled into preparations. Raiders-to-be set to melting lead in the fireplace, molding bullets, and readying their weapons.

Onboard the *Gaspee*, sails furled for the night. Lt. Dudingston strode impatiently on deck as he viewed the last red glow of sunset.

"Sailor's delight be damned," he scoffed. "We sit perched like a plump goose for the taking. Damn this wretched bay," he cursed. Shaking his fist at the sunset, he threatened, "I shall have the pleasure of seeing that scoundrel hang from the gallows on Long Wharf. I shall enjoy my gaze upon the foul stench of Newport snobbery. I shall! I shall, indeed!" he snarled as he hacked the deck with his saber.

Growing increasingly impatient, he yelled, "Bo'sun!"

From overboard, Boatswain Johnson answered, "Aye,

Captain."

"Have your dubbers scrape the hull well, for we shall set upon them on the morrow with the speed of the fisherhawk."

Johnson climbed the rope ladder hanging over the gunnel, "Beggin' yer pardon, sir. We've tried hard to pull anchor to get us off the sand, without success. And we've scraped the barnacles off all around, twice at yer command, sir. Me men, sir, well, we be wet an' the chill be upon us. I fear Caple's already got the cough, an' Cheever, sir, he's overcome with a mighty shiver. We are of no more benefit to the hull. Beggin' yer leave, sir. A spot of tea to warm the soul be a fine reward for our labors."

"Yes, yes. As you will. A fine job, I am sure. Double grog for the crew. Tomorrow we shall feast upon mutton fresh from the pens of Providence Plantations." Turning aft and yelling, "Dickinson!" brought the young midshipman muttering to the deck.

"Set the watch, Mr. Dickinson," Dudingston ordered.

"Aye, sir. Dublet, sir?"

"Yes, yes.... Nay, a single man-o-the-watch should be sufficient." He grasped the starboard railing with both hands and spit onto the sand below. "Damn this god-forsaken bay."

"The tide will set us aright by the new day, sir." Mister Dickinson offered.

"Indeed. Waters will return and then this colony will see my wrath." He stomped away. "I shall be in my cabin."

Muttering aside, Dickinson mused, "With good riddance."

Dudingston stopped and turned, "What was that, Dickinson?"

"Good readings to you, sir."

Soon, the night calm set in. Well after darkness, far down the bay, oarsmen in a long boat pulled hard against the receding tide to make their way up river from Bristol Bay. Captain Potter's crew made good time.

"Brinley, what do you make of our mission now?" Thomas whispered. The bearded oarsman beside him leaned near to his ear and whispered back, "I fear not what may come, for we now row to our liberty, striking back at the contempt the Crown holds over us. Keep yer face down, lad, an' offer no voice."

Soon, they came upon a double line of boats going the opposite direction and silently fell in line. Midnight darkness masked their progress as the flow of the outgoing tide and current made quick work of speeding down the channel. Shore lights in the distance spoke of the nearness of land, yet the longboats glided silently and unnoticed toward their quarry. Within minutes, the captain signaled for the two lines to merge into a single file; the *Gaspee* lay ahead, and heightened excitement ran through each man in the longboats. From his position, oar in hand, Thomas strained to see into the night, then made out the lights of the schooner. He elbowed Brinley and pointed toward their objective. Brinley returned a confirming nod, then silently dusted the remains from his pipe and stuffed the empty pipe into a coat pocket. He positioned his knitted watch cap securely on his head low to his eyebrows, and checked the inside pockets of his coat, each with its belaying pin in place. Thomas did the same, insuring that his similar foot-long clubs were also in place.

Their approach brought the *Gaspee*'s lights steadily nearer as Dudingston's stern visage emerged in Thomas' thoughts; fear of what lay ahead swept over him. He had given the devil the slip just that morning and had pledged to remain clear of him forevermore, yet here he was among those set upon capturing the beast. Vivid imagery overwhelmed him. If their mission failed, the Lieutenant was sure to exact revenge doubly on him. Suddenly overwhelmed with longing for the warmth of Molly's hearths, he yearned for the taste of her warm biscuits spread with butter and pozzie of berries. His body pulsed with imagery as a certainty of being captured took hold, and he ached. If only he was at the White Horse where he should be. If only he had listened to Aunt Nettie and not gotten swept up into the doings of the sea. Yet here he was among the Sons of Liberty with Brinley. "Liberty boys" they called themselves, but images of being hanged on Long Wharf, his carcass pecked by crows and birds, brought a dryness to Thomas' mouth as never before, the same as "seeing" Bonny Mary at the well. A cold shudder swept up his spine. He dipped his hand into the surf and brought a palm-full to his mouth. The chill as the cold water went down his throat made him shudder, then he coughed and spit the salty taste from his mouth, drawing stern glances from the others.

Brinley whispered, "Yew be the namesake of sech actions, Thomas. Yon crew awaits. We shall soon learn our fates, sure to make fine scribblin's fer the tellin' someday."

Onboard the *Gaspee*, seaman Bartholomew Cheever walked the mid-watch on deck. He tucked the lapels of his coat around his neck and buttoned the overpiece in place against the chill of the night. Keeping warm during four hours of watch was his main intention, still with the shakes from getting cold during scraping the hull earlier in the day. Once relieved by the morning watch, he would get only a few hours of sleep before being rousted out for the new day of duties at Captain Dudingston's beck and call. With lantern in hand, he walked from port to starboard around the bow, slowly back and forth along the deck, occasionally looking out into the night at the lights on distant shores.

Act 2

Chapter 9

Captain Whipple, standing tall in the bow of the lead longboat, was determined to seize his quarry. He guided the raiders toward the faint image of the *Gaspee* ahead; soft sounds of oars dipping regularly into the Bay behind him accompanied his firm resolve and clinched jaw. The sixty-five men in all the longboats were of equal resolve, some with muskets, others with pistols, most with clubs of various sorts. The line of longboats rapidly approached by the bow as planned.

Onboard the *Gaspee*, watchman Cheever carried a saber and a pistol in his belt, never suspecting to be confronted with their imminent use. Checking a starboard stay, he glanced off into the night and was startled by what he saw; a flotilla of longboats nearly at hand. He called out frantically, "Who comes there?" but got no response. "Who comes there?" he called again, then ran aft to the captain's cabin. "Captain Dudingston! Sir. Intruders!"

Lt. Dudingston, about to settle in for the night and dressed only in his blouse and trousers tight at the knee, quickly donned his boots and ran up on deck with his saber and pistol in hand.

"Off the starboard bow, sir!" Cheever pointed.

Lt. Dudingson ran forward to the bow, grabbed a stay and called out firmly, "I order you to stand off at your peril!"

Oarsmen in the boats quickened their pace and closed rapidly on the *Gaspee* as Cheever yelled toward them again, "Stand off and identify yourself!"

A firm voice returned, "I wish to come aboard," and received Cheever's equally firm response, "You cannot, sir!"

Now with longboats nearly at the schooner, a strong voice shouted, "I am the sheriff of County Kent. I am come for the captain of this vessel, and have him I will."

Lt. Dudingston shouted commands. "Battle stations! Sound the alarm."

Cheever grabbed the battle rattle from its perch on the mainmast and gave it repeated twirls as he fired his pistol in the direction of the raiders, immediately receiving return fire. Overwhelmed by the sudden onslaught in such great numbers, Lt. Dudingston fired his pistol toward longboats, then had only his saber for defense. Other crewmen from below scrambled on deck to the sounds of battle as raiders, with blackened faces, climbed up the ship's anchor and bowsprit lines over the freeboard, quickly pulling themselves onto the deck. More shots streaked the night and left an acrid pall of burnt powder further obscuring the raider's approach.

Off the starboard bow, Ephrain Bowen sat on a thwart of his longboat, adjacent to Captain Whipple's boat, waiting his turn to board. Beside him lay his father's musket. His companion, Joseph Bucklin, standing just ahead made out Lt. Dudingston's figure on the freeboard holding onto a standing line, left-handedly swinging his saber with dispatch and yelling at raiders to, "Stand off, vermin, or receive the fine edge of my saber."

Bucklin yelled excitedly back to his young friend, "Eph, reach me your gun, and I can kill that fellow."

The long barrel of the musket aligned with Dudingston's figure outlined in the dim light as Captain Whipple once again bellowed his intention to seize the captain. Dudingston swung his saber at a raider, missing by a hair's breadth, just as the flash from Bowen's shot lit up the action and sent its lead ball flying toward the British commander. Instantly, Bucklin jumped down into his longboat and ducked under the smoke to see the effects of his shot.

The ball passed through Dudingston's lowered left arm, then penetrated deep into his left groin. He collapsed onto the deck and shrieked in pain, "Good God, I am done for!"

Hearing Dudingston's cry, Bucklin jumped up and yelled excitedly, "I HAVE KILLED THE RASCAL!" Cheers erupted among raiders still in their longboats and those onboard the *Gaspee* as it was quickly overwhelmed, the British crew now leaderless. Dudingston stumbled his way aft, leaving a trail of blood on deck and made it to the protection of the companion way to his cabin. Using the tail of his shirt as bandage, he lay helpless and bleeding as the Rhode Islanders swarmed over the ship and its crew.

Dr. John Mawney was the first from his longboat to board. Falling first into water up to his waist, he then clambered over the freeboard leaving a trail of watery footsteps. Once onboard, another raider handed him a belaying pin for a club that he attempted, in the darkness, to use immediately.

"John! Don't strike!" a familiar but alarmed voice requested. In rapidly increasing numbers, the raiders poured over the freeboard on both sides, pushing the overwhelmed British sailors back along the deck until some jumped down into the hold. The hand-to-hand battle raged, and Dr. Mawney followed those into the hold, ordering, "Yield and ye shall not be harmed but set ashore."

A commanding voice shouted through the night, reminding the raiders of their mission without brutality, but ransacking the *Gaspee* began immediately.

John Brown quickly set upon the Lieutenant as he lay trying to hold back the bleeding from his groin. "You piratical rascal, we have got you!" he scowled. "We shall have you dead, if that be the case, shot by your own people."

A second raider glowered, "Stand aside! Let me dispatch the sea dog!" and raised a handspike over Dudingston's head to deliver a fatal blow.

Desperately, Lt. Dudingston appealed to Brown. "Sir. Quarter, sir. Spare my crew, if we should yield, sir?"

"Damn you and your crew!" Brown snarled back.

"No gain of law exists in slaughter, sir. We shall surrender to you."

The British crewmen nearby dropped their weapons and quickly repeated around, "The captain yields! The captain yields!" but Boatswain John Johnson, wanting no part of it, fiercely fought on. Set upon by several raiders, he was beaten with staves and belaying pins that quickly overpowered him, driving him to the deck. All others hastily dropped their weapons. In the hold, Dr. Mawney commanded, "Fetch cords for binding, and ye shall not be harmed but set ashore."

A crewman offered tarred cords with which the doctor and other raiders bound their captive's hands behind their backs.

On deck, Dudingston pleaded for his life. "Please, sir. I beg of you. I am much weakened from loss of vital fluid. I cannot last much longer without attention. Please, sir, allow Mister Dickinson to attend my immediate need."

John Brown stood over Dudingston, the wounded man's mid-section covered in blood. In a fetal position, holding his penetrated left arm tightly with his right hand, he pressed both to his groin in a desperate attempt to reduced the bleeding.

Brown, disgustedly, vented his sentiments. "You are best left to die on your own accord, you worthless scoundrel."

The Lieutenant pleaded with Brown, "Decent men of your

means would not let a poor man die. Please, sir, search yourself for kindness. Allow my servant to assist me."

Reconsidering, Brown yelled through the night. "Dickinson! Identify yourself." From the darkness came the man's answer from one of the boats, followed by Brown's relent. "Assist your captain here."

Dickinson was cut from his binding and quickly came to attend his captain. He assisted Dudingston to his quarters as Brown turned to searching out Dr. Mawney, whispering, "Our surgeon. Where is our surgeon?"

From the hold, Dr. Mawney was helped up on deck and answered. "Mr. Brown, sir. You requested my presence?"

"Don't call names, sir. Go immediately into the cabin. There is one wounded who will soon bleed to death. If I should have my wish, he will."

Dr. Mawney hastened to the cabin below, with Bucklin in tow. They stepped into the dimly lit cabin where Dickinson assisted his captain, having now removed the man's trousers that were used as a compress. Dudingston reclined to the left on his bunk covered with a white woolen blanket that already showed splotches of red. Without a word, Dr. Mawney threw off the cover and pulled off Dudingston's efforts to reveal the dark hole in his groin made by Bucklin's shot, a dark hole that immediately filled and oozed with the officer's blood. Not taking time to scrape lint, the surgeon threw open his waistcoat and ripped his shirt to the waist to make a compress bandage of white cloth and firmly pressed it against the wound with the heel of a hand.

In extreme pain and not at all certain that he would survive, Dudingston carefully observed the surgeon who made no attempt to disguise himself, other than black smudgings on his face. His actions and attire were not those of a pirate or rogue and revealed Dr. Mawney to be a learned man of medicine. Other raiders soon filled the cabin and gathered around the captain's sea desk going through his papers and murmuring among themselves. Unlike Dr. Mawney, they were careful to keep their backs to Dudingston, although revealing that they, too, were men of means as shown in their clothing and manner. With Bucklin standing near at hand observing his quarry's apparent decline into death, and with Dickinson behind them, there to assist if requested, Justin moved quietly with frightened Thomas at hand. Dickinson was immediately ordered to hand over the ship's papers and commission which he struggled to do in the faint light. Thomas pulled his cap low over his brow keeping his face from Dudingston and his crewmen as he pulsed with fear of being recognized, but with Justin beside him rifling the Lieutenant's effects, he did the same and soon came upon a brass barreled pistol that captured his attention. From the corner of his eye, he noticed Justin whisking Dudingston's brass parade cap and its plum into a canvas ditty bag he had with him. So inspired, Thomas slid the pistol under his coat and suddenly felt the elation of following his forbears' pirating footsteps. Justin fetched item after item into his bag.

Lt. Dudingston blurted, "Pray sir, do not rip your clothes. There is linen in the trunk there," he pointed.

Turning to Bucklin, Dr. Mawney told him, "Break open that trunk and tear linen. Scrape much lint. Quickly, quickly." Bucklin did so, but the linen was new and little lint could be scrapped.

"Slide your hand under mine," Dr. Mawney directed Bucklin. "Press the ball of your hand hard as I am to stop the effusion of blood." Bucklin did so, now attempting to salvage the life of the man he so excitedly proclaimed to have killed just a few minutes earlier. Hunter and hunted, victor and vanquished, were now in a race against death, the very objective that the raiding party wished to confer upon the dastardly British captain.

Dr. Mawney scraped again and again but was equally unsuccessful; the new linen was nearly lint-free. Folding the linen instead, he made six compresses, the first he applied to Dudingston's forearm wound, wrapping it rapidly. The captain helped tie the bindings in place with his free hand. When ready with the other compresses, he commanded Bucklin, "Raise your hand," and he slid them in place over the groin wound, pressing firmly once again, then began wrapping the bandages tightly, binding them around Dudingston's body. The flow of blood continued but slowed.

Over by the Captain's sea desk, lit only by a single lanthorn, John Brown, Captains Whipple, Hopkins and other leaders of the raid scoured the ship's papers, careful not to reveal their blackened faces. Short commands were delivered to Dickinson regarding official documents as a familiar voice admonished everyone, "Move quickly. Dawn fast approaches."

Thomas did so. He and Justin went through Dudingston's belongings, steadily tossing those things of no interest overboard from an open sea window. Not only was the *Gaspee* being stripped of her fittings topside, out from the portals of the Captain's quarters went most of his belongings.

When told to let events overtake Dudingston, Dr. Mawney refused and continued to attend to his patient's bandaging. "We shall properly dress his wound to transport him from this ship as planned," he said. In due course, but taking much longer than the leaders felt comfortable, the flow of blood was finally stopped. Relieved, Dudingston fumbled through a drawer adjacent to his bunk and extended a gold buckle to Dr. Mawney. "Please, sir, do me the honor of accepting this gold buckle as a measure of my gratitude for your most kind service."

"I think not, sir," Dr. Mawney said cooly, purposely avoiding eye contact. "I am in need of no offerings from the likes of you."

Returning the gold buckle to the drawer, Dudingston offered a silver buckle instead. "For your clothing damaged in my service then. Think this not as a gift, but for replacing your frock, sir."

Dr. Mawney reconsidered. "Very well then." He slipped the buckle into a waistcoat pocket, then directed Dickinson, "Move your captain to the deck for transport off this vessel." Dickinson and Bucklin complied, wrapping the injured man in another blanket and his long coat against the chill of the night. Using a second blanket for a sling, they moved the wounded man along the passageways toward topside.

Having studied the captain's log and the ship's papers, taking some with them, the leaders reminded Dr. Mawney of the approaching dawn and their need to leave the ship. Feigning to toss more items overboard, Justin covered his actions from view as he slipped the gold buckle into a pocket, then he and Thomas followed Dr. Mawney out as other raiders burst into the cabin and further ransacked the place. Breaking into the Captain's personal locker, they took bottles of brandy and other items of worth.

Smoke wafting into the Captain's cabin spoke of the need for a speedy retreat. Raiders had succeeded in tossing the ship's arms overboard and had set her alight. Returning to the location of his longboat, Dr. Mawney met his friend and boat captain, Joseph Tillinghast. Assuring that Lt. Dudingston was properly handled into a longboat, Dr. Mawney followed with Justin and Thomas behind. Suddenly, Thomas realized that he was in the wrong boat; his destination was Bristol, not where this boat was headed. Without a word, he scrambled back up the schooner's freeboard onto the deck and searched along the gunnel for his boat. Coming upon Brinley, who motioned him to get aboard, Thomas monkeyed his way down standing lines and plopped onto the thwart beside his companion, then breathed a sigh of relief. Captain Potter checked to see that everyone was aboard and commanded, "To the oars, mates."

As their boat eased away, the last of the raiders onboard the *Gaspee* whooped at the flames beginning to make their way into the hated ship's rigging. Then, quickly, the last of the raiders clamored over the side. Each boat's oarsmen soon put distance between them and the burning ship. British seamen, captured and bound in various longboats watched in disbelief. The raid and destruction of their ship was fulfilled before their eyes.

The Bay was slowly filling with incoming tide, soon to join the approaching sunrise, but on this new day, the *Gaspee* would sail no more.

Flames crackled up tarred rigging lines and shot skyward as the *Gaspee's* canvas and varnished wood erupted in flames. Longboats pulled further away as the night lit in the red glow that rapidly engulfed the ship. A cannon fired its charge wildly into the night, followed by a succession of discharges from fused shot on the main deck. A large explosion was the first in succession that ripped the ship apart. Still hard aground, the schooner became its own funeral pyre as burning debris successively belched upward in explosion after explosion that arched through the darkness in flaming displays. A massive succession of sizzling whistlers that fizzed and barked their presence and quick demise told that a small arms magazine had exploded. Nearest longboats were showered in sparks. In one, Dudingston brushed sparks off his blanket.

With his back to the ship and silhouetted against the flames, John Brown vehemently made his case against Dudingston. "I have you Dudingston, a most vile and disreputable creature you are. It is upon your person to pay for the hogsheads of rum taken unjustly from our good merchant Mr. Greene, and others, to be sure, on your long list of persons wronged by your dastardly ways. No personal belongings shall be returned until consent to payment is made. For me, I pray that the court determines that ye shall never see such things again, and I shall have the pleasure to witness your hanging, a great pleasure to be sure."

Just as contemptuously, Lt. Dudingston replied, "Whatever reparation the law would give, I am ready and willing. For my things, do with them as you please. We shall see by law who hangs, sir. You shall be the dangler, not I."

Brown pointed out into the bay. "Leave this despicable vermin on that spit of land where the incoming tide will resolve his fate."

Among five bound *Gaspee* crewmen, one assisting the forward oarsman, Dudingston scowled, "Why wait for the tide, you coward? I am unable to fight the surf if you throw me overboard here and now."

Others among the raiders concurred and came near to rolling Dudingston off into the water from his aft position in the boat when Dr. Mawney intervened. "Gentlemen, stop this madness. We are civil beings. We shall off-load our cargo on shore in the company of his men as prescribed."

Shortly, the longboat slid up on the beach, and Dr. Mawney cut the bindings of the prisoners. "Attend to your captain," he commanded. "Carry him among you. His wounds do not permit walking."

One *Gaspee* crewmen stumbled over the forward oarsman and nearly landed on him, a man wearing a red and white spotted bandana around his head. Regaining his balance, he assisted other crewmen who carried Dudingston off into the night as captives were prodded along by raiders toward prearranged confinement. Behind them, a massive explosion ripped through the *Gaspee* as its main powder magazine erupted in a giant fireball. Dr. Mawney and Captain Tillinghast turned to watch the debris cascade back into the Bay as flaming splinters. A sense of sadness welled up in both of them to witness the schooner burn, hated only because of its captain. Their hastily planned raid a complete success, the housing of captives also went as planned but posed innumerable possibilities that could lead to their identification.

One by one, the longboats turned out into the Bay, most returning up-river toward Providence while one vanished into the night toward Bristol. Dr. Mawney and Capt. Tillinghast continued their walk up the gentle hill leading away from Namquit Point, stopping frequently to see the ship behind them wither in the flames. "Joseph," Dr. Mawney said, "I believe a hearty breakfast has been earned by our night's work."

Tillinghast smiled as another powder keg exploded, producing a great shower of sparks from what had been the Captain's cabin. "Quite right, my friend. Perhaps we shall return later to review our handiwork? I wonder, though, our blackened faces will do little to prevent Dudingston from identifying you. And that buckle he insisted you take, it could be the thing that puts a hangman's noose around your neck."

Dr. Mawney stopped in his tracks and withdrew the buckle from his waistcoat pocket. Flipping it successively in his fingers, he recognized that it was, indeed, a turning point in his life. What to do next was not so clear, the moment then accented by another explosion that sent more flaming bits of the burning schooner skyward, one a cannon ball that exploded into a shower of fiery sparks like festive Chinese fireworks. He felt the smooth workmanship of the buckle. "Finely crafted, to be sure, certain to replace my garments rent for a scoundrel. But, alas, I suspect that you are quite correct, my friend."

Looking to the east at the faint light of dawn on the distant horizon as if to toss the buckle out into the bay, he reconsidered. "A new day is upon us, Joseph. What shall we see in our tomorrows for such an act as we have perpetrated?" he asked, while turning the buckle over and over again in his fingers.

Chapter 10

Always an early riser, John Andrews was up and setting about returning home to Cranston just south of Providence. He and fellow men of law, having completed their duties in the Court of Common Pleas, had spent the evening at Sabin's Tavern as was customary following close of the court. During their dinner the evening before, he had noticed the drumming and assembly of boys marching about and asked about the nature of the commotion, dismissing it as frolic of Training Day. He had not more than dressed when he heard a murmur of talk unusual so early in the morning. Hearing the name *Gaspee* spoken excitedly, he went to a window, threw open the shutters, and looked about the street below. A small gathering of men had assembled at the head of Fenner's Wharf across Main Street.

"You there," he yelled. "What is the talk of the *Gaspee*?"

"Burnt, sir," one of the men replied. "Seized during the night an' put to the torch."

"Good God!" Andrews exclaimed, envisioning all sorts of Royal retributions. "Are you certain?"

"Aye. 'Tis the talk o' the marnin', sir."

Hurrying to finish dressing, he skipped breakfast and set foot on the street seeking the Chief Justice of Common Pleas. Mister Jenckes was already about the morning, having just left the Deputy Governor's home from taking word of the events to the surprised official.

"Mister Andrews, sir," Justice Jenckes called out to him from some distance. Andrews hurried to him.

"What of the *Gaspee*? Have you heard, sir?" Andrews asked.

"Indeed. I have just now informed the Deputy Governor of

this most unpleasant turn of events. The *Gaspee* lies upon the sands of Namquit Point smoldering about her waterline as we speak. I have just now recommended to his honor that he and you, sir, the site being within your purview, should retire to Pawtuxet immediately, where, I am told, the crew has been confined. I regret to inform you that the captain, Mister Dudingston, has been wounded and may already have expired."

"God help us!" exclaimed Andrews.

"Aye, sir. The perpetrators have thrust upon us a most unwelcome confrontation with the Crown."

"What of the attackers?"

"Nothing is known of them at this time, all the more reason to go with haste to Pawtuxet to inquire of the captives, should any remain alive." Justice Jenckes shook his head slowly and despaired. "I fear that the wrath of the Royal Navy will be set upon us, John. A most terrifying vision."

"Similarly in my mind as well, Daniel. I shall inquire of his honor forthwith. A good day to you, sir."

With a few quick steps, Andrews was at the Deputy Governor's home and rapped on its door. When opened, he met the shocked expression of the man struggling with his tie. "Sir, I am at your service," he said.

The Deputy Governor invited him in.

"What do you make of this, John?" Deputy Governor Sessions asked.

"I have yet to learn many details of the event, if, in fact, it is true. Yet, sir, I am quite certain that the King and his court will use just such aggression as this to dissolve any hope of independence in our lives. I fear martial law with posting of troops in our homes."

"Yes," the Deputy Governor said, thrusting his arms into his frock. "I imagine the same, I am afraid. We must make haste, John."

Soon the two of them were astride horses galloping the few miles to Pawtuxet. They arrived to find the village filled with the scent of burnt wood and spent gun powder. The pall of smoke on the horizon told the tale.

Earlier, *Gaspee* explosions had roused some of the town's people from their beds, and just as the day broke the eastern horizon, while scurrying toward Namquit Point, the villagers had met a strange cavalcade of bound British prisoners, one shivering and carried in a blanket sling, all marched under guard to captivity. By sunrise, men in small boats were salvaging the wreck.

Tying their horses at the Commons, the Deputy Governor and Andrews made quick strides about the village while they exchanged concerns over what may or may not be true and where each circumstance might lead. Approaching a man, Sessions asked of him, "You sir. I am Deputy Governor Darius Sessions. I am told that captives are confined hereabouts."

The man pointed to a house toward the Bay. "Yon home of Joseph Rhodes. Find them there, you will, that villainous one wounded."

Sessions' hard knock on the front door of the house brought no response. Impatiently, he knocked again, harder this time, and roused a disgruntled voice. The door squeaked open slowly.

"I am told that one William Dudingston, wounded, is in this residence. Is that true, sir?"

Still in his nightshirt, Joseph Rhodes, was suspicious of his early callers. "What be yer business with such a man at this hour?"

"I am Deputy Governor Darius Session and with me is Justice John Andrews. It is my most disagreeable duty to find Mister Dudingston, whom, I am told, has been rendered near death, if not passed from us already, the result of a most unfortunate gunshot said to have originated from one of our citizens. I trust that I am not too late. Is Mr. Dudingston in your keeping sir?"

Satisfied, Rhodes opened the door and led the pair to a bedroom. There, lying on his back, covered for warmth, the young Lieutenant moaned in pain. Just in front of them, the lady of the house curtly placed an urn of water in a bowl with a towel on the table by the bed, her scowl showing her displeasure at having such a contemptuous person in her home. Upon exiting, she nearly collided with Sessions, then, noting that he was a man of stature, she confronted him.

"You will take this vile creature from our home, sir?"

"Begging your pardon, madam. I must learn the details of this most foul deed. Mister Dudingston is but one of the crew members, and I know not the fate of the others as yet."

"Free yourself of the thought that our home is for board, sir," she said. "The price of the tavern be his charge, and more if I had my way."

Sessions agreed. "Yes, yes. Quite so," and handed her a coin to hasten her exit.

Approaching the wounded officer, Sessions came face to face with the man to ascertain how near death he may be. The Lieutenant opened his eyes, and, showing substantial vigor, scowled, "Who might you be, another of these villainous colonists?"

"I am Darius Sessions, Deputy Governor of this colony, sir. I regret this terrible injustice to you, Mister Dudingston. Should you require money, surgeons, or removal to a place more convenient, please allow me to assist in any manner in my power."

Dudingston scowled, "I am in need of no favors, sir. I do, however, fear for the safety of my crew. I would request that they be collected and transported to Admiral Montagu in Boston or to Captain Linzee of the *Beaver* in Newport."

"Rest assured, sir. I shall see that it be done. If you will, sir, respecting your condition, I can offer little relief from your circumstances. However, it is my intent also with this visit to learn more of the attack on your person and upon your vessel."

The lieutenant replied contemptuously. "I shall give no accounting of the matter for details will escape me in my weakened condition. I must forebear as well for being duty bound to report to my commanding officer at court martial, for which, if I survive, I am certain to be called. If I should die, as I suspect I shall, I will take the affair with me."

"Leaving you to God's care, I shall move to locate your men as requested."

"You can be trusted to do so?"

Offended and surprised at the inference, Sessions rebuffed Dudingston. "Most certainly, sir. From whence is that remark? I come to aid, not to have my intent questioned."

"Who among you can be trusted?" Dudingston snarled. "I lay here near death due to those of your ill-begotten citizenry who, most cowardly, lay siege to my vessel under the cover of night to fire upon us at close range."

"Sir?"

"Two surgeons were among my attackers, much to my benefit. And able bodied seamen were among them, captains to be sure, all who knew the workings of a ship, ship's papers and captain's log; all certainly destroyed by now. Does such a crew not seem odd among *peaceful* citizens?"

"Odd, sir? How so?"

"Such an organization reveals the high level with which this most illegal assault was planned and carried out, and with the expectation of bloodshed, I might add, proven by the presence of surgeons. My present condition points to that fact without doubt. To have surgeons in their company was purposed preparation for injurious assault, was it not?"

Implications that the raiders were of the ranking citizens of the colony, including surgeons, took the Deputy Governor by surprise. "I do not think it odd at all. Searovers...." He paused in thought.

"You see as well that this action was contrived and planned in detail. I am convinced of it. These men were not pirates but seamen of skill and men of quality. Men of your kind."

Insulted, Sessions objected. "Surely, sir, you are not so brash as to suggest that I was among the perpetrators of such a foul deed."

"Must you be coy, *Deputy Governor*?" Dudingston scowled. "Men of measure are well known to be villainous in this colony. I have sailed these waters from four years past, sir. I have seen your violators of the sea laws, thieves and bootleggers of goods past the King's authorities while they swagger and flaunt their wealth, their fine homes in Newport, Providence, throughout this enclave of wickedness. These 'gentlemen' are the same cowards who cover their acts with darkness as they care not to be identified, admitting their guilt, and show face paint for disguise. Others among them displayed attire of the common man. Perhaps so, but rabble just the same, enlisted to their cause."

Sessions turned abruptly to leave, then snarled in return, "I can offer no more than assistance to you and your crew."

Dudingston waved him away. "My ship, sir, I and my crew, we are victims of treachery, not of sudden passion, sir. That is clear to me. If I should recover from my wounds, I shall have the pleasure of seeing a captain among you, and one so loathsome to claim himself the high sheriff, hang before me."

Further insulted, Sessions departed without another word to Dudingston. He inquired of Rhodes of a physician, to learn of a man so trained locally. After giving instructions to seek the man, once outside and incensed by Dudingston's remarks, he confided to Andrews. "Never have I met so contemptuous a man. Such imperious arrogance! To merely suggest my involvement... me, deputy to the Governor. I have never been so offended."

Along their way through the village, the pair came upon another man whom they asked if he knew the whereabouts of the confined British sailors. Without a word, the man led them to a gambrel roofed house on Peck Lane. Still smoldering over Dudingston's remarks, Sessions muttered, "I fear this man will not pass from us soon enough. Such a grudge as he carries against us will become his sole passion. What will become of our colony if his men have been slaughtered? Surely the same contempt will be displayed by the King's magistrates. God help us. The King's dragoons will see that we all hang."

Behind the house, Sessions was relieved to find the *Gaspee* crew confined in a low overhead cellar but unharmed, other than Boatswain Johnson whose cuts and bruises on his face and head were reminders of the previous conflict. Immediately releasing the men, Sessions and Andrews began taking statements. Each crewman told the same story, with personal recollections added, each telling of such a large number of attackers in many longboats that both Sessions and Andrews were skeptical. When asked if any of the raiders were recognized, not a single crewman admitted to recognizing anyone.

Afterward, Sessions was puzzled and mused to Andrews saying the facts added up to a strange set of circumstances that were nearly unbelievable. The *Gaspee* had been seized and burned, the acrid odor of burnt gun powder, wood and tar in the morning's air attested to that fact, but having time during confinement to resolve their story, it being so consistent from man to man, led him to wonder what portion of the action they may have contrived. Once the statements were collected, and to complete his promise to their captain, the crew was led the short distance to Benjamin Smith's boatyard where they came upon Samuel Aborn attending to his sloop, the *Sally*.

"Hail, good citizen. I am Darius Sessions, Deputy Governor of this colony, and I am in need of your services."

Aborn, a gruff, white bearded seaman, eyed the British sailors without a word, then turned back to his work.

"I am in need of transport of these seamen to his Majesty's sloop of war, the *Beaver*, in Newport Harbor. I commission you, sir, for the duty."

Standing erect in defiance, Aborn snarled, "What be the nature of yer commission for the *Sally*?"

"Transport, sir, as previously stated. To the *Beaver* in Newport Harbor, with proper pay, sir."

Aborn held a hand to his ear, "Aye. Newport?"

Sessions drew nearer and spoke loudly and more slowly. He motioned to the men behind him. "These crewmen are to be taken to the *Beaver* in Newport." He motioned out in the direction of the Bay. "The *Gaspee* lies off Namquit Point, burnt I am afraid. Collect from her whatever of the King's goods that can be salvaged for transport, also to the *Beaver*, but at a later time."

Aborn recoiled. "Need not yell, sir. I can hear."

"Indeed," Sessions smiled. "With proper pay, sir. For now, ferry services for these seamen."

"So be it." Aborn motioned for the seamen to come aboard his craft.

As the *Sally* eased off from the dock in Pawtuxet village, Sessions, distraught, confided to Andrews his concerns of what this attack on the King's revenue service would bring. "We must see the evidence, the smoldering ruin of the infamous *Gaspee*, I fear… I fear… many things to come."

Stepping quickly, they soon arrived at Namquit Point among the scattered curious and salvagers to find the wreck shrouded in smoke, a burning hulk near to the waterline.

From a distance further up the shore, having returned after breakfast, Dr. Mawney and Joseph Tillinghast witnessed the same, noting the presence of the Deputy Governor and the Justice.

"What shall we make of this, John?" Sessions asked of Andrews.

"I suspect that the King's fury will be mightily provoked. Indeed, mightily provoked."

"And here we stand, having come upon the scene of a crime perpetrated, as claimed by that vile Lieutenant, by our very own friends and neighbors, wondering as I do if the man should have been left to die, incinerated with the ship that he commanded to such contemptuous repute in our fair colony. Yet, as his ship dies, he lives! If he survives, he will, no doubt, seek his own revenge at the lead of the King's marines who will certainly ravage among us and send... Who, I wonder in the depths of my pained stomach, will he send to the gallows."

"'Tis a ponderable point, my friend."

"I am not at all certain that he will live. Perhaps I should wish for the contrary. However, I have provided for the care of a physician."

"And if he does, sir? His dying will free you of the dread of facing him at some future time in the courts. What of his surviving? Is he not in debt to the duo of surgeons he claimed to be among the raiders? Will that not soften his resolve to some degree?"

"I think not, Mister Andrews, fearing that he has no sense of indebtedness, only overwhelming contempt for all of us Rhode Islanders, even to the extent of implying that I was among the untrustworthy lot who perpetrated this... this.... I cannot bring myself to call it a crime."

"Troubling, that. Troubling, indeed. How are men of law to handle resolution of this matter, I wonder? Who will be implicated? How will we prosecute them, if indeed they are our friends and neighbors? Who will try and sentence? Hanged most probably, it seems to me? For the defense, how will implication of individuals, so far unidentified, be defended? Charges will, most likely, be brought by mere accusation, particularly so with vengeance on the mind of the King's prosecutors, who will, no doubt, supersede our courts of law. What evidence can be brought to bear other than affidavits and testimony? What reliable evidence?"

"Aye, you are a good friend, indeed, John. One can see how men of law would be troubled with this matter, but I fear not what may transpire in our own courts but that what is likely to come from British home courts where suppression of our trade for the benefit of the King's commerce is likely to sway all reason away to fulfill the lust of vengeance."

"Perhaps so, Darius. Troubling indeed. However, identifying a perpetrator is mere accusation. Proof of involvement comes with evidence. What evidence can be offered? The facts are clear; there burns the remnants of the *Gaspee*, its captain wounded seriously, if not mortally, and we have nothing other than sworn statements from a confined crew who identified no one and whose stories may contain elements of concoction."

Sessions thought for a moment. "I fear the lust for revenge much more so than the proceedings of court, my friend. What has been touched off here will, I fear, result in one after another British Man of War anchored in our harbors off-loading dragoons, the King exercising his will against the perceived ne'er-do-wells said to thrive in this colony. A lesson in abiding with kingship, not law, may become a lesson demonstrated here for the benefit of the remaining twelve colonies, each shown how the King's courts maintain discipline... by our whipping. Law is not the issue, John, unless we are prepared to uphold our own standards...." The Deputy Governor paused at the thought. "God help us. Have we touched off rebellion? Rebellion against the mightiest empire on earth?"

Andrews thought a moment. "The stew that boils among us pits Tories and Patriots as adversaries...."

"TORIES! PATRIOTS!" Sessions blurted. "My god, John. Have we come to such unresolvable differences as to... as to...?"

Andrews pointed out towad Namquit Point, "There lies your answer, Darius, smoldering in our bay."

Chapter 11

Further inland, Dr. Mawney and Joseph Tillinghast stood above the burning wreck and wondered what the Deputy Governor and the Chief Justice were talking about.

Tillinghast mused, "Are we looking upon our prosecutors compiling evidence against us, those who will take up the charge for the benefit of the King? Are they the magistrates among our own kind who will permit Dudingston the satisfaction of seeing us hang, our rotting flesh picked to the bone by the crows and gulls…? Such a troubling image."

"If I alone should hang, you, my good friend," Dr. Mawney said, "should be the recipient of that most despicable of relics of our escapade into history, that very same cold, silver buckle worth more than my life." He handed the buckle to his friend, who declined. "I should like to think it brings you the finest of brandies to toast in my honor. Perhaps I shall become of value after all, Joseph. As the last vestiges of life twitch from my body, I shall become testimony prominently displaying to one and all the very behavior the Crown does not tolerate. Will the masses cheer before me, then return to their lives of subjugation?"

"The will of the people is to see you hang, John? I think not."

"Our favorite Lieutenant and his Admiral… certainly. Our People? We shall see, shall we not? We shall see whose fate will be determined by the quantity of gold offered for our identities. Gold, that eternal temptress, determines the will of man, so the philosophers say. I suspect that the will of the Crown will be mightily provoked by our actions, and a proclamation of worth to make a man rich may seal my fate, and yours, perhaps."

"A reward of death for saving the life of your accuser?"

"Hmmm. Interesting thought. Perhaps Mister Brown was right; let him die of his own accord. I wonder though; as a gentleman, will he value his life more than his duty? Or, is his pride so piqued that revenge at all costs will be his mettle?"

Unexpectedly, a small arms powder magazine in the forward hold of the burning ship erupted into pops, crackles and firey whizzes that belched puffs of smoke skyward. Everyone around the wreck stopped what they were doing to watch the fireworks. They stood in rapt delight when the foremast leaned further astern, moaned under its now unsupported weight and fell against the mainmast, the two of them then crashing onto the deck sending blazing debris in all directions.

Dr. Mawney continued with his observations. "To hang is a dreadful thought, Joseph. 'Tis the reward fit for a pirate, as I am not, only a surgeon interested in lives that I may better. However, I am well aware that no thanks is given in the eyes of the law for such deeds. My transgressions, our transgressions, I might add, have now made us enemies of the Crown and Dudingston my accuser. I have no doubt that he will speak to the willing ear of Admiral Montagu, who, seeing our handiwork from afar, will seek bloody revenge for such an affront to HIS dignity. Being a military man by profession, he will, no doubt, seek a military solution."

"And I, and whoever else can be brought to the bar of HIS justice," Tillinghast mused.

"Yes, indeed. Here we stand, comrades in treachery, we two. Some say patriots to the cause of the colonies, though with little power to back such words. Others scorn and say brigands... they being Tories who have power behind their words. The law and such...." Dr. Mawney paused to reflect further. "A sense of the criminal is new and quite foreign to me, yet I find my position most intriguing, fascinating, as it were. I have committed myself to a cause that is quite unclear to me. Mine is a sense of the fox as the hunt begins. Where shall I hide while the hounds pursue?"

"Quite so, my friend. I, too, see the fire of freedom burning in the hulk that remains of the *Gaspee* and wonder what the future will bring."

"Joseph, will a countryman or two among us answer the call to loyalty for their gain, or shall we unite in a cause that now shapes our destiny, so many of us who are now known to so many? And each as guilty as the next."

"Perhaps, therein lies the strength to prevail, my friend. So many of us hanging from the yardarms of our seaports would be a dreadful rape of the good families of our fair colony, eight longboats full of men who provide much commerce to the benefit of both the colonies and the Crown. Their loss... quite an impact on this colony.

Perhaps our number is sufficiently large to provide some assurance of anonymity."

"I can only hope that you are correct. The Crown is, I suspect, sufficiently unconcerned of our fate to use all of us for examples, hung en masse to the joy of Dudingston and consummation of Montagu's will, and the minions of the Crown's as well, not to mention the King himself. All delivering their views that the criminals of Rhode Island have been purged."

Captain Tillinghast paused in thought, then said, "If such a rape of Rhode Island occurs, I suspect that we shall all become of value. Known far and wide as the Sons of Liberty, our hanging may become the fire of freedom that kindles far from this place a spirit that the Crown cannot suppress. We of this colony have enjoyed a taste of self-rule and independence in our little democracy... quite extraordinary among these thirteen foundlings of the King's empire. We shall have freedom or die. That, I am certain." Pointing to the remains of the *Gaspee*, he continued, "There lies the testimony in flames."

Dr. Mawney was surprised. "Joseph Tillinghast! You, a political firebrand? A man with a cause? How have you managed to arrive at such a state of mind?"

"The taste of freedom is sweet, ever so sweet, my friend."

"And this? This is a quest for freedom in our actions, taking and burning a ship of the Crown?" Dr. Mawney paused to consider the revelation of his friend's strong feeling. "Indeed," he said. "We have made a remarkable coincidence here, of time, of place and of the human spirit in these waters, have we not? You may be quite right, Joseph. This may very well be the initiation of a quest for freedom often talked of, freedom and liberty among a people committed to a common cause brought on by that smoldering ruin before us." He paused. "My mind wanders. What we have here is merely another of the ever so common disputes on the high seas, to be prosecuted in the courts."

"Just what are we looking upon here, John?" Capt. Tillinghast asked. "Here is the temper of our time, not just another conflict on the sea. There lies a dying ship not to be confused with mere buccaneering, but the combined efforts of a people of like mind with motive of justice. As our quarry burns, the flames within us seek release as free men... free of the King and his ministers who rape our very existence."

"Joseph! You are quite the revelation this morning, a man of conviction I see. Are you not speaking, nay, questing for revolution? I was simply swept up in an adventure of the moment foisted upon me by a chance encounter with Captain Whipple. Now I see, as you already have, far-reaching consequences of our night's escapade."

Tillinghast continued firmly, "Revolution is pressed upon me, my friend. Pressed upon all of us in the spinning of wills into the fabric of our lives. It is our will, our choice, to be free and self-directed, is it not? We now look upon another thread being laid in the fabric of our colony, woven since Roger Williams and Ann Hutchinson and William Coddington and all of our forebears who established the mode of our existence of self-rule and free expression, to choose our paths for ourselves, as inalienable rights!"

"An inalienable right? Who ever heard of such a thing? Certainly not the King. Joseph, you speak of actually being free of the Crown? What a novel thought! No sovereign! We have talked of such things as mere ideas of politics far remote from reality, yet here before us is, as you say, actions of a people committed to rebellion to achieve that very aim."

"And, my good surgeon, you are the focus of our endeavor."

"Me!? The focus! What on earth are you talking about?"

"If left to natural consequences and the will of our cause, young Dudingston would now be dead, bled to death from a gun shot, would he not? Some say that very gun shot was from his own people. Regardless, a shot from a raider will always be told as its origin. Nay sayth surgeon John Mawney, answering to a higher conviction. Yours was to attend to his wounds to prevent the natural course of events, thus shaping the future with the survival of a man who is certain to be our accuser, one who has both authority and legal footing, if only military in nature, to see that his accusations are acted upon in court, leading, most certainly, to hanging all of us for sedition, our efforts coming to naught. You could have let him die, but you did not. You even prevented our leader from having the man dumped overboard, to drown in the surf, his voice muted forever. You did not permit that, either. Yours was answering the cause of civility and respect for life while the will of our cause was not so clear in the minds of others. Our actions were revenge born of hatred of Dudingston's ways. Your actions, like it or not, became the focus of the consequences of our raid. Your will prevailed in attending to the wounded man and set the tone of what is to come."

Dr. Mawney shook his head in disbelief. "I was only doing what came naturally to me, a man of medicine."

"Yet, now we face a most troubling time because our accuser lives. He, the man who looked closely and repeatedly upon your face, only smudged with blackening, and your hands, showing no camouflaging and bearing the ring of your family crest… He is the man who can determine your fate, and ours."

Dr. Mawney turned suddenly, hiding his hands, and walked

abruptly off toward Pawtuxet village. "Good Lord! What have I done, Joseph?"

"What have 'we' done, my friend," Tillinghast said, following closely.

After a few steps, Dr. Mawney stopped. "So be it then. I shall retire to anonymity, and my future will be of this land." Fetching a long splinter blown from the *Gaspee*, he shoved it deeply into the soft sand shaping a hole. Into it he dropped the golden ring, a family heirloom from his father, and pushed sand over it. "I am from this day forward John Mawney, Rhode Islander, American... A man of this soil."

"Bravo, my friend, Sons of Liberty one and all. In these perilous times, we can survive as individuals only in anonymity, yet we must tell of our actions to others of like mind in order to transcend mere individual acts and form a binding of cause for everyone everywhere in the colonies."

"The shaping of history..." Dr. Mawney mused. "How quickly our destiny was set this night past. And I, just twenty-two years upon this land, will live with these events for all my years to come. We must now hide in anonymity, you say, and I agree. Yet I wonder, my friend; how will our actions become known to others of the colonies if we are to remain anonymous? Who among them will our acts of sedition inspire?"

"Our friends, John. We have friends. Others of like mind. We shall endeavor to write of these events in correspondence with others in the colonies."

"We two, simply good citizens yesterday, revolutionaries today. It is now upon us to fan the flames of freedom far from these shores. What a difference a night can make."

"Indeed!" Captain Tillinghast said. "We are but two among a host of brave men who have taken the first steps for liberty in this raid, and face the same prospects, hanging as pirates, our lives lost, our families disgraced while the King's officers crack the whip of bondage."

Dr. Mawney was amazed. "Such visions you conjure, Joseph. Perhaps you should inquire of the poetic arts."

Tillinghast smiled. "Where do you suppose the poets draw their inspiration? From human endeavor, just such as this. If we succeed, our actions will become the inspiration of poets long into the future. If we fail, we will be soon forgotten, as would be the case in the normal course of events. Instead, our names and actions will be carried forward from this place as subjects of history in founding a new nation, America."

Dr. Mawney shook his head in disbelief. "The ideas you speak, Joseph, how very classical. Having read Homer's *Iliad* and envisioned from his words the battles between noble adversaries for fame and glory hand-to-hand as did opponents Achilles and Hector, each with deeds surviving time, these thousands of years hence in story and rhyme, I am most gratified to think of our names and actions joining such illustrious themes of literature."

"Rather than each man hand-to-hand, we are bound by like convictions as one and cheer the symbols of our actions as inspiration to others to bind similarly."

"Yes! Indeed. I see clearly now. You are quite right," Dr. Mawney agreed. "And if you are further correct, that there are more, many more of like mind, we must let them know that we have taken the first steps. We must let them know that we chose en masse to fire upon the King's appointed, taking captives, and burning his craft in a display of combined wills. Inspiration lies in events known, the further afield the better. I see that anonymity lies in individuals unknown. Tell me, Joseph. How will we insure anonymity and fan the flames as well?"

"Frankly, John, at this moment, such is not entirely clear to me. I can only trust that the will to protect the identities of so many will prevail, and prevail at high levels to stave off powerful prosecutors. Only one person stands the likelihood of identification, and that one must be kept clear of all possible accusation." Tillinghast pointed at his friend.

"Aye! For certain. I wish not to experience the noose. So, what now?"

"I propose that we retire to our desks, John. We have letters to write while we two begin our lives of anonymity, good citizens openly abhorring the actions we have perpetrated while clandestinely fanning the very flames of rebellion that we have, ourselves, committed."

"And I? How shall I conduct myself?" Dr. Mawney thought a moment. "I suspect that conducting my affairs in complete openness as normal, while professing to be unaware of our little endeavor, except knowledge by hearsay. That shall be my way. And you?"

"I, sir, Captain Tillinghast, have shipping for Mister Brown to attend to."

Chapter 12

Two days later, Thursday, Darius Sessions sat at his desk writing a letter to Joseph Wanton, Governor of Rhode Island.

"Providence, June 12, 1772
"Sir: I have received the advice of all the civil authority in this town, as well as an application in writing, signed by a great number of the most reputable inhabitants, who are unanimously of opinion, and earnestly desire that Your Honor forthwith issue a proclamation, with proper reward, for the apprehending and bringing to justice any and every person that was concerned in destroying the schooner *Gaspee*, or in assaulting and wounding William Dudingston, the commander of said schooner...."(2)

He sat back in his chair and spoke to his mind's eye, "My god, we have done the most preposterous thing imaginable."
Later that day, just before dusk, Dr. Mawney strode briskly along the town Commons with his friend and fellow raider, John Howland, when they came upon a group of boys laughing and parading playfully. Two of the boys seemed to be leaders, one wearing a Naval officer's brass parade cap, its plume flying. The two men stopped in their tracks with disbelief. The boys were somehow familiar to Dr. Mawney; a vague recollection of the dim confines of Dudingston's cabin returned. Then, the cap suddenly fixed his attention as with the clap of bell. He and Howland looked at each other and paled with the horror they recognized in the tales spun by the two boys loudly proclaiming how "we" took the *Gaspee* by storm, wounded the notorious captain, stripped the schooner of her fittings, flung the crew's goods overboard, set fire to the ship, and made off with Dudingston's parade cap among

other treasures. As Dr. Mawney and Howland came closer, the deeper their horror sank with the loud bragging. Their alarm was emphasized when the setting sun glinted off the brass officer's cap. Thomas and Justin were enjoying their new-found fame and following, and in the midst of another brag, Howland collared Justin.

"Move along, boys," he commanded the others. "The time is near to the evening meal. Go along home now."

Their play interrupted, the boys dispersed, except for Thomas and Justin. Howland pulled Justin aside to beyond the others' hearing, and sternly, without question, told him, "Get yourself hung with this foolishness, boy!" He yanked the cap off Justin's head and thrust it into his mid-section. "Rid yourself of this thing forever! Never speak of it or what you know of the *Gaspee* again, you hear!? Never again! Speak of that raid as only hearsay you've come upon, or you'll have the Crown's magistrates down upon you and this town with such stupidly rash displays as this. Think, lad. Others are with grave concern over this matter. If not the magistrates, your carcass may wind up in the drink, drowned to keep you silent, lost in the sea forevermore."

Justin paled at the imagery and, wide-eyed with fear, he grabbed the ditty bag in his back pocket and stuffed the cap back into it, then ran off.

At the same time, Dr. Mawney sternly told Thomas, "Ye tempt the hangman's noose with such display, lad. Torys seek ye this very moment! Give them no reason to speak for the Crown, just what this display attracts, or a tight noose around your neck will be yours." He squeezed Thomas' neck for emphasis. "Never let another soul see or hear such bragging again, and never mention any association with the *Gaspee*, lad. Keep your distance from its captain and crew as well and conjure association elsewhere. Play this foolishness no more, lad. Always declare to know nothing but hearsay or your play will provoke troubles for one and all."

Thomas knew all too well what was being said, knowing the wrath of Dudingston learned firsthand from the morning past. He had wanted to run through Newport streets yelling to the top of his voice about giving the hated Lieutenant the slip, but Brinley's admonishments kept him silent, advice that he now understood far better. He had wanted to show off his brass pistol taken from the Lieutenant's quarters but wisely kept it well hidden, its taking remaining unmentioned. The events of the day past were firmly burned into his mind, thrusting the need for keeping secrets deeply within him.

Thomas jerked free of Dr. Mawney's grip and ran off after Justin.

Assessing the moment, Howland said, "Displays such as this are all that is needed to unravel this affair, John." They looked around to see if anyone was watching and were relieved to see no one. "Fortunate," he said. "We are indeed fortunate to have no audience, but I cannot comprehend the complications these boys have now unleashed. In how many homes will the affair be told by excited boys? In how many homes will their tales be strictly forbidden? I cannot imagine a worse situation to be in, John. Only one of those homes need be Tory, and it can begin the trail that will lead to each of us being set upon by the King's vultures." Howland shook his head in despair. "Alas, I fear that what we have done will return to us from boy's play."

Dr. Mawney breathed deeply. "My friend, we can only hope that in each home this very evening, stern warnings will be spoken. The passing of each day henceforth will tell the results of our chance encounter, perhaps nipped in the bud."

In deep thought while continuing on toward the wharf, each man glanced around for whomever may have seen their actions and wondered what was about. Shortly, they entered the business office of John Brown. Captains Lindsey, Hopkins, Whipple and Tillinghast were there, meeting secretly. Dr. Mawney and Howland were welcomed in.

John Brown continued, "Gentlemen, our strategy has worked so far. In being concerned citizens abhorring the conflict surrounding the *Gaspee* and committing to our Deputy Governor our statements of unanimous need for immediate action, Governor Wanton has today issued a proclamation with reward for arrest of the perpetrators. One hundred pounds sterling now rests on each of our heads."

Someone muttered, "A mere one hundred pounds! Insulting," he laughed.

"Continuing our strategy of cooperation with the authorities," Brown continued, "but with no direct knowledge of the affair, we protect ourselves and all concerned. The deed is now done, and I offer my reassurances that we shall remain free of the hangman's noose only if we remain together, calmly, coolly, even in the face of accusers. Only if we are identified by crewmen are we likely to endure harsh treatment, and thanks to the deep darkness of the night, I suspect that our actions will remain hidden. Even if accused, we stand the advantage of credible testimony amongst ourselves for being elsewhere. Only the name of Mister Brown was uttered in the presence of the crew, and, I suspect, Doctor Mawney encounters the most risk of being identified by Lieutenant Dudingston."

Dr. Mawney offered his observations. "It is my intention,

Gentlemen, never again to set eyes on Mister Dudingston, barring a chance encounter that I will certainly try to avoid. Although I am not certain that he will survive his wounds, I hear that he is still breathing."

Someone quipped, "The rascal should have died on his infernal boat, the better for us and everyone."

"Perhaps," continued Dr. Mawney. "I am committed to uphold my anonymity and yours. Unfortunately, in a moment of nonsense, 'twas I who uttered the name 'Mister Brown.' I hope that, should the need arise, the number of Mister Browns in Rhode Island is sufficient to confuse the person, and further, I hope that number holds our subterfuge as its use, the name of so many, could be said to simply be code for someone not of that name at all."

Everyone agreed and liked that line of reasoning. Captain Tillinghast took up the thought. "Rumor tells of the attacking boats leaving the scene easterly, toward Bristol and Newport, further confusing the direction from whence the attackers originated, although approaching from the bow much implies Providence as the point of origin. However, with no bow guns, clearly known by everyone, logic dictates, I believe, that any attack, from wherever it originated, would be from the bow. I hear from rumormongers who assert that the attack did originate from Newport, others say with certainty that it was launched from Bristol and Warren. Further, locating the prisoners in Pawtuxet village appears to have been a fortuitous choice that has focused pursuit of the 'gang of pirates' in that location." He paused and grinned. "But Pawtuxet has no such boats nor the numbers of souls to man them. Gentlemen, I believe further subterfuge is in hand in every direction."

Abraham Whipple chuckled. "The Deputy Governor has seen to that diversion, unknowingly perhaps," then added, "I am uncertain about who should be credited for the ploy." He pointed upward, "Perhaps Providence?" Everyone expressed the same hope. "The Deputy Governor and the Governor and all their kind must fulfill their official functions, if the King and his dogs are to be satisfied. A show of great zeal in this matter is a statement of loyalty to His Britannic Majesty that adds its own layer of subterfuge, further diluting the prospects of pursuit. God save the King!"

Everyone laughed.

"Quite so, Abraham," confirmed Brown. "We are counting on quick action on the part of our local authorities to appease the contempt that will, no doubt, rise in Parliament. Such a pity, a heinous act is performed by persons unknown, and Parliament will, no doubt, enact another Maritime law." More laughter confirmed his insight.

Tillinghast added, "I was told by one of the men in my company that he was, as a young man, involved in the burning of the *Liberty* some years ago in Newport harbor and none were apprehended for that action. I am reasonably certain that we shall benefit from the same guise, dark of night and silence and knowledge only by hearsay, similarly for this event now known throughout the colony and beyond."

"However," cautioned Brown, "should there be trouble from someone wishing to advance his lot with reward money, it is upon our heads as prominent citizens of the colony to provide each other's defense. Without accusers who point at us directly, we simply know nothing of the incident other than, as you say, hearsay. Should accusers point at us, we remind them simply that we were in the company of one of us, each providing an alibi for the other, beginning with Training Day assembly at Sabin's Tavern, then confining ourselves to the evening here, pursuing business plans as is our regular mode and to be continued as usual."

All agreed. "So," he continued. "There are those who can confirm our attendance at that time and place. With no record kept or roster completed, our exercises were purely among volunteers and went to melting lead and molding shot, also incontestable and reasonable to anyone who might inquire. Discussions and actions pursuing how to defend our town is the purpose of Training Day, and, due to being witnessed manning longboats, our exercises were of the nature to defend by sea. Those things happened under the cover of night that further hides our identities. Should the occasion arise, however, we need only repeat what happened. Should there be no need, the matter simply goes unexplored. We shall see in the unfolding of events where inquiries lead. So far, no inquest has been called and with Newport seemingly the focus, we shall see if Providence is spared. And, as each of you is well aware, our meeting here is also the norm in conducting regular business."

Further discussion among them settled on exchanged alibis.

Dr. Mawney was troubled. "What of the outside, sir, some unexpected revelation. A boy, perhaps. One or two among us who made off with items of boast and bluster that can, quite possibly, become sources of prosecution if identified. Bragging of his involvement then leads to others and the plot is revealed."

Each man contemplated the thought, then John Brown offered his view, "A boy? Perhaps, as a boy, little stock will be put in his story."

"How does one circumvent overwhelming evidence, such as the captain's parade hat?"

"Hmmm. Certainly a sticky wicket, that," Brown continued. "Who is the boy? Does he know of us? Do we know him? What is to be done with items of identification?"

"Such a boy exists, my friends. On our walk here just now, Mister Howland and I happened upon such a display. One lad paraded about the Commons, playfully among others, wearing Dudingston's brass parade hat. Another who was among us was with him. The two among some half dozen or more boys were seen, presumably, by a number of citizens before we arrived. However, I suspect that no one recognized the officer's parade hat or its association to our nefarious deed. Further, I saw no one paying particular attention to their boasts. I believe that we collared the incident, sending the boys packing without identifying ourselves, or themselves, and with serious admonishments never to reveal the cap or mention involvement with the *Gaspee* affair for fear of hanging."

Someone asked, "Mere boys were raiders among us who took artifacts? Such things cast a chill over me, the very items that can unravel this affair. Do you think the fright of hanging will be sufficient to contain the potential of their knowledge expressed in bragging, as boys are wont to do?"

Dr. Mawney rubbed his chin. "I recollect that the lads were in the captain's compartment with us and can likely identify me, although I do not know either of them nor did I ask their names or where they lived. I thought it prudent not to delve into such particulars. My admonishment to stay hidden did, however, seem to be sufficiently frightening to gather some measure of confidence that the lad I admonished will do so. I believe Mister Howland's did the same."

"Troubling, that," confirmed John Brown. "A wild card, as it were. Well, gentlemen, we know not where such events may lead. I suspect, though, that mothers and fathers will recognize the serious nature of the matter and see the potential of their child hanging, thus reinforcing the need for silence. If revealed, however, perhaps from a Tory household that may be near to volunteering their obstreperous youth for the Royal Navy, we may face serious charges. Further, if they should be seekers of wealth seen in an unwanted boy, I suspect that we will have to provide for our own defense. Until then, anonymity has hidden us and, hopefully, will continue to do so."

Chapter 13

A few days later, Joseph Bucklin was walking along a Providence street near Sabin's Tavern with Lieutenant Dudingston on his mind. No word had come to him of the officer's fate, and he was troubled with the thought of possibly having killed a fellow human being, even one so hated. The elation of the moment had faded into the burden of reality. He knew well that his shooting the captain had to remain unknown, as was his participation in the raid, yet he was about to burst to go running through the streets yelling to everyone that he had shot the devil. Even though, some days past, Dr. Mawney relayed from Dr. Sterling assurances that the wounded man would survive, Bucklin itched to learn what had become of Dudingston since. Unable to free himself of the many conflicts brought on by his actions, as if a God-send, but one dangling a noose, he recognized Midshipman Dickinson stepping off the coach from Boston, having just returned to Providence from giving his report to the Admiral. Bucklin risked his fate, and those of every raider, to seize this chance encounter.

"Sir?" he asked, stopping Dickinson who tugged his uniform into order.

"Yes," the Midshipman responded, his eyes growing larger upon recognizing Bucklin's heavily pock-marked face.

"Are you, perhaps, acquainted with the fate of that Lieutenant of the *Gaspee* what was wounded in the raid?"

"Yes, quite so."

"Could you tell me his condition?"

"I believe him to recover fully, sir."

"Thank you for your time, sir. Good day," Bucklin said, then hurried off as Dickinson's eyes followed his every step until out of sight.

Two weeks later in early July, after dark one day, the *HMS Beaver* lay at anchor just above Prudence Island. The watchman hailed an approaching skiff being rowed by a lone man who swung a lantern upon close approach. "Stand off and identify yourself!" the watchman commanded.

"I 'ave need o' yer captain," the young man yelled back.

"My captain is not available. Stand off I say!"

"I wish to come aboard yer vessel an' await 'is presence."

The watchman called below for the duty officer who arrived quickly and took command of the situation. He rolled down a rope ladder to allow the young man to climb aboard. The watchman grabbed the tossed line from the boat and tied it off.

The duty officer accosted the young man. "For what purpose are you in need of coming aboard this vessel?"

"I wants to talk with yer captain."

The duty officer noted the young man's attire as a commoner and addressed him as a servant attempting to flee. "You are attempting to secure your passage aboard this vessel, are you not?" the officer questioned sternly.

The young man hesitated and gave no answer.

The officer stepped forward, backhanded him and commanded, "Speak up, negro!"

"I am in wait o' yer captain, sir," he blurted, now not so sure of his actions.

Angrily the officer commanded further, "Answer me or I shall have you flogged, slave!"

The young man attempted to escape by jumping over the side but was grabbed by the watchman. Another seaman joined in as they wrestled him to the deck and into irons.

"All I wants, sir, is to talk with yer captain," the young man yelled. "I ain't done nothin'."

"Take him below," the officer commanded.

The next day, lashed to the mainmast, the young man's shirt was stripped off his back, Captain Linzee ordered the Boatswain to ready the cat-o-nine-tails.

"I ain't done nothin' fer a whippin', sir. I ain't," the young man repeated.

"Running from your bondage, are you? Speak up, negro!"

The young man, his plan thwarted and suddenly in the throes of receiving the lashings of the whip, grappled with what to do to save himself.

"Bo'sun! Ready your whip," Linzee ordered.

The bo'sun loosened its tails with a swift flick of the wrist. Each tip cracked the air and told what was about arrive on the captive's back.

"Speak up, negro! Running from your master, are you not!?"

The young man burst into tears. "I ain't done nothin'. Please, sir, don't lay yer whip to me."

"Well then, tell me of your cause to be here and do so immediately!" Linzee motioned for another crack of the whip, duly answered by its raking the air.

The captive shuddered with fright.

"What is the nature of your need to speak with me? Speak up!"

"Please, sir. I jes come so's to be a man o' the sea... in the Royal Navy, sir."

"The Crown does not take accept runaways from bondage, slave. We shall teach you a lesson for running."

Another crack of the whip terrified the young man. Desperate and in tears, he blurted, "I knows them what torched that ship, sir. Please don't lay the whip to me, sir. I'll tell all I knows. Please don't whip me."

Surprised, Linzee commanded, "Bo'sun, hold your whip." Assessing the moment in disbelief, a slave involved in the raid seemed most improbable. He scolded the captive. "The *Gaspee*? What could you possibly know of that ship?"

"Them what took her, sir."

"The leaders of the raid?"

"Yes, sir. I knows who they wuz."

Soon confined in chains under the forecastle, the young man muttered to himself, "Done got into troubles thick, a den plum full o' vipers."

Sailors, some from the *Gaspee*, came to look at the captive as he moved about his low confines, yanking his chains to no avail. Seaman Patrick Earle exchanged stares with the young man and fixed his eyes on his red and white headscarf. Suddenly, Earle stood erect, nearly bashing his head on a low boom, then ran to get Boatswain Johnson.

"Tis 'im, I say," Earle said, pointing to the prisoner. The two British sailors talked excitedly, then departed in quick step to return shortly with Captain Linzee.

Earle, finger pointing, accused the young man. "This negro is one o' them what took our ship, sir. I am sure of it. Negros was in that company, an' this one still has the same wrappin's on 'is noggin. 'E was the bow oarsman in the longboat what put us and Cap'n Dudingston ashore. Me own 'ands took to the oar with him, upon the order of the boat cap'n. Sat beside 'im for the time, I did. Nearly broke me leg over 'im when I slipped upon departin' the boat. Put ashore, we wuz, captives."

Infuriated, Captain Linzee took up the line of questioning.

"So, runaway. You are also a traitor to the Crown and a mutinous rebel." He had the young man dragged upon deck and backhanded the prisoner with more commands. "Tell of your loathsome compatriots or I shall have you strung from the yard arm immediately. If you do, you will not be harmed."

Chapter 14

Admiral Montagu sat at his desk penning a letter.

"Boston, 11th July, 1772. To the Earl of Hillsborough.
"My Lord: Since I had the honor of writing to Your Lordship last, I have received an express from Capt. Linzee of His Majesty's sloop *Beaver*, at Rhode Island, informing me he has discovered and detained an indented black servant, who was in one of the boats that boarded the *Gaspee* schooner.

"I beg to observe to Your Lordship, that... the Browns, of Providence, are principal people of that place.

"It appears to me, My Lord, that these people were the ringleaders in this piratical proceeding. I have, therefore, written to Governor Wanton, of Rhode Island, and begged his utmost exertions may be used for the apprehension and bringing to justice the people mentioned...."(2)

Meanwhile, Deputy Governor Sessions left the door of a house on Brenton's Point near Newport where Lieutenant Dudingston had been moved for greater safety, still under the care of the aging Dr. Sterling. Stopping to talk with the marine guard on duty, he said, "Do your duty well, young man, and be ever so vigilant."

"Yes Sir," the marine answered.

Sessions motioned inside the house, saying, "I fear for your Mister Dudingston's recovery. If I read the rancor of the citizens correctly, they would have him pulled from his bed and hanged from the nearest tree, with no regard for the grievous nature of his wounds or their actions. Grave circumstances have beset us."

"I shall do my best, sir."

"I am not at all certain that this new location is of benefit to him," Sessions continued, motioning toward the ships anchored in the distance. "Even though his being closer to your ship, the *Beaver*, now with the threat of a frigate such as yon *HMS Lizard* and its company of marines as well, such may not deter another raid. Defense from that distance in sight of this house will not prevent ending of your Lieutenant's existence if he is not properly protected. I trust that this message will be conveyed to your Captain?"

"I shall see that 'e is duly informed, sir."

Onboard the *Beaver* at that moment, Captain Linzee, seeing through the long brass tube of his telescope, made note of the visitor talking with his marine. He did not know the man but recognized him to be a person of quality from his attire. The young captain set his jaw with determined hope, knowing that he would be placed in command of a landing force should an attempt be made on Dudingston. He savored the thought; he would lead in exacting revenge upon the impudent Rhode Islanders, rabble one and all, so brazen as to attack and wound a fellow officer of the Crown. Linzee relished bringing the guns of the newly arrived *Lizard* to bear, the crown's answer to rising arrogance of the colonists, and he would take great pleasure in delivering the King's revenge.

Inside the house, Lt. Dudingston sat propped up in a bed in an austere room writing another letter to his commanding officer.

"July 1772, Brenton's Point, near Newport.

"To Admiral Montagu.

"Sir. This day I received yours of the 8th past, and am hardly able to give answer, from the painful situation I am in; nor is it possible, at present, for me to be of the least use in respect to the negro.

"I have no doubt of his being in the boat with me, and it is what I expected, that the Governor would say he was an imposter; and I cannot help telling you, that, without I was able to retire to a ship, I should not exist one night on shore, if I was capable to make oath to any one of the people mentioned.

"I beg this may be private, till I can be moved; as the copy of the former letter, being made public to the people by the Governor, puts me in great danger.

"I am, sir, W. Dudingston."(2)

Dudingston called out for the guard and handed him the letter. "Take this letter to Captain Linzee of the *Beaver* for delivery to Admiral Montagu, to Linzee alone."

121

"Aye, sir," the marine complied.

In Newport at the Colony House, a thin man opened the door to the Governor's office. "Doctor Mawney to see your, sir."

Governor Wanton did not look up from his work. "Yes, yes. See him in."

Dr. Mawney strode in, somewhat apprehensive about being summoned. Suspecting that the Governor might have learned details of the raid, he was not certain how to handle the possibilities of this meeting.

"John, so good to see you. It has been much too long since your last visit to Newport."

"Good afternoon Governor," Dr. Mawney responded, looking behind him to insure that the doors to the office were closed and that the two men were alone.

Governor Wanton smiled. "One cannot be too careful in covering one's tracks, my friend. Please, sit down. We have much to discuss."

"Really? You must enlighten me, sir." Dr. Mawney pulled a chair close to confine the carry of their voices.

"I believe the good surgeon's skills attending to our Lieutenant Dudingston has given the man a new lease on life, so Doctor Sterling tells me."

Careful to remain noncommital, Dr. Mawney said, "An unfortunate happenstance, so the rumors fly. Has the wounded been able to identify his assailant?"

"No, not as yet. However, he remains unable to get about. However, one of the raiders has been taken into custody by Captain Linzee, and that person, one Aaron Briggs, a negro servant from Prudence Island, has identified such a person."

Containing his surprise and the sudden elevation in heart beat, while racking his memory for a negro among the raiders, without success, Dr. Mawney kept his composure within the perspective of a non-participant. "Most interesting. You must tell me the name of the guilty party."

"That is why I have asked you here. If anyone should know these persons...." The Governor paused. "Forgive me, I should begin by restating the claim of Lieutenant Dudingston that two surgeons attended him. I am sure it is you," coughing politely for emphasis, "among surgeons whom I know, who may know of these persons," he said with a smile.

Remaining noncommital, Dr. Mawney fought his urge to flee by feigning the need to know the time, withdrawing his timepiece from his waistcoat pocket. "I shall do my best, sir. However, in doing so, I soil my own profession. After all, as you indicate, the surgeon provided sufficient care that our Mister

Dudingston survives. Such a person deserves gratitude, not the gallows, does he not?"

Governor Wanton smiled. "Indeed, sir. However, in his affidavit, Aaron Briggs has named the lead surgeon as one...." He stopped to light his pipe, taking a puff or two, then went on, "...one Doctor Weeks of Warwick. Do you know of such a man?"

Relieved but still containing his nearly explosive emotions, Dr. Mawney took time to think, time to settle his mind. "Weeks, he says. Weeks of Warwick?" Feigning further thought but near to bursting with laughter for relief, he kept his actions and voice contained. "Sir, I may not know every surgeon in the surrounds of Narragansett Bay. However, I know, or have heard of most, certainly around Warwick, so near to my own residence. I am certain... yes, quite certain, sir... there is no Weeks, a surgeon, in Warwick."

The Governor smiled. "As I suspected."

"Sir?"

"I have suspicious thoughts of Capt. Linzee's prime witness. It is not obvious to me why a servant would be rowing alone at that hour miles from Prudence Island, as Briggs tells the story, even if to visit some maiden, which he does not claim. Then to have an accidental encounter in the midst of the Bay, well into darkness in which the crafts could easily have passed near but unknown to each other, and then have himself taken into the confidence of one Captain Potter of Bristol. Such a Captain Potter of Bristol exists, and is said by some to be a rogue of a pirate. In reality, the man is a member of the council of that city, not a rogue or pirate at all, a man who has no knowledge of the affair. This man, who is described by Briggs as bent upon capturing and burning an armed ship of the line with attackers numbering one hundred twenty or more in twelve or fifteen longboats.... Then, the said Captain Potter, knowing that his actions would be unlawful, having made no attempt to hide his own involvement, forces Briggs to become a participant. Then afterwards, pays Briggs for his services, presumably to buy his silence, after which the said Briggs has not been silent. What sense can be made of it all, especially when considering that the servant has to accomplish all this and return to the residence of his indenture for chores prior to the rise of the sun the morning immediately following the raid?"

Increasingly confident that the Governor was not a Tory, in spite of being an official of the Crown in both dress and manner, Dr. Mawney inquired, "Please, tell me more, sir. I find this very intriguing."

"The testimony of Mister Briggs makes no sense of purpose or time, other than a man bent on capturing a handsome prize of wealth, perhaps his freedom, or perhaps simply having fallen in with events beyond his control.

"However, a warship is certainly no prize of wealth, particularly so if burned to the waterline. And taking of the crew as prisoners without significant harm, other than the captain, for whom a great distaste resides in every citizen, each knowing his name upon first mention. What would the good citizens of Bristol, in numbers of one hundred and twenty, a number that certainly exceeds the quantity of able bodied seamen of that town, gain by taking a revenue vessel and its crew? And why would they confine their captives in Pawtuxet village? Would their goal be only to sack the ship?" The Governor drew deeply from his pipe and continued.

"These events certainly transpired, drawing the conclusion that the ship must not have been the object of the raid in which Briggs claims to have become swept up. Whoever the raiders may be, originating in Bristol, Pawtuxet, Warwick... who knows... the Lieutenant claims without doubt that the raiders and their leaders originated in Providence. Why so escapes me. If the ship's crew were the object of vengeful action due to some transgressions, why did the raiders not slay the crew? The ship, a fine schooner, most surely was not the object of any presumed gain; it was set afire and consumed, unfortunately. Just as surely, any motivations in response to individual transgressions would be directed at the crew, perhaps for no more than some action their captain committed, who is, as always, responsible for his crew. Yet, only the captain was wounded significantly, apparently much to the satisfaction of our citizenry, seemingly to point out the objective of the raid: the captain himself. Briggs, however, claims no knowledge of anyone from the *Gaspee* or any contact, having simply stumbled into the affair. The man's story makes no sense whatever."

Dr. Mawney smiled. "A remarkable sequence of events, sir."

"Indeed. Furthermore, the Lieutenant attests to the raid being well planned and well orchestrated, as demonstrated by having two surgeons among them. This demonstrates, without doubt to him, that the raiders set about to perpetrate the deed with bloodshed, rather unlike pirates who would simply have abandoned their victims to their eventualities. Was the object of the raid simply the captain? If so... and with much consterntion from his abusive behavior that is known to me from my own encounters with the man... permitting him to live from a gunshot wound that would otherwise surely have been fatal seems quite odd to me."

"Fascinating, indeed. That is the servant's story, sir?"

"Quite so. A most foul deed, this, implicating honest citizens such John and Joseph Brown, a family that my brother and I, and our families, have done business with for a generation or more and that I know well. Also, a surgeon, whom I now learn does not exist by the name provided, along with an unnamed companion of medicine, leaves me questioning both the motives of Briggs and the methods employed by Captain Linzee in extracting the man's confession as highly questionable."

"What of John and Joseph Brown, sir? I know the brothers Brown of Providence well, fine merchants in that fair town. What need would merchants have for taking the *Gaspee*? As I recall, Jacob Greene and Company have litigation in the courts charging Dudingston of unlawfully taking their goods and having their sloop forfeited, just recently recovered, I understand."

The Governor nodded with satisfaction. "Ah. I suspected as much. I suspect that an indentured servant such as Aaron Briggs would have had ample occasion upon attending to his master's business in Providence where he could well have heard these names, perhaps having been treated badly at some time. Certainly, he had ample opportunity to learn of the talk of the colony, the raid being the subject on everyone's lips for weeks now and surely brought to his master's home by visitors. Then we have his master, Samuel Thompkins, and other servants of that house, Somerset and Jack, appearing before me and giving solemn oath of the presence of Briggs at all the appropriate times of day and night, even to the statement that he slept the very night of that raid between them in the same bed. Such sworn testimony contains no hint of deception. All proclaim Briggs to have been on the island the entire night of the raid... and present for chores as usual on arrival of the new day. And of the boat he claims to have rowed well into the bay? It is affirmed by its owner, Mister Thompkins, to have been in such disrepair as to have been unserviceable."

"Most interesting... and rather entertaining, I might add," Dr. Mawney replied.

"And now, with all the repetition of the story flying about, it is no wonder that someone, even a house servant, could grasp a name or two for whatever motive. I think it reasonable that among so many raiders, at least one hundred twenty strong as said by Briggs, some among them should surely have been known to each other. Do you not agree, Doctor Mawney? A slave who became involved on a chance encounter, who knows no one, is a most remarkable coincidence."

Dr. Mawney smiled and nodded. "Well done, sir. A lesser man would spring to action without such facts for guidance."

"Action is, indeed, widely called for these days, what with the Greene's securing their vessel due to bidders holding their purses so that the craft goes to its rightful owner for a pittance. And to have won their proceedings against Dudingston in court....

I hear cheers from colonists, some calling themselves 'Patriots' now, who claim to have begun righting great wrongs as they thumb their noses at the King and his people, even taking on an armed vessel of the line. I hear also from loyal voices who speak of pirates among us who perform most unwelcome atrocities against the civility of our colony, who advise me that the King is certain to post his dragoons among us for this atrocity. I fear that these times do not bode well, my friend, for the King is certain to be spurred to action by his advisors."

"And for the perpetrators? What is known of them, sir?"

"No direct evidence against anyone as yet, although those named appear to me to be so unlikely to be mere fabrication. However, I remain fearful that those doors will open and bring damning testimony into my hands, thus compelling me to act in accordance with the law I am sworn to uphold. Such are the bindings of law, yet I am in a quandary as to which law I am to uphold; our own civil law that has been in place now for a century, or the Admiral's law that he dictates to me as if I am his servant, or the King's law that continually seeks wealth at our expense. I am faced with answering to three competing bodies of law."

"Hmm," Dr. Mawney mused. "Quite the sticky wicket, sir. Without damning testimony, are the assailants likely to avoid such bindings of law, whatever its direction?"

"Admiral Montagu has conveyed to me by letter, nay, commanded if he had the right, to apprehend these men so named. Those who do not exist, I cannot. And in affidavits sworn by Aaron Briggs, I find great flaw. Similarly, affidavits from *Gaspee* crewmen do not agree in numbers of details. Thus, I believe I have acted responsibly to all bodies..." He paused and grinned, "although the vagabonds and rogues who caught our infamous Lieutenant off guard and embarrassed him remain at large. Or, perhaps they were neither vagabonds nor rogues but a selection of our good citizens acting at the behest of the sheriff... within our civil law. Yet, the High Sheriff knows of no such acts and was far from the scene."

"An intriguing state of affairs, to be sure, sir."

"Further, I question the Admiral's jurisdiction in the matter, having taken place some thirty miles inland, yet involving one of his ships which he assumes infers jurisdiction. There are, however, several other points of concern. That of Patrick Earle, a *Gaspee* seaman, has sworn an oath that Aaron Briggs is positively the man he saw on the night of the raid, at an oar in the boat in which he and some of the crew were taken ashore. Notwithstanding the honor of the negro, I have attempted to acquire the lad to stand before me to ascertain the story from him first hand."

"And did he oblige?"

"No, not as yet. Captain Linzee refused my sheriff and sent him away from his ship empty-handed only to present the witness to Admiral Montagu in Boston. Even upon invitation of his presence during an examination of Briggs before me, Captain Linzee refused. I perceive the man to be the equal of Lt. Dudingston in measures of contempt. He utterly dismissed as meaningless the request of this high office. And now I hear from the Admiral that Mister Dudingston rings in with no doubts that Aaron Briggs was an oarsman on the same boat that took him ashore. Yet his correspondence with the Admiral is inconsistent, having stated the man to be Aaron Bowler rather than Briggs at times, perhaps an oversight of name, yet without doubt in the Lieutenant's mind, whatever the name. Confusion, I think... nay, grappling for straws to get into the matter regardless of effect... simply to get someone, anyone, I think. These things I have put in writing to the Admiral who has become so infuriated with me that he has broken off all communication."

Dr. Mawney wondered aloud, "Pondering the point of not permitting access to Mister Briggs, sir.... The matter suggests contrivance, does it not?"

"Quite so, quite so. Perhaps to rattle the threat of accusation at the lesser of perpetrators to arouse one or more to come forward with a sense of being pardoned upon identifying the leaders. A most fearful prospect, I might add. Yet, I conjure in my mind a certain resolve among the raiders, first to act together in perpetrating the raid, then to vanish into the night with new resolve now binding them in plain sight, rather like a band of brothers, with much satisfaction for their actions, I suspect. The very thing that the Sons of Liberty profess... to be among those willing to throw off the yoke of royal bondage by force."

"Sons of Liberty, sir? Who might these persons be?"

Governor Wanton smiled at the opportunity he had made to straddle his political fence. "They are us, among us, around us, whispering voices who speak of common interests in opposition to the Crown... sons of Rhode Island soil who champion the cause of liberty from actions taken by an increasingly oppressive King. They are among us, they are us, but unknown."

"Well then, Governor. If I may be so bold, for the time being, the matter appears unresolvable."

"For now, seemingly so. Yet this office continues its investigations."

"You seem doubtful, sir."

"I have suspicions that this office is likely to be circumvented on the matter as I strongly suspect that the Earl of Hillsborough and Lord Dartmouth will set about securing a King's

Proclamation and the appointment of commissioners to carry out further inquiry."

Dr. Mawney acted surprised. "A King's Proclamation, sir! Really?"

"However..." the Governor paused for emphasis. "I recognize two items of importance... I shall insist upon, by virtue of my office, being the senior commissioner attending to the Proclamation, and winter is likely to be upon us before other commissioners arrive with royal privileges conferred. Consequently, travel by then is likely to be quite difficult for those called for testimony, don't you agree Doctor Mawney?"

"Sir, I do believe you will be proven correct, given the ferocity of our winters."

"Further, Mister Franklin's almanac is calling for a severe winter. Should that prediction bear out, travel to Newport from Providence and elsewhere in the colony will be quite difficult indeed."

"To Newport, sir?"

"To this very office."

Dr. Mawney thought for a moment, recognizing the Governor's alluding to a plan to obstruct further investigations. "I see. Yes, impossibly difficult, to be sure."

"Lord Dartmouth is quite certain that our port is the focus of inquiry, given his outrage over past actions against the King, the *St. John*, the Stamp Act riots and the burning of the *Liberty* in particular, the latter I acted upon during my first year as Governor, providing no outcome. Lord Dartmouth's conclusion is no doubt based on the supposition that the raid, once again, took place in or near our harbor. I have informed his Lordship by letter that the affair was well inland from Newport and could not have been perpetrated by citizens of this town. However, Dudingston has no doubt that Providence was the point of origin. The man exhibits, I might add, a most reprehensible manner, seconded by Mister Sessions who has also been the object of his insolent behavior."

"Regard for the man seems consistent among everyone, sir."

"Rightly so, I am certain. Consequently, the belief that the *Gaspee's* assailants walk among Newporters is, no doubt, discussed among the King's men of state. With Dudingston championing the view that Providence is the point of origin and John Brown the leader, I suspect that the Crown will inflict its own fatal wound upon inquiries from such presumptions, perhaps furthered along with confusion of facts."

Dr. Mawney smiled and nodded agreement.

"And, my young friend, you may find the following entertaining. I have recently learned that the Lieutenant regards conduct of our affairs in the Assembly to be so democratic and devoid of authority that he cannot trust his correspondence to confidence through me, for fear that every word he writes will become a matter of public record that further escalates rancor against him. He now employs couriers, ship's crewmen. Furthermore, Lieutenant Linzee keeps watch upon the Brenton Point house that now contains Mister Dudingston. Isn't that fascinating? Keeping watch for what reason, I wonder? Would it be to launch a reprisal attack manned by his marines upon anyone attempting to bring further harm to Dudingston? Would not such an event be an excuse for armed reprisals, perhaps seeking justification as we speak? Another attack upon Dudingston would certainly precipitate such, all the more reason for leaving Mister Dudingston in our midst rather than under the care of a ship's surgeon, don't you think?"

"Indeed, sir. I quite agree. Your allusion that Dudingston is bait in a trap set for springing military action against us is a most interesting thought, Governor."

"Many possibilities come to mind, John. For my purposes, my hope is that no such action should be forthcoming. Otherwise, the perpetrators will, most likely, play into martial law imposed by the Admiral who will conduct the affairs of this colony thereafter. A most frightening prospect."

Dr. Mawney blinked at the suddenness of the thought. "Sir, I do hope your purposes are fulfilled. Such action would be most unwelcome."

The Governor stood up and offered a hand to his friend and messenger. "I extend my thanks for your long journey, John. Please convey elements of this conversation to our friends in Providence and that their Governor sends warm greetings."

"I shall indeed, sir. This has been a most pleasant exchange."

Just as Dr. Mawney was about to close the doors to the Governor's office behind him, the clock struck its reminder that evening was nigh.

"Oh, John!" the Govenor called out. "Given this late hour, would you join me at the White Horse Tavern for a spot of tea and Molly's famous bouillabaisse?"

"I am most delighted to accept, your honor."

"Very well then. As an aside, have you heard the tale of our nefarious Lieutenant Dudingston attempting to press her young dusty into his service?"

"No, sir. I am not aware of it. Pressed, you say?"

"So I hear. Perhaps we shall have the occasion to chat with the lad."

"I look forward to making his acquaintance."

"What is more, and most entertaining, the lad descends from our own infamy, both our pirates Thomas Tew and William Mayes the younger. Quite a storied lineage; I am told that the lad is known to many of our seafaring men, from the Tavern, no doubt, and for having sailed to the islands in years past with two of our finest captains, their cabin boy. The lad already has marvelous adventures for one so young, about fourteen years of age now, I believe. And with this new tale... of having squirted from the clutches of Dudingston's grasp... the lad...." The Governor hesitated in a moment of thought. "I believe the timing to be of interest. As I recall, the tale dates from the day of the last great fog. Hmmm. That places the lad on our wharfs the morning before the *Gaspee* was torched that evening. Oh, well. Of no importance."

"Fine adventures, indeed, Governor. I shall make an effort to meet this lad of yours."

"And John, should Captain Lillibridge, our good sheriff, be of similar mind this evening, you shall have the opportunity to hear him confide to you the evils of the Crown and Linzee and Dudingston and God knows who else."

As they left the building and stepped onto the cobblestones of the short walk to the Tavern, the Governor offered a suggestion. "By-the-by, John. One can always count on some patron of the Tavern to entertain with recitations of tales, particularly those from its own hallowed walls, within which remains Newport's very own, quite legendary pirate who owned it not so long ago, a fine man whom I recall from my youth, the quite famous William Mayes the younger. He, the notorious great-grandfather to Molly's dusty, I believe, is said to remain in ghostly residence within the structure to this day. His sister, the bonny Mary whom I can attest was a most striking woman, having married into the Nichols family, is said to be the candle that wanders the darkened tavern late of night. Imagine that, brother and sister ghosts who remain in legend and tale. Most fascinating!

"Anyway, the Nichols family has been the Tavern's proprietors since their time, leading to the current Benjamin and Molly who have been known to show, on rare occasion, one of those large gold coins that their forebear took directly from Grand Mogul's treasure. Quite a sight to have such wealth in one's hand, I can tell you. Such wonders! I find the Tavern and all its pirates, ghosts, and gold taken on the high seas more intriguing than book stories. Who knows, perhaps another chapter is being written in the Tavern's legacy with the *Gaspee*. Alas, I remain quite certain that those of us who live common lives can only wish for such notoriety."

Chapter 15

The warm months passed into winter. On a cold day of wind and snow, Admiral Montagu sat at his desk penning a letter to Joseph Wanton, Governor of Rhode Island.

"Boston, 11th December, 1772
"Sir: Last night an express arrived, with dispatches from the Right Honorable My Lords Commissioners of the Admiralty, by which came under cover to me, the packet I send to you, herewith."(2)

The next day, his letter with the King's Proclamation, Royal Commission, and Royal Instructions lay before the Governor, having also arrived by express overnight. As the Governor read the Royal Commission, he shuddered at its implications, reading:

"...And for the better execution of our royal will and pleasure therein, we do hereby give unto you, the said Joseph Wanton, Daniel Horsmanden, Frederick Smythe, Peter Oliver, and Robert Auchmuty, or any three of you, full power and authority to receive all such informations and advertisements as shall be brought unto you, by or from any of our loving subjects or others, touching the premises; and also, to inquire, by the examination of witnesses on oath, which oath we do hereby give you or any of you, full power, warrant and authority to administer, or by such other ways and means as you, or any three of you, shall, in your discretion, think fit, into the premises, or any of them.

"And we do further give you, or any three of you, full power and authority to send for such persons, papers, and records, as shall be useful; to you, for the better carrying on the service hereby intended, willing and requiring you, the said Governor...."(2)

Governor Wanton sat down slowly as grave thoughts passed through his mind. He mused aloud, "More than a century has passed since Roger Williams and his followers brought religious and political freedom here, much to our benefit since, now these documents are set to sweep away everything before them."

As he read Article 5 of the Royal Instructions, his heart sank.

"And whereas, there may be reason to apprehend, from the outrages which have been committed within our said colony of Rhode Island, by numbers of lawless persons, that insults may be offered to you, it is therefore our will and pleasure that if any disturbance shall arise, with a view to obstruct you in the execution of your duty, and any violence should in consequence thereof, be offered to you, you do, in such case, give immediate notice thereof to the commander in chief of our forces in North America, and require of him to send such a military force into the colony, as you shall judge necessary for your protection, and for the aiding the civil magistrates in suppressing any tumults or riots, and preserving the public peace."(2)

These words rang clearly in the Governor's mind; the King and his ministers were posturing a military takeover of the colony. He recognized that once military forces were requested, what lay thereafter would be beyond the colony's control, and being charged with seniority among the commissioners, he knew that his direction of the proceedings must result in no military action. How to do that, given the outspoken and volatile nature of his citizens, was not so clear. Seeing the certainty of dark days ahead if the *Gaspee* investigations were not handled carefully, further darkened by visualized consequences of another uprising, he paced the room trying to determine a way to warn his citizens of the dangers, but doing so without bringing his position into question.

Two weeks later, he sat reading the latest edition of the Providence Gazette.

"Saturday, December 26, 1772

"To be, or not to be, that's the question; whether our unalienable rights and privileges are any longer worth contending for, is now to be determined. Permit me, my countrymen, to beseech you to attend to your alarming situation....

"A court of inquisition, more horrid than that of Spain or Portugal, is established within this colony, to inquire into the circumstances of destroying the *Gaspee* schooner; and the persons who are the commissioners of this new-fangled court, are vested with most exorbitant and unconstitutional power. They are directed to summon witnesses, apprehend persons not only impeached, but even suspected! and them, and every of them, to deliver them to Admiral Montagu, who is ordered to have a ship in readiness to carry them to England, where they are to be tried..."(7)

The Governor shook his head slowly as he read, his jaw set firmly as he read further.

"To be tried by one's peers, is the greatest privilege a subject can wish for; and so excellent is our constitution, that no subject shall be tried, but by his peers.... The tools of despotism and arbitrary power, have long wished that this important bulwark might be destroyed, and now have the impudence to triumph in our faces, because such of their fellow subjects in America, as are suspected of being guilty of a crime, are ordered to be transported to Great Britain for trial, in open violation of Magna Charta.
"Thus are we robbed of our birth-rights, and treated with every mark of indignity, insult and contempt; and can we possibly be so supine, as not to feel ourselves firmly disposed to treat the advocates for such horrid measures with a detestation and scorn, proportionate to their perfidy and baseness?..."(7)

Those words struck deeply within the Governor's heart. As lead commissioner, thoughts raced through his mind; how to convey to his subjects what they must do was not at all evident, and recognizing the inflamatory nature of the words he was reading, words certain to capture the talk of the colony, he was faced with daunting prospects that could easily erupt into conflict and derail the delicate course he must steer.

"...Her colonies loudly complain of the violences and vexations they suffer by having their moneys taken from them, without their consent, by measures more unjustifiable than highway robbery; and applied to the basest purposes, - those of supporting *tyrants* and *debauchers*. No private house is inaccessible to the avarice of custom-house officers; no place so remote whither the injustice and extortion of these miscreant tools in power, have not penetrated....
"To live a life of rational beings, is to live free; to live a life of slaves, is to die by inches.... AMERICANUS"(7)

Bitter winter winds blew about Newport and whipped across the Bay with each snowflake a stinging missile flung upon unprotected faces. Governor Wanton sat by his warming fireplace contemplating the words he read. He must carefully wade through the growing indignation of the colonists to give Patriot and Tory alike a sense that their causes were being furthered. But how?

Long conversations with his sons, Joseph the younger and William, with their loyalist views, had sharpened the Governor's thoughts. Joseph, having taken up arms as a Lieutenant Colonel in the French and Indian War and a leading member of the Newport Artillery Company, had twice been Deputy Governor, the second just five years earlier. He spoke forcefully of the need to defend Rhode Island and its causes but yielded on points of authority to the King's Proclamation. William, having been appointed by his father as Customs Naval Officer of the colony, was just as forceful for quick action in the name of the Crown. "After all," his words rang in his father's memory, "when will we Rhode Islanders rise above being called pirates and brigands if we do not exercise justice of law in this and all matters?"

The Governor sat alone thinking over past conversations and could not agree with his sons. More was at stake than simply bowing to the King's authority and rounding up his citizens on mere suspicions. That, he could not allow. He must hold the reins of power given in the Proclamation by firmly guiding both the process of law and the letter of the King's will, avoiding every opportunity for proceedings to leap beyond his control. A knock at his door roused him from thought.

"Yes, enter."

His tall, thin secretary opened the door. "Doctor Mawney to see you, sir."

"Oh, yes. Please see him in."

Dr. Mawney strode in with his hand extended to the Governor. "Good to see you again, sir."

"You are a brave man, John, having taken on the weather to confer with me."

"I bring seasonal tidings of good will, your honor."

"Yes, yes, and to you, too… and to our friends to the north, as well. Seat yourself, John. We have much to discuss."

"The affairs of state are on everyone's lips these days, sir. How do you read the times?"

The Governor spoke carefully. "As you know by now, the charters we commissioners must act upon are in hand and have been read publicly, stimulating much discussion. Having read the charters carefully, I must relay to you to carry to our friends both dire warnings so stated in them, that care must be exercised this happy time of year and beyond not to allow cheery carousing to erupt into riots. Secondly, respect for the proceedings and those involved must prevail as I guide toward desirable outcomes bound within the documents of instruction."

After further discussion, the Governor asked, "Have you read the Gazette?"

"Oh, yes. It is high gossip. The entire colony is abuzz with AMERICANUS. What do you make of it, sir."

"The words speak well, a kind of foment that, if handled properly, can be of great strength. However, we must pass along to everyone not to play into the King's hands with violence, for he is set to spring martial law upon us that will very likely preempt our Commission with a military court."

Further discussion of the *Gaspee* led into late afternoon, and, as had become their custom, the two men retired to the White Horse Tavern for their evening meal. Crossing the Commons from the Colony House, they stomped off the snow and ice from their boots and stepped into the warm and inviting public house. Its broad fireplace adorned with holly was their first stop. A small cedar tree with a glistening star on top stood in one corner. A man with a newspaper in hand raised his voice to welcome the Governor. "'Ave yew read the Gazette, Guv'ner? A letter from Boston...."

Another man interrupted gleefully. "The Admiral is to set sail with his fleet to impound our harbor before the new year. In this weather!"

The patrons laughed heartily, each knowing that sailing the worst time of the year invited disaster. A third man stood up and read from his Gazette, "The admiral is in very high spirits on the occasion, and cheerfully undertakes an expedition which promises to gratify his rancor against your colony. It is hoped, from his avowed disposition towards our Rhode Island brethren, that he will meet with a proper reception among them."(2)

The first man burst back into the conversation. "Give 'im the flamin' end o' me musket, thet be the reception I'd give the bloomin' Admiral."

The crowd roared its approval.

"Now, now, gentlemen," the Governor cautioned loudly. "We must not resort to such an invitation for the Admiral to declare martial law. We do not want that, not at all. Imagine the whole of the Admiral's Royal Navy lying at anchor in our harbor... if the fleet makes it in this weather." Everyone laughed at the thought of the Admiral's ships foundering in a winter gale.

The second man mused, "'Spect ol' George the Third hisself will be comin' next." Tauntingly, he scoffed, "'Is Grace of Great Britain, France and Ireland, King, Defender of the Faith an' only the Almighty hisself knows what more the King claims. God save the King!"

Laughter rolled again, inviting the third man's reply with further reading.

"The high commissioned court, especially appointed, with novel, unconstitutional and exorbitant powers, for the trial of the persons concerned in burning the schooner, are forthwith to repair to Rhode Island for that purpose; and are to be accompanied with His High Mightiness the Admiral."(2)

Everyone laughed again as he continued. "And listen to this letter from a gentlemen of character in England, Guv'ner. 'Our tyrants in the administration, are greatly exasperated with the late maneuvers of the brave Rhode Islanders…'(2) We're all bloody 'eros over there."

Governor Wanton raised his hands to quell the laughter with his own knowledge. "Ah yes, gentlemen. But we must be wary, particularly, that officials of the Crown may intend to vacate the charter of our colony if we do not conduct ourselves civilly. Martial law will prevail in that event, and we will have ourselves not only beset with the Navy's presence, but British regulars at every turn."

Grumbling replaced laughter. The third man asked, "The King can't do it, can 'e, Guv'ner? We got laws."

"I'm afraid the King can do whatever he wishes, and quite independently of our law. We are, after all, his colony and his subjects. For now, my friends, our best ally to avoid such things is the weather and conducting ourselves civily."

Amid the quiet that followed, someone muttered, "Damn cold out."

Mumblings of agreement arose, and patrons returned to their own warm bowls Devil's root chowder as the Governor and Dr. Mawney took seats cleared for them near the fireplace. Thomas hastily delivered more bowls of soup and bread loaves to a table nearby.

"Well, well, John. I believe the evening has brought the opportunity you've long sought during past visits. Our young adventurer is within the premises. Perhaps you will have the pleasure of making his acquaintance."

Dr. Mawney had only a glimpse of the boy hurrying about his duties, returning to the kitchen through the doorway on the opposite side of the fireplace. The lad was familiar, somehow, but the surgeon dismissed the notion and motioned for the keeper. Benjamin Nichols stepped over to their table. "Good evening, gentlemen. Keeping warm and dry, I trust. Ale to warm you?"

"A fine evening to you Benjamin. Ale, John?" asked the Governor.

"Rather a warm mead, if such is available, Mister Nichols."

The keeper smiled, anticipating Dr. Mawney's usual request

beyond the ordinary. "Mead it is, sir. Be along shortly. Ale for the Guv'ner, sir?"

The Governor agreed, and as everyone settled back into their evening, he and Dr. Mawney returned to their earlier conversation. "I see good cheer among us, John. But danger looms on the horizon."

"How so, sir?"

"The King's Proclamation has put such an immense ransom on the heads of the raiders that I fear the unscrupulous can be bought and that they will contrive circumstances to their benefit. Sifting through the chaff for the grains of truth has been difficult enough, much credit to my Deputy, Mister Sessions, for his efforts. Now the prospects of having the Admiral in residence looms large, yet I have much doubt that he has jurisdiction, due to the *Gaspee* affair taking place well within the confines of our Bay some thirty miles from its mouth and open sea. Due to that fact, I have related to the Admiral my conclusion, and that of Chief Justice Hopkins, that by reason of *infra corpus comitatus*, he has no jurisdiction.

"Regardless of my efforts, the Admiral has assumed supreme authority and imposes upon me to respond to his will. I am, however, reasonably certain that sufficient truths and doubts have revealed themselves to further entangle any prosecution, particularly so should the Admiral remain in Boston. If he should come here, it will, hopefully, be at our behest making him answerable to our civil proceedings, something I feel that he will find strongly objectionable. You may recall from an exchange back in September, at the behest of Lord Sandwich, General Gage was notified to ready his troops for our colony. We have succeeded these three months hence to see no such movement, although I perceive that both the King's land and sea forces are set to move to impose the Admiral's will."

Thomas placed a tankard of ale before the Governor and a similar tankard of warm mead before Dr. Mawney. "Always a pleasure to 'ave yew at the White Horse, Guv'ner," he said.

"My pleasure indeed, young man. I trust that chowder and bread pudding are on the menu again this evening?"

"And beans of the Boston variety, sir. Slow cooked with molasses. Molly's kept me shackled to the hearth all day for fear I'd be about boastin' o' takin' that *Gaspee* an' 'er crew an' drivin' the Lieutenant to his madness by me own self."

Both men laughed at such an out-spoken admission, and the Governor seized the moment. "Thomas Mayes, have you met our fine surgeon, Doctor Mawney from Warwick?"

Thomas had already recognized Dr. Mawney, and being quick witted, he extended his hand to continue the moment's passing influence. "Damn fine cap you be wearin', Doctor. Lost mine... back summertime it were."

Dr. Mawney's normal courtesies took him to his feet, giving him an interlude to gather his thoughts, having now recognized Thomas. "So, we meet at last, young man. A pleasure it is, indeed," he said, shaking Thomas' hand. "Our fine Governor has told me much about you and, of course, this old tavern with its legacies, saying that its destiny appears set to gather more."

Thomas stepped closer to Dr. Mawney and spoke in a hushed voice. "I seen 'er with me own eyes, I did."

Dr. Mawney was intrigued by this unexpected turn in the conversation. "Saw her? Whom did you see?"

"She who walks the night, the candle flame what lives within these walls, what ever'body says is the ghost of Bonny Mary, me very own kin. I seen 'er, I did. In the marnin' mist one day. Dressed all in white and carryin' water buckets from the spring, she was. Give me the chills, it did. Gives me willies now, thinkin' 'bout 'er."

Dr. Mawney grinned. "We must speak further, young man...."

"Thomas!" Called Benjamin from across the room. "Be needin' yer 'elp in the kitchen."

With Thomas' departure, Dr. Mawney took his seat as the Governor mused, "Lost his cap during summer? A strange thing to say. Who loses their cap in summertime? What on earth?"

"Fascinating lad.... Just boy talk, I presume, probably a tussle among the lads, or some such."

Shortly, Thomas returned with an urn of chowder, then a bowl of beans and fresh baked bread. Next came bowls and spoons, along with a grin and a wink at Dr. Mawney. "Bein' just a dusty 'ere at the White Horse, all I gets is what's told. Are sayin's right, Guv'ner? Ol' George hisself'll be droppin' anchor right 'ere to Newport?"

"I suspect not, young man. But if he does, we'll send you to entertain him."

Thomas returned their grins and went back to work as the Governor returned to the thought of the King's Proclamation and chose his words carefully. "My opinion, John, is that winter and distance from this place is of greatest advantage. The Lord High Commissioners will soon be in residence here, and I shall inform them of the details as they are known. However, I perceive that the Proclamation itself holds the key that will lock the case away."

"How so, sir? I am intrigued."

The governor looked around to insure that no one was eavesdropping and lowered his voice still further. "The Royal Commission is to reside in Newport, a stroke of great good fortune to place the court far from the act. Secondly, the Admiral is named in all cases as receiver of those arrested. If he cannot travel to the court, or chooses not to travel, no warrants can be issued for he would be unable to take them, as directed by the King. In that case, the High Commissioners have little to act upon. I shall hold to the Proclamation as point of law, regardless of appointees by the Admiral, and request likewise of the High Commissioners, that the Admiral should be in residence at this place to conform to the King's decree, but having no other function of the Commission."

Dr. Mawney recognized the ploy. "Ah, such fortune, indeed. And of the winter, sir?"

"Unfortunately, winter can hold him away only until spring warmth."

"What then? Should the Admiral choose to sail, bringing his might would be further cause for concern, would it not?"

"Perhaps. Those of his majesty's warships lying anchored in our harbor now, each covered with snow and ice, confine their crews aboard. The same for all such ships further north, none capable of bearing the weight of ice topside in gale winds, winds likely to blow up at any moment making their captains uneasy about putting to sea, regardless of what is said of the Admiral in the newspapers. Our severe weather has not permitted sailing, so far, and with crews confined to quarters, unwelcome ashore most everywhere, tense times are upon them. We are, for the moment, free of their marauding for supplies that spring will bring, as is their usual. My hope is that no wild card pops up somewhere to upset the balance that seems to prevail. Each day without inquiry is another day further away from the act."

"I see," Dr. Mawney agreed. "Winter an ally... an interesting thought, particularly with this one being such a fright."

"By spring, having endured the rigors of winter, the age of the Commissioners and their need to return to home and business interests may then be such that pursuit of their commission flags. I suspicion that most, if not all of them, are disgruntled to have been picked by the King to perform such an unwelcome task this time of year, and, if I judge the King's methods correctly, each of them will be expected to bear all expense themselves; plucked by the King, as it were," he chuckled. "That should suffice to parry a great deal of their attention."

Dr. Mawney chuckled, "Most interesting developments, sir."

"As the Commission's chief prosecutor, I perceive that advantage is gained by the Commission proceeding forthrightly, yet conforming strictly to point of law. Responsibility assigned to the Admiral is likely to be in conflict with his interests of pursuing the good life he enjoys in Boston, and, without his presence here, proceedings of the Commission are likely to become rather frozen with little progress other than correspondence. Speaking of which, I am told of correspondence now being shared among the colonies, a most interesting prospect with potential to unite with a common cause, the very thing lacking so far."

Dr. Mawney smiled. "I understand, sir."

"We shall see how events unfold, perhaps with some direction in shaping to come."

"Indeed, sir. An admirable crafting."

The Governor grasped the surgeon's play on words and nodded agreement. "An admirable crafting, indeed. Well said, my friend. Shall we meet again a month hence, at your discretion, Doctor Mawney?"

"Certainly, sir. And I shall convey sentiments of the day to those in Bristol, Warren, Providence and Warwick who may have interest."

"Rather good chowder, don't you think, Doctor?" the Governor said, lifting another spoonful to his mouth.

A tall sailor stepped from a nearby table over to the fireplace and lit his pipe. Taking a draw and blowing a cloud of smoke into the air, he gathered everyone's attention to his baritone voice when he loudly said, "Jack, am I, a sailor so bold, an' sea tales 'ave I often told.

An approving voice rose from the patrons. "Shoot us a line, Jack, a right fair one 'bout some place warm."

Everyone agreed with added mumblings about the cold.

Extending his hand toward the distance, "So, a tale ye seek of places warm. Me thinks, yes, there's ol' Nassau town." And he began another recitation of the kind to which the Tavern was accustomed.

> Come along, me 'ardies; a tale I aim to tell,
>   Of old Nassau town an' ridin' sea swell.
> The lay of me ship, cloth full with stout wind,
>   No finer day could be sailin' with Brethren.
>
> Bright twinklers overhead fade to oblivion,
>   As sunrays break night on distant 'orizon.
> Awake greets cool morn an' hails new sun,
>   All hands rousted to man each ship's station.
>
> Blustered salt spray roils off Poseidon's deep,
>   Breathed briney prickled on weathered cheek.
> Wind through lashings sing our day's reward,
>   O'er yon vista Nassau lay to starboard.

Hard tack soaked in ale eases sore teeth,
    Amid yearns of empty belly soon to pique.
Belt tightened an' cinched over a-gain,
    Awaitin' Nassau's bounty to ease the pain.

Yearns for bangers an' pozzie an' fresh soft tack,
    Then floaters in snow to bring me back.
She-crab soup with shrimp and corn pie,
    Rhubarb crumble and plum duff to sigh.

Tankard of grog in lee o' Maggie's Mad Hare,
    With fiddleheads, cowslips and greens so fair.
Empty Horse-Necks of rum left bye the bye,
    Better in Snake's Pit than ship's pig stye.

Month's long sailin' a barber to seek,
    An' bathin' an' shavin' so fondly I speak.
Clean outers me long overdue treat,
    Then come pleasures for this man o' the sea.

Pockets thin o' jinglers, scrimshaw to trade,
    I seeks me pleasures in sun an' shade.
Fine sands to lay at waters warm edge,
    A den and a lass, what more to wage?

Stories rum honed for all to bray an' boast;
    Hard rains whipped by fierce gale me toast.
Squall's wind song a wail through tight stays.
    Tales of the bold an' daring e'er so brave,

All hands stationed amid decks held on,
    One and all shiverin' to wind's cold song.
Breathin' hopes for our Cap'n's good will,
    That a new sun would find us in mornin's still.

Calm seas warmed under the new day's sun,
    Speaks no hint of what we've seen an' done.
Many a stout 'earted seaman rode in tall sail,
    Lost to Davy Jones' deep tolls our bell.

Sad song for shipmates among timber so tall,
    Then near isles feed yearns for that call.
"Land Ho!" turns eyes 'cross ship's freeboard,
    Welcomed Nassau rises off to leeward.

Good ale and fine eats once again to rejoice,
  Among fragrant trollops my treasure of choice.
O'er strumpets and cheer me 'earties will boast,
  Till dry spendin's sends me back to our boat.

Grand Nassau how you e'er tempt me so,
  How you fill me up and leave me low.
Need I of prairie-oysters for mornin's after,
  Chin in hand from gun'l I stare so plastered.

A hearty round of laughter and cheers told Jack that his tale was well received, and with the offering of a tankard of ale his reward, he rejoined his companions as someone bellowed toward the Governor. "Hail, Guv'ner. Shoot us a right fair line, sir."

Governor Wanton, taken by surprise, dismissed the request saying, "Now gentlemen, well known is the complete lack of such tales among politicians. My duties, dull and laden with details, afford no such entertainment for narrations." Then seizing the moment, the thought struck him that the young dusty among them might oblige. "Perhaps our very own Thomas Mayes, a lad of great adventures, I'm told, will provide us entertainment."

Both Dr. Mawney and Thomas were surprised. Thomas, having been the teller only among the lads, always the listener among seasoned sailors, was prepared and quick to take the moment to his own. He stepped to the hearth saying, "Captain Swan of Bristol put to pen this," and he began with the limping gait of a familiar tavern song. Soon, patrons began swaying their mugs in time with the tune.

'Twas in the reign of George the Third,
  Our public peace was much disturbed,
By ships of war, that came and laid,
  Within our ports, to stop our trade.

Seventeen hundred and seventy-two,
  In Newport harbor lay the crew,
That played the part of pirates there,
  The Sons of Freedom could not bear.

Sometimes they weighed and gave them chase,
  Such action sure were very base.
No honest coaster could pass by,
  But what they would let some shot fly.

And did provoke, to high degree,
   Those true born Sons of Liberty;
So that they could not longer bear,
   The sons of Belial staying there.

But 'twas not long 'fore it fell out,
   That William Dudingston, so stout,
Commander of the *Gaspee* tender,
   Which he has reason to remember.

Because, as people do assert,
   He almost had his just dessert;
Here, on the ninth day of June,
   Betwixt the hours of twelve and one.

Did chase the sloop, called *Hannah*,
   Of whom, one Lindsey, was commander,
They dogged her up Providence Sound,
   And there the rascal got aground.

The news of it flew that very day,
   That ship on Namquit Point did lay.
That night, about half after ten,
   Some Narragansett Indian men.

Being sixty-four, if I remember,
   Which made the stout coxcomb surrender.
And what was best of all their tricks,
   They in his breech a ball did fix.

Then set the men upon the land,
   And burnt her up, we understand;
Which thing provoked the King so high,
   He said those men shall surely die.

So if he could but find them out,
   The hangman he'll employ, no doubt;
For he's declared, in his passion,
   He'll have them tried a new fashion.

Now, for to find these people out,
   King George has offered very stout;
One thousand pounds to find out one,
   That wounded William Dudingston.

> One thousand more, he says he'll spare,
>   For those who say the sheriff's were;
> One thousand more, there doth remain,
>   For to find out the leader's name.
>
> Likewise, five hundred pounds per man,
>   For any one of all the clan.
> But let him try his utmost skill,
>   I'm apt to think he never will.
>
> Find out any of those hearts of gold,
>   Though he should offer sixty-fold.(2)

Thomas bowed as cheers erupted. Dr. Mawney's dry mouth left him speechless, his heart beating violently in his throat from expecting at any moment to have himself exposed in the rhyme. His sigh of relief was lost in the moment's high candor, and both he and the Governor kept silent. Thomas seized the moment and gave Dr. Mawney a sly grin as he ran off into the kitchen. The surgeon abruptly returned to his chowder and beans.

The Governor, not suspecting the subject and hiding his eyes, regretted having asked to be entertained. Thomas' recitation was much too close for comfort. "My God!" he whispered. "Narragansett Indians, Sons of Liberty. The taking of that ship is still upon us, and our citizens make light of it?"

"Hail, Guv'ner," a patron asked. "Wot be the state o' thet schooner these days? Wot with Dudingston shipped off to England?"

The room quieted for his answer, just the turn of events that the Governor hoped would not occur.

"Dudingston shipped off to England?" he asked, unaware of that event.

"Aye, sir. Seen them what took 'im to the *Lizard*, I did. On Brenton's Point, I wuz. Off to England they took 'im."

"I must consider that, an interesting turn. As for the matter of destroying the ship, investigations proceed as we speak."

The man elbowed his friend seated next to him. "Jes like the *Liberty*. Jes like I said. Burnt that bastard out and, whisp, right out into the night they went. Jes like the *Liberty*. Ain't nothin' to come of it. Aye, Guv'ner?"

"I suspect that a good deal is to come of it, my friend. The King's Commission, soon to be convened, is to look into the matter."

"An' wot do they 'ope to uncover what ain't already knowed?"

"That, sir, is yet to be resolved. Perhaps, what is assumed known may not become the results of the inquest. Perhaps?"

Act 3

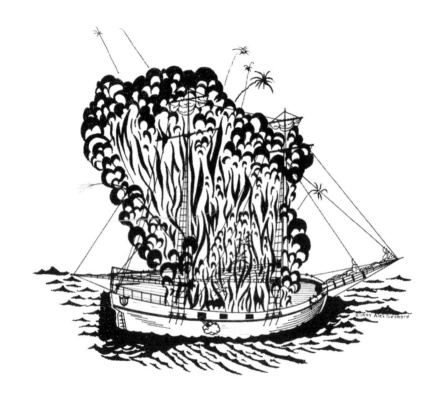

Chapter 16

A month later, along a Newport street, the crunching of ice under foot as Dr. Mawney hurried along ended with a knocking at the door of the home of the Governor. The door opened, he was invited in, and the door quickly closed behind him.

"A pleasant good evening to you, John," the Governor said.

"And to you, sir. I shall be only the night in Newport, and take this opportunity to visit."

They sat by the fireplace, its warmth welcoming the new arrival. "The fires are aflame about us, my friend," the Governor said.

"Yes, I am aware and bring news of rebellious risings, sir."

The Governor handed a small glass of cognac to the surgeon. "I am told of such. I fear that events are near to escaping my hand. I was, just now, going through the number of dispatches that have collected about the *Gaspee* affair. Allow me to read a passage from Lord Dartmouth in a letter arrived some three months past.

"' ...The particulars of that atrocious proceeding (referring to the burning the *Gaspee* schooner), have, by the King's command, been examined and considered with the greatest attention... and taking all the circumstances together, the offence is, in the opinion of the law servants of the crown, who have been consulted upon that question, of a much deeper dye, and is considered in no other light, than as an act of high treason, viz: levying war against the King.' (2)

"This passage, John, I have often pondered. Nay, it is with me at all times, and I believe it to be the very basis of the military posturing to assail our colony. Within the same letter is the notice to General Gage to ready his troops, the same that I have mentioned in our past meetings."

The Governor handed the letter to Dr. Mawney who read the lines, then thought for a moment. "Are we near to war with the mother country, Governor? No such appearances have I seen."

"Not as yet, but I fear that those who champion the cause of war, as both a way of throttling this colony and, being the smallest among the thirteen, the most likely to receive the wrath of the crown as a demonstration to the others. What troubles me so is recently learning that my counterpart in the Massachusetts Colony, Governor Hutchinson, has cast his lot with the Crown."

Dr. Mawney was shocked. "Really! Sir, I find the sentiments in that colony just the opposite."

"Perhaps not within official circles. Read this private dispatch that arrived today. Note the date and location, late August of the year past and from Boston."

Dr. Mawney's eyes widened as he read. "The persons who were the immediate actors, are men of estate, and property, in the colony. A prosecution is impossible. If ever the government of that colony is to be reformed, this seems to be the time; and it would have a happy effect in the colonies which adjoin it. Several persons have been advised by letters from their friends, that as the ministry are united, and opposition at an end, there will certainly be an inquiry into the state of America, the next session of Parliament. The denial of the supremacy of Parliament, and the contempt with which its authority has been treated by the Lilliputian Assemblies of America, can never be justified or excused by any one member of either House of Parliament."(2) Stunned, he sat down in a chair.

"Appearances, seem to me, John, that our neighbor to the north has designs upon expanding his holdings with quests for the removal of our 'Lilliputian Assembly', taking our charter as well, to be joined in the 'happy' unification of that colony's ministry, saying nothing of the sentiments of this colony that Mister Hutchinson appears to dismiss out of hand. These times are our most dangerous, particularly so if our actions are perceived to be in opposition to the Crown. We may stand alone in an unwinnable contest. To preserve our colony, we must present the appearance of civil respect, and the Commission must present a thorough investigation with concern for justice, without confrontation. This you must relay to our friends to hold what wills may be set to take up arms. We must step lightly and carefully."

Dr. Mawney nodded agreement. "I find these events most troubling, for I have come from a similar discussion to bring news of Massachusetts standing with us."

"Oh! That would be most welcome. What news?"

"A good friend, who sits on the council of the town of Ipswich, relayed to me that the council is mightily alarmed at the appointment of your commission. Furthermore, the council, supported by a host of citizenry, condemns this method of proceeding as an infringement upon liberty and our established legal structure, a most dangerous consequence of imposed outside authority. That council, as does every council throughout the colonies, operates on its own proceedings without need for outside meddling by the King or anyone."

Governor Wanton sighed. "I can only say, with great satisfaction, that I am most relieved to learn this. This reassurance calls for another cognac. Yourself?"

After some moments to reflect, he continued, "How to proceed is clearer now. We have a list of names from the Admiral, with expectations that each of them will put some portion of the puzzle in place such that prosecutions will result. The method of individual inquiry seems appropriate."

"Individual inquiry, sir?"

"Each witness alone. That process will inhibit the potential of emotional blurtings between witnesses, one against the other."

Dr. Mawney smiled. "May I ask what you have learned?"

"What do you know of one Stephen Gulley?"

"Stephen Gulley, sir? I know of no such person."

"In days just past, Mr. Gulley was called before the High Commissioners and gave a deposition stating that he had been onboard His Majesty's ship, *Lizard*, for some days for fear of his life."

"Really? On what account?"

"He stated that he happened upon Mister Borden's public house just north of Newport some time back...."

A smoke-filled tavern known to Dr. Mawney emerged in his mind's eye. Men carousing and gaming away a cold winter's evening were disturbed with the arrival of a man who called out in a boisterous voice, "Who is the proprietor of this establishment?"

"'Tis I," the innkeeper replied from across the room.

The man shuddered from the cold and made his way directly for the fireplace. "I am in need of me evenin' meal and lodgin's, and I have silver to pay," he bellowed.

"A bed for the night and soup to warm thee, sir. Ten shillings."

"Ten shillings!" blared Stephen Gulley. "You rob a man!"

"The price of keep overnight, sir," the keeper replied, recognizing that his new patron was laden with rum.

Gulley responded with a sweeping gesture, "I shall pay no more than half-crown, a fair price, I should think."

"Warm by me fire and partake of me soup pot, but no bed for the night for a mere half-crown. The road awaits yew, sir."

Gulley glared at the innkeeper. "You are a hard man, sir, no friend of the common man."

"These times are hard for one and all, sir. Mind yew, other patrons are about."

"Ten shillings for supper, the night, and me breakfast in addition, an' me 'orse in yer stable with grain," grinned Gulley.

"Ten shillings, no less, for yew alone, sir. Oats for yer horse and mornin' oats for yew as well, along with yer berth in the stable for yer ten shillings, not in this house."

Gulley became angry. "Swine, I've a mind to...."

Two patrons assisted and persuaded Gulley to sit by the fire and warm himself. He complied, then slammed three crowns on the table, each silver coin making a metallic whack recognized by everyone.

"This should bear the expense, innkeeper. A mug of ale if you will, and be quick about it." Gulley banged his fist on the table. "By the morrow I shall have a king's ransom."

As the following moments settled with Gulley gathering warmth by the fire, a patron unknown to him approached and asked quietly, "Wot be yer destination, friend?"

"Newport and the high court. What of it?" Gulley snapped.

The innkeeper placed a large bowl of hot soup and a chunk of bread before Gulley, who took to the meal as if starved. When the keeper took his coins and moved off, the man continued. "A matter of grave concern to yew, my friend," he whispered. "A body of twenty armed Indians await yer passage along the road. Yer presence is known, sir, and they aim to leave yew dead in a ditch somewhere, as if done in by highwaymen."

"Indians!" Gulley scowled. "Nonsense."

"Indians in fact or by dress alone, yer passage is known. They lay in wait to do yew harm."

The revelation caused Gulley to regain a bit of his composure, and while he finished his soup more slowly, the two men talked until Gulley rose from his chair showing need to relieve himself and went outside, as did his companion. The innkeeper quickly locked the door behind him, having noticed other patrons making gestures toward Gulley, seeming to plot trouble. Soon, Gulley returned to find himself locked out. He beat on the door and yelled, "I have paid for me own keep, you rogue. Let me in!"

"Only if yew takes the remainder of yer meal in me back room an' retire for the evenin'," warned the keeper.

"Scoundrel! That you be, sir! A scoundrel o' the first order. LET ME IN!" Gulley demanded as he beat on the door.

"Ruffians like yew, sir, break up me own establishment, an' I won't 'ave it. Yew 'ear?"

"Damn you, innkeeper. I shall freeze in this cursed weather."

"Only into me back room, sir. Do yew agree?"

"So be it. Open this damned door, you cursed brigand!"

"Round to the back with yew, sir. To the rear door."

Gulley, cursing all the way, led his horse and tramped through the snow around the tavern to the rear door of a large porch packed with stored goods. The innkeeper met him. "Yer talk, sir, speaks that yew 'ave set yer way to Newport to give information about the *Gaspee* burning. 'Tis not the truth, sir?"

"Where I venture is me own business. Aside with you," he demanded. Handing the reins of his horse to the keeper, he continued, "Bed me 'orse, an' feed as well. Yer own bargain, you scoundrel."

"Nay, sir. Not a scoundrel, but a friend what sees yer steps into grave troubles. I fear that patrons within plot against yew, friend. Knives they 'ave, hidden under coats. Please, sir, keep yer voice low, an' the night may see yew through 'till the morn for yer noble quest."

"Nonsense you speak, man. A plot against me?"

"Aye. 'Tis true. I fear that yew 'ave fallen in among those cursed Sons o' Liberty what 'ave gathered within. Yew be warned already by a good friend o' King George. Take heed o' another, sir. 'Tis good advice, the likes o' which may permit yew to see another sunrise."

"Out o' me way, scoundrel. Trust is not upon you... you... scoundrel. Bed me 'orse for the night an' show what be me own. Damn cold out."

"The appearance of bad blood between yew an' me patrons implores me to tell yew o' the lower road to the Newport ferry, sir. Yew must leave immediately. I fear for yer life. They will lay in wait fer yew throughout the night. Yew shall not rise to another day, I tell yew. Take the low road, now, sir. Go with haste, I implore yew. The low road by the Bay, a bit rough but passable; it will take yew to the ferryman's stable fer yerself an' yer 'orse. Go now, quickly, an' speak not o' yer mission to anyone or troubles aplenty will be yer reward. Yew must keep yer intent private. Listen carefully an' take heed to me words, sir."

Gulley acquiesced and swung up on his horse, shuddering at the cold saddle suddenly in his crotch. The innkeeper motioned him toward a narrow, overgrown road leading by the barn. He grasped Gulley's hand and placed two of the coins in his palm, making a fist of the gloved hand. "Two crowns for yer journey, sir, for King and country. God save the King. Go quickly, now. The low road will take yew to the ferry clear o' yer pursuers on the main road, one with two brass pistols, I am told. Me thinks such weapons are not the sort to be among Indians or common thieves; these are men of purpose. If yew value yer life, sir, ride clear o' the main road. Yew now know of highwaymen in wait for travelers to Newport on missions such as yers. Make no mention of *Gaspee* in any way, sir, an' yew might arrive in Newport on the morrow."

Gulley rode off into the night.

Governor Wanton continued with the story. "Stephen Gulley told of such harrowing exploits, then arrived before the court the next day to swear to his affidavit. He claimed before the High Commissioners to have been taken into the confidence of a good friend in Providence who told him the names of the leaders of the raid. We are left to presume that those leaders, attempting to protect their identities, dispatched accomplices to intercept him. Mister Gulley claimed to have no more than consumed his meal when warned of men wielding knives and guns. He was provided a means of escape...."

The Governor paused and shook his head with concern. "I fear that division has taken hold, John, Patriot-Tory, Tory-Patriot, to use the inflammatory words of Boston's firebrands, those Sons of Liberty, Liberty Boys... I fear the growing swell of contempt on both sides." The Governor gazed into the flames of his fireplace and added, "Particularly so such inflammatory proceedings as fostered by the likes of Samuel Adams and Joseph Warren, whom I do not know nor need their influence that was so well received by the Assembly. The names of these two Bostonians lay on an article from a "Committee of Correspondence" originating in that colony that was recently presented to our Assembly with claims of "common cause." I see the rise of a new stage of confrontration in this affair that we certainly do not need. We must resolve the pressing matters of the Commission without highwaymen bearing knives and firearms."

Dr. Mawney offered his view, "I receive your warning, sir. I shall be wary of my stops in passage back to Providence with your recommendations. And all travels henceforth."

"Oh! My apologies, Doctor Mawney, I digress. However, I should think it wise to be wary while traveling our roads. To continue, Gulley claimed no direct knowledge of the *Gaspee* incident, second or third hand at best. Of the leaders, all are new names to me except for the Browns. He claimed his source to be a shoemaker in Providence at the time the ship was burned, one Saul Ramsdale. He says the man claimed near to being inducted into the escapade, but being faint of heart, he declined participation only to become the one voice in this affair, if in fact such a person exists, that could tip the anonymous to infamy. Gulley stated that the shoemaker learned the identities of the leaders, and fearing for himself afterwards, returned to Mendon in Massachusetts Colony, whereupon one Captain Thayer learned of his story, then passed it to our Mister Gulley. Ramsdale has not been located. Thayer, however, is due to testify."

"These and other persons have been sought?" asked the surgeon.

"Indeed, perhaps others hide in anonymity for fear of their lives. Gulley's tale tells me that the times grow increasingly tense each day, yet I am troubled by his statement. If such a Thayer exists, who must know that Gulley will identify him, would not the person seek the ransom for himself, particularly if a Tory? And particularly so if a resident of another colony, the very same in which the King's Admiral conducts his court? Why did he not appear before the Admiral himself? Gulley told of learning the particulars, having befriended Thayer who divulged his knowledge while well into an evening of ale, a most suspect circumstance, I must say. Gulley has also made no mention of sharing rewards with anyone, presumably intending to keep all proceeds for himself. I find the situation most suspect with this thought; if information passed to him is of such value that simply making statement with accusations is sufficient to secure the King's ransom, would not the man Thayer or Ramsdale have made their own statements, most probably to magistrates in their own colony for they must surely know that they are named by Gulley? If the facts are known to them and actually told to Gulley, would they not wish to share in its prize as well?"

"Sounds much of story-making to me as well, sir," Dr. Mawney confided.

"Such testimony is certainly not prime evidence, but it is the sort to keep the Commissioners looking elsewhere. By Gulley's accounting," the Governor laughed, "the High Commissioners are now in pursuit of between three hundred and four hundred raiders. The story grows with each telling, and my fellow courtsmen have commented despairingly that all of Rhode Island appears to have been in on the incident, yet no one knows anything but hearsay."

Chapter 17

As frigid, mid-January winds blew snow upon windows hung with icicles outside, in the court of the High Commission the five appointees of the King pursued the inquest of Aaron Briggs. The sixteen year old's muscular build spoke of his physical abilities, but not knowing what was to become of him in the company of such powerful men made him fearful.

Daniel Horsmanden, Chief Justice of the Province of New York, demanded, "How much money?"

"Cap'n Potter give me two dollar for me own services, sir," Briggs said nervously.

"What services?"

"Mannin' a oar, sir. Rowin', what 'e paid me fer doin'."

"What time of the night did your encounter with Captain Potter take place?"

"I reckon the time, sir.... It were... I reckon it were... it were nigh on to midnight."

"Where were you rowing at such an hour?"

"I wuz, sir, takin' me master's skiff 'round Prudence Island to the east side, gettin' it ready fer takin' Mister Faulkner to Bristol the next evenin', sir. I wuz gonna ask Mister Tompkins fer its use the next evenin', sir."

"Samuel Faulkner, a hired hand?"

"Yes, sir."

"And, Mister Briggs, you put the skiff into the water when?"

Briggs eyes enlarged, and he thought quickly. "It were a little after sunset, sir. A bit later, I reckon."

"Not yet in the darkness of night?"

Briggs thought a moment. "It were dark then."

"When was it dark?"

"When I run in with Cap'n Potter's boat."

"Now, Mister Briggs. Let me see if I understand. You launched your master's skiff of two oars shortly after sunset, then met Captain Potter's longboat deep into the night, about ten o'clock? Is that correct?"

Briggs recognized the point the Commissioner was making and stumbled, "I weren't in no hurry, sir. An', the tide were thinnin', too. I wuz restin' out on the Bay, sir."

"So, no more than two miles or so of rowing took you well into the evening, as you have stated. Further, you say that you rested along the way, presumably rowing only enough to keep ahead of the out-going tide such that you advanced up the Bay a half-mile or so beyond Prudence Island, whereupon you met a longboat rowed from Bristol?"

"Yes, sir."

The lead Commissioner, Governor Wanton, interrupted. "For the record, gentlemen, Mister Briggs should clarify the geography as he knows it. Namquit Point, Mister Briggs. Isn't that spit of low-water land a goodly way *upstream* from Prudence Island, about ten miles or more? And isn't Bristol Bay to the northeast of Prudence Island about five miles by water?"

"Yes, sir. That be 'bout right."

"So the geography implies that both your small boat with a single oarsman and the longboat that you say came from the town of Bristol filled with oarsmen, the same containing oarsmen with sidearms, knives and clubs... that both boats had the disadvantage of the out-going tide?"

"Yes, sir. The tide weren't yet even."

Horsmanden was not pleased with the interruption and continued his questioning. "Now, Mister Briggs; you have stated that you knew of Captain Potter, recognizing him from having the man pointed out to you on Bristol wharf by Mister Faulkner the year before when the two of you purchased rope at Potter's ropewalk for your master. Is that correct?"

"Yes, sir."

"And that he commanded eleven persons in the boat, eight of them manning the available oar locks...." Horsmanden's voice trailed as he searched for his next thought. "Mister Briggs, if more than enough oarsmen were in the boat, for what purpose would Captain Potter hire you to row?"

Briggs had anticipated the question and had his answer ready. "I reckon the Cap'n wanted me on a oar so's to free up the man what had it fer fightin', sir."

Believing that he had led Briggs' testimony to firmly identify one of the raid leaders, Commissioner Horsmanden sat back in his chair, satisfied, and turned the proceedings over to Governor Wanton.

"For further clarification, I have some questions," the Govenor stated. "Mister Briggs. Are you in need of relief at the moment?"

"No, sir."

"We shall proceed. In your previous statements, you have said that the time you met Captain Potter's boat was about a half-hour after putting your master's skiff into the water. Is that correct?"

"Yes, sir."

"And during that time, you progressed against the tide about one or two miles, to the point of meeting Potter's boat?"

"Yes, sir."

"That would place the time of day, in darkness, about nine o'clock in the evening. Yet, testimony from *Gaspee* crewmen confirm the time of attack at just after changing of the mid-watch, after midnight."

"I reckon that be 'bout right."

"Yet, your statement for the record to Admiral Montagu says that you rowed alongside the longboat until near where the *Gaspee* was grounded. Is that correct?"

Briggs hesitated. "I reckon it were like that, sir."

"You 'reckon', Mister Briggs? Now sir, please tell this court; Is your statement correct or incorrect?"

"I... I reckon, sir."

"You 'reckon' again, Mister Briggs?"

Briggs, unsure of where the question would lead, became exasperated. "The Admiral, sir.... When me words got writ, they wuz sayin' the main things... but didn't get all the partic'lars what went on. It were dark, too, an' I wuz right scairt...."

"Mister Briggs, collect yourself, sir. I am merely attempting to clarify that you rowed single-handedly for some twelve miles or more, against an out-going tide, while the encountered longboat was rowed by a full compliment of oarsmen, eight or more, and that you kept pace with them for that distance. That is some feat, isn't it?" Governor Wanton was pleased with the testimony, having placed several elements of doubt about Briggs' statements.

Briggs sensed a compliment and was relieved. "Yes, sir. I got right tired...."

"Thank you, Mister Briggs. I turn the inquiry to the right honorable Judge Smythe."

Frederick Smythe, Chief Justice of the Province of New Jersey, continued the line of questioning. "Whereupon, as you say, Captain Potter told you to take up a weapon and do as the other men did once aboard the intended vessel. Is that correct?"

"Yes, sir. An' 'e say they wuz goin' to meet sixteen or seventeen boats comin' from Providence. Weren't but eight boats what we met 'bout a hour later, I reckon. They was full of people."

Commissioner Smythe knitted his brow. "Mister Briggs, would you clarify for me, please; you were in the water more than an hour going a mile or two when you met Potter's boat at about a half-hour after darkness, sometime before mid-night according to your testimony to the Admiral, then rowed beside a fully manned longboat going twelve miles or so against the tide in about an hour when your assembly met eight or more boats about half mile above the *Gaspee*. The timing says that all the boats were within a half-mile of the schooner at that time. Is that correct?"

"Yes, sir."

"The time at that moment was, by your accounting, about eleven o'clock in the evening. How long after that, sir, did the attack take place?"

Briggs stumbled for thought. "Cap'n Potter an' them two leaders what come from Providence, they wuz both called Mister Brown, talked about the best way to attack the ship."

"How long did they talk, Mister Briggs?"

"Weren't long, I reckon."

"And then the attack began?"

"Yes, sir."

"So, the assembled boats met in the bay and oarsmen kept the boats at that location for a short time while the attack was planned. Is that correct?"

"Yes, sir."

"I am curious, Mister Briggs. In your previous statement to the Admiral, you gave the exact number of longboats as seventeen, each filled with men with weapons. Now you say eight longboats, making a total of nine counting the longboat from Bristol. And that immediately upon meeting, the assembled boats, '...we rowed towards the schooner...' to quote you, sir. How is it possible to have counted exactly eight or seventeen boats in the darkness? Can you count to seventeen, sir?"

"Yes, sir. I counts right good, learnin' at me master's work."

"In the darkness of a very dark night as well, sir?"

"Right many boats, sir. They wuz rowin' hard with locks muffled. Right quiet like, an' fast, so Captain Potter tol' me to get in 'is boat so's I wouldn't be makin' no noise with me own oars...."

"Mister Briggs! Please return to the question of counting the boats. Which figure in your statements is correct? Eight boats? Seventeen boats? And if so, how did you arrive at such a figure?"

Robert Auchmuty, Judge of the Vice-Admiralty Court for the surrounding colonies, interrupted. "Allow me to interject, gentlemen. Affidavits have been taken as records of the facts in this case. If we pursue each detail, we will not likely arrive at the goal of our inquiry. I recommend that we pursue the main events such as the leaders of the raid and who shot Lieutenant Dudingston. Once those goals are achieved, other participants will fall in order. May I take the floor, Judge Smythe?"

The commissioner yielded.

"Mister Briggs, in your statement you have identified John Brown of Providence Plantations as both the leader of the raid and the person who fired upon Mister Dudingston, have you not?"

Briggs knitted his brow, hesitated, then blurted, "I seen the man what shot Mister Dudingston, I did. An' I seen Mister Dudingston fall, howlin' thet 'e wuz kilt. Seen it, I did!"

"And you declare that it was John Brown of Providence Plantations who fired the shot?"

"Yes, sir. Seen it, I did."

Governor Wanton did not permit these slights of the facts pass and interrupted. "Mister Briggs, would you describe the person whom you declare fired upon Mister Dudingston?" he asked.

Briggs looked off into space. "He were slight o' build, sir. 'Bout as tall as me. Wearin' a frock what come down his legs like usual, buttoned tight agin' the cold. I wuz wearin' two frocks, me own self."

"And you could see the man clearly in the darkness, a very dark and cloudy night, according to the affidavits of Seaman Bartholemew Cheever and other *Gaspee* crewmen?"

"Yes, sir. Dark night it were, but some light from the ship cast about. 'E was standing in the boat right near to me own.... I means, the boat what Cap'n Potter put me to rowin'."

"So you were near enough to unmistakably make out the identity of this person, even in the darkness and within the rapidly unfolding action of the raid, rowing, tying up, men with weapons clambering off the boat you were in?"

"Right good, sir. I seen 'im right good."

"What sort of hat was he wearing?"

Briggs thought for a moment. "I reckon it were a knit cap, sir."

"You have met Mister Brown, perhaps in conduct of your master's business?"

Briggs hesitated. "No sir. Don't reckon so."

"You 'reckon', sir? Do you mean that you have been in close company with John Brown in Providence, or elsewhere, sufficiently to know him well enough to recognize the man in total darkness?"

"I reckon...."

"Sir," Judge Auchmuty interjected. "Mister Briggs, please

step out of this chamber with the sheriff."

Once the doors closed behind Briggs, the judge continued. "Gentlemen, Briggs has made his affidavit of record, stating under oath that John and Joseph Brown of Providence, Simeon Potter of Bristol, Doctor Weeks of Warwick and a Mister Richmond of Providence were involved in leading the destruction of the *Gaspee*. So named are five individuals among some one hundred and thirty-six individuals if we count eight for each of seventeen longboats that Briggs originally professed to have perpetrated the raid, some seventy-five if in nine boats, or sixty-four or so men if we count the seven or eight boats as stated by Mister Cheever, the discoverer of the impending raid. How many boats were involved in the attack is not an issue. Also, how Mister Briggs may have come to know these people is also not at issue. Mister Briggs has been clearly identified as among the raiders by both a crewman and the captain of that doomed vessel. How they should come to know him is not at issue as well. Each has been identified. Our charter, gentlemen, is to apprehend these individuals and bring them to justice."

"Quite so," Governor Wanton agreed. "However, in the case of Doctor Weeks, certainly a person of prominence who would be widely known in the surrounding area, my inquiries have returned the fact that no such person exists. No Doctor Weeks is known anywhere in our fair colony, according to surgeons to whom I have personally spoken. That being a fact, such a person cannot be apprehended. That fact leads me to question the veracity of Mister Briggs' statements as a whole, originating with the opening sentence of his statement referring to rowing from Providence...."

Judge Auchmuty interrupted. "A simple matter of incorrect transcription, or not being fully aware of the timing, and of no significance. Mister Briggs cannot write, nor does he speak with perfect clarity. The transcriber simply mistakenly wrote 'Providence' for 'Prudence'."

Governor Wanton conceded the latter point. "You are likely correct in the matter, sir. However, if we are to judge the correctness of all matters of question in the various affidavits before us, dismissing those elements within them that we choose as simple errors, then we are faced with disconcerting matters of determining what truthfully occurred from mere interpretation of statements and their surrounding events. Do we seek truth, sir? I believe that is our goal, certainly not to extract only those elements that fit a forgone conclusion to aid in prosecutions. We must be careful not to dismiss all others, seeming to relent upon the facts such that any prosecution will do."

Judge Auchmuty showed his displeasure at being confronted and replied contemptuously, "The truth of the matter is clearly laced with deceptions at all turns, whether sixty-five raiders or one hundred sixty-five, eight longboats or seventeen. The acts were committed and perpetrators remain at large, so named in affidavit after affidavit before us. Debating who was or was not involved is not our charter. Ours is to arrive at sufficient conviction to issue warrants for arrests."

"Quite right again, sir," Governor Wanton confirmed. "Our guidance remains the King's Proclamation in giving authority to this inquiry to proceed forthrightly. I believe its reading compels us to charge those proven to be involved, as stated clearly in its opening sentence, offered here for clarity, I quote, 'For the discovering and apprehending the persons who plundered and burnt the *Gaspee* schooner, and barbarously wounded and ill-treated Lieutenant Dudingston, commander of the said schooner.' We are, as yet, seeking discovery of these persons. They are the targets of this inquiry, yet to be identified."(2)

"Indeed," grumbled Judge Auchmuty. "Proceed."

"Very well, sir. Commissioner Smythe led us to the realization that significant timing problems exist in conflicting testimony from Mister Briggs. In both statements, previously to the Admiral and now to us, he relates the sequence of events to have transpired well prior to midnight, yet crewmen Cheever's testimony, having just assumed the mid-watch, fixes the time of the attack after midnight."

Judge Auchmuty dismissed the conflict. "As I have said, Governor, the man could easily not have had a grasp of the time. Again, the time of the attack is not at issue."

"Point well made, sir. I concede to you on the matter. The question of identities is not so easily dismissed, however. Mister Briggs stated to the Admiral that John Brown led the raid. Now to this proceeding, Joseph Brown has been added. The fact that John and Joseph Brown do exist and are well known as among the finest and most prominent citizens of this colony brings significant points to mind. Firstly, their names are certainly known throughout our colony and could easily have been mistaken or inferred by someone with a grievance, or any number of other circumstances, with themselves having no involvement whatever. Secondly, being among our most prominent merchants, I question what benefit would accrue their commerce by seizing a ship of the line and wounding its commanding officer? Thirdly, a number of families by the Brown name exist, but whether or not another 'John Brown' exists elsewhere in the colony has not been determined. I might add, fourthly, since 'John Brown' is a well known name, the raiders, who have given all appearances of detailed planning, may have contrived the name for their leader as simply a code for identity in the darkness, similarly for the high sheriff.

"Regarding Simeon Potter, whom I also know personally, I know him to be a fine man who sits on the town's council, an upstanding citizen and merchant whose accusation I find most questionable, particularly so when recognizing his infirm physical condition, leaving him a person not likely to be sufficiently agile to participate in the raid for he is a man who walks but slowly and with a cane. Note also that thorough inquiry has, as yet, revealed no Mister Richmond within the confines of Providence or surrounds.

"Knowing these things, I believe, gentlemen, that only with the truth can we identify the actual suspects subsequent to apprehending them. Our charter is not simply to apprehend people and charge them with crimes, mere scapegoats; ours is to identify the actual perpetrators and bring them to justice. Furthermore, given the fact that the King's Proclamation extends one thousand pounds sterling for identifying the leaders of the raid, five hundred pounds for participants, I am certain that our mission is further complicated by quests for sudden wealth among the unscrupulous, quests that we must ferret out if we are to arrive at truth. Otherwise, this inquiry will unjustly accuse. Pursuit of the various truths, and honesty in revealing them, is, I believe, our charter as clearly stated in the King's Proclamation, having superseded my own Proclamation."

The commissioners sat quietly for a moment, each contemplating more clearly the difficulties illustrated in pursuing their charter.

Governor Wanton continued, "These many complications I find troubling. So far, gentlemen, we have only Mister Briggs as positively identified as among the raiders. Yet that identification seems to revolve about his wearing a red kerchief with white dots on his head, so recognized by a member of the *Gaspee* crew in the dead of a dark night. Many of the same headware have I observed among our seafarers and laborers, a common element of attire among those without means for a hat or the need for one."

Judge Auchmuty sighed disgustedly. "Shall we proceed with the facts, Governor, and rest speculations?"

"Indeed, sir. This council has, no doubt, noted in statements by his master, along with two servants of that house, Somerset and Jack, that Mister Briggs is solemnly sworn by them to have been at his assigned duties, as usual, on waking the morning after the night of the 9th of June past when the *Gaspee* was seized and burned. In addition, his master affirms that the skiff said to have been so masterly rowed by Mister Briggs was in such a state of disrepair that it was not seaworthy. What are we to make of these testimonies?

"Further, his master's father-in-law, who also resides within that household and has done so for many years past, has affirmed that Mister Briggs had not been off the island within the preceding twelve months prior to the second of July when he approached His Majesty's Ship, the *Beaver*, in the skiff recently repaired from long disuse, thus beginning the sequence of events leading to his standing before us as an identified assailant of the *Gaspee*. These persons solemnly swear that it is impossible that Mister Briggs could have been anywhere near the site of the raid, and at no time subsequent gave any hint of knowledge of the raid. These affidavits, gentlemen, are before us to consider as well. Are they to be dismissed?"

"I believe Governor Wanton to make valid points," confirmed Symthe. "If we follow the Admiral's simple directive to arrest the so-named individuals, even if only those real persons, if in error, what will become of respect for pursuit of law? Is law simply to act upon accusations? I think not. Law must proceed upon pursuit of truth. Otherwise, our courts, this proceeding as well, become nothing more than rituals acted out against the accused at the behest of anyone who chooses to accuse. We should be well informed of such diabolical consequences as illustrated during the age of the Inquisition. I believe, and have for my entire career, that law must reside above being nothing more than a tool to administer damnation at the behest of the powerful. Law must exercise its power forthrightly as fair and just. We have a servant before us, identified and accused of participating in high crimes of treason against the Crown. Is he to receive more or less consideration than anyone else?"

Judge Auchmuty took issue with the ideas expressed. "Are you suggesting that colonial law stands above the King, sir? Horrors at the thought! The King *IS* the supreme law by divine right. It is the duty of law, our duty, to administer the King's will."

Governor Wanton was secretly pleased at the course the investigation had taken. "To whom do we administer the King's will, sir?" he asked. "Anyone accused? In our colony, sir, from the very beginning as established by charter from our illustrious founder, Roger Williams and his associates, one Chad Brown was among them, forebear of the brothers John and Joseph Brown named in affidavits within these proceedings. That charter, having remained in force since, was granted by the reigning monarch of the time. Within our charter are cornerstone elements including respect for the individual, each protected against false accusation, each protected by proceedings of law among peers. Our colony rests upon fair and just adjudication of law, as does our assembly where voices are regarded as equals, giving no one greater influence than others, regardless of their station. I expect this proceeding to be so conducted."

Judge Auchmuty recoiled from the statement, clearly offended, and blurted, "You speak of democracy among equals, Governor. I assure you, sir, that His Britannic Majesty and his court, which includes this body, I might add, are not among equals. It is our duty to exercise due process as directed by the King and no other body! Whatever construct this colony may have arrived at for its own administration is no more than that, a construct to aid in administering day-to-day affairs. This colony is a dominion of the King, forever and always, and each person is his subject, forever and always. We are not debating the basis of equality in law, sir. We are pursuing the King's directive!"

Governor Wanton suppressed his urge to leap with rejoicing. The exchange could not have gone better for his intentions. "Quite right, Judge Auchmuty. We have the King's Proclamation as our guide and follow it to the letter we must."

Judge Auchmuty snorted. "Indeed!"

With the direction of the inquiry now firmly established, Governor Wanton requested the return of Briggs. "Mister Briggs, please excuse our debate of points of order. I am interested to know how you know Mister Brown was the man who fired upon Captain Dudingston. Tell this court how the surrounding events proceeded, please."

"The man, Mister Brown, what got in our boat done it."

Governor Wanton was surprised. "What? Please restate that sequence of events. Begin, please, with the meeting of your boat and the others from Providence."

"Yes, sir. When we come together there, an' Cap'n Potter an' them Browns talked about the best way to attack, one o' them Browns got in our boat an' the attack started."

"Without delay?" the Governor asked.

"Yes, sir. Right quick after that, the man on the ship hailed us to stand off. Mister Brown said to row up. Then, right quick, I seen the cap'n o' that ship come up. He shot his pistol at us."

"Was anyone hit by the shot?"

"Yes, sir. The shot hit one o' the men."

"Where?"

"In a thigh, sir." Briggs patted his left thigh.

"Was the injured man an oarsman?"

"Yes, sir. Sat right ahead a me," then quickly added, "on t'other side."

"You have told of being the forward oarsman in that boat, which would imply that the shot must have come close to you. Were you hit by the shot?"

"No, sir."

"Go on. Tell us what happened next."

"Mister Brown raised his musket an' shot the cap'n what cried out 'e was kilt."

"Mister Brown fired the shot from your boat, is that correct, Mister Briggs?"

"Yes, sir."

"Did you participate in the attack, boarding, taking of prisoners, capturing the ship and burning it?"

"Yes, sir. I means, no, sir. Didn't set no fire."

"What about taking the crew?"

"Weren't no more shootin' after the cap'n was struck down, an' we wuz quick on 'em so's they wuz pushed back...."

"How many defenders, sir, at that time."

"I reckon... Weren't but four or five, sir. They was comin' up out o' the hold by then. Talk was to knock 'em down an' kill 'em no matter what."

"And you could see all this well?"

"Yes, sir."

"By ship lights? By moonlight? By lanterns carried with you? How did you have light?"

"It were the moon, sir. Right good."

"To clarify, Mister Briggs, this was after Lieutenant Dudingston had been wounded, a shot from the longboat in which you were a bow oarsman. Is that correct?"

"Yes, sir."

"That shot must have come from further back in your longboat in front of you, your back to the bow, and passed over your head. Did the flash of the shot not affect your sight?"

Briggs stumbled for words. "No... sir. Don't reckon."

"By the time the captured crewmen were in the longboats, and you pushed off from the *Gaspee*, what was the time of the morning, about?"

"I reckon it were 'bout... three o'clock, I reckon."

"Now, if I understand correctly from your testimony, the assembly of boats met about eleven o'clock. The raid began immediately with the captain of the *Gaspee* quickly wounded and the crew captured shortly thereafter. What would be the time at that point, approximately?"

"I reckon... It were 'bout... nigh on to midnight."

"Please describe for us the progression of the raid."

Briggs thought for a moment. "I reckon, sir, it went right along the way what Mister Brown ordered."

"How was it that a member of the ship's crew came to identify you?"

"I reckon it wuz when they wuz put in the longboat, sir. Tied up, they wuz."

"Who was placed in your boat?"

"I reckon it were five or six."

"So, if the longboat had eight rowing stations and contained eleven persons originally, twelve counting yourself, when five or six more were placed in it as prisoners, that would make at least seventeen men in the boat. Is that right?"

Briggs looked troubled. "I reckon."

"That would make a very crowded longboat, would it not, particularly considering that you have already told us that the boat was fully manned when, as you say, Captain Potter directed you to tie off your skiff to it, and to come aboard just prior to the attack?"

"Rightly so, I reckon."

"Mister Briggs, please tell this court about Doctor Weeks."

"'E wuz in the boat, too."

"Doctor Weeks was originally in the boat from Bristol, or did he get into the boat you were in after the raid?"

"No, sir. I don't recollect if'n he wuz in the boat to start with."

"What did Doctor Weeks do once in the boat, after leaving the *Gaspee*?"

"'E tended to the Cap'n's wounds, sir."

"On the longboat in which you were oarsman?"

"Yes, sir."

"So... Allow me to think this out. Counting yourself, your longboat contained twelve men at the point of attack, a full complement. Five or six *Gaspee* captives were brought into it, one the wounded captain, and Doctor Weeks as well? That makes at least eighteen men in that boat. Is that correct, Mister Briggs?"

"I reckon, it wuz like that, sir."

"When the boat arrived at the shore, what happened?"

"The men, they wuz untied and let loose. They carried their cap'n off to a house."

"Then...?"

"Cap'n Potter give me the two dollar 'e said 'e would, an' I got in me own skiff what was tied off onto the longboat an' rowed home."

"Did you know Doctor Weeks, perhaps having seen him before or after the raid?"

"I reckon... I reckon 'e might a come to me master's 'ouse, once, I reckon. Don't rightly know fer certain."

Seizing the moment to place all future testimony in doubt, the Governor continued, "Widespread hearsay of a most excited kind has circulated the Bay for these months past, since the ninth of June extant, that the wounded captain, unable to make his own way, was assisted by unbound members of his crew and was laid out on oars upon thwarts of a boat, his length sufficient to span three oar stations and consume three or four oars. Is that correct, Mister Briggs?"

"I reckon." Then Briggs almost derailed the Governor's line. "But me longboat, sir, it were right long."

"But fully manned prior to the attack, regardless of the boat's length. Is that correct?"

"Yes, sir."

"What time of the night or day was it when you departed from the burning ship?"

"I reckon it were 'bout four o'clock of the morning, still dark. Weren't long to daylight, so's I had to row right steady to get 'ome."

"And you have us believe that you rowed your skiff singlehandedly twelve or more miles to arrive at Prudence Island, then that you made your way across land, in the darkness, to your master's house, then slipped through a lower window, then went to your berth as if having been there the entire night, and your two compatriots did not wake upon your return to bed, the same bed that they were sleeping in? Is that correct, Mister Briggs?"

"I rowed hard, sir. I was affeared the light o' dawn would catch me. The current 'elped....." Briggs winced at that slip and caught his breath.

Speaking more firmly, the Governor demanded confirmation. "Is that correct, Mister Briggs?"

"Yes, sir. That be 'bout right. I recollect that's the way it 'appened."

The fourth commissioner, Peter Oliver, Chief Justice of the Province of Massachusetts, offered a friendlier tone. "Let me see, now, if I may, Mister Briggs. If I understand the lay of the Bay correctly, Namquit Point is well up the Bay from Prudence Island, some twelve or more miles from your master's house?"

"Yes, sir. Right far."

"And you rowed hard *against* the incoming tide. You rowed down river as the tide came up river, and you say that the current was swift and helped you?"

"I didn't pay no attention. No sir. I rowed 'ard, real 'ard, a right long way, sir."

"You must be quite an oarsman to have made such distance so quickly against the tide."

"Yes sir. I rowed 'ard, what bein' a right good 'and rowin' me own master an' 'is goods all the time."

"Show the court your hands."

Briggs stepped near the commissioners and displayed his callused hands.

"You certainly appear to have oarsman's hands, young man."

With a sense of relief, Briggs smiled. "Yes sir, I rows all the time. I'm a good 'and with one oar or two."

"What sort of crafts does your master maintain?"

"'E got a two-master an' the skiff."

"A two-master is a sailing craft, is it not?"

"Yes, sir."

"Do you row that craft?"

Briggs stumbled with his reply. "No, sir... I rows the skiff, mostly, but there be other crafts on Prudence what I rows."

"I see. Thank you, Mister Briggs. I return the proceedings to Governor Wanton."

"Thank you, Judge Oliver. Now to continue... you rowed hard back to Prudence Island, arriving in time prior to daybreak to return to bed with Somerset and Jack, fellow servants of that household for some years, without waking them, then rose as was your usual custom to do your morning chores, beginning with fetching the cows."

"Yes, sir. I recollect thet 'bout right."

"Are you aware, Mister Briggs, that both Somerset and Jack, along with Mister Thompkins and Mister Thurston, his father-in-law, with whom you have lived these years passed, have declared before this commission that you were not at any time off Prudence Island in many months preceding the raid upon the *Gaspee*, and that you had given not a hint of knowledge of the affair until your arrival at the *Beaver* some three weeks after the incident, taken prisoner?"

Briggs stuttered. "I.... It weren't...."

"How long did your chores take?"

"All morning, sir, right up to mid-day. Summertime, there be lotsa work to do."

"And you do your chores by hand, correct?"

"Yes, sir. All the time."

"Your master declares that the skiff said to have been rowed so handsomely the night of the raid was not seaworthy. Somerset and Jack, along with Mister Thurston, similarly affirmed under oath that you had not been off the island in many months. Could your callused hands be the result of your chores and have nothing whatever to do with rowing?"

Briggs was stymied, seemingly caught in a web of untruths of his own making.

"Mister Briggs," the Governor demanded, "Captain Linzee

has reported that you were seized aboard his ship during the evening of the second of July past, seized for being identified as a runaway, subsequently identified as a *Gaspee* raider. Yet, all your associates state that you were on Prudence Island during the time the *Gaspee* was burnt. Only one or the other is possible. Being in two places at one time is not possible. How do you explain this discrepancy?"

Briggs was troubled. "No sir, weren't…. I recollect it were… it were…. I reckon… I….

Commissioner Oliver interrupted. "Mister Briggs, tell us again, carefully please, leaving nothing out, about your encounter with Captain Linzee of the *Beaver*."

"I didn't want to go back to Prudence Island, no sir, but I reckon now that I shoulda tol' all I knowed when I first got aboard the *Beaver*. They put me in irons an' wuz near to whippin' me at the mast. Then I wuz chained under the foc'sul."

"Were other seaman about?"

"Yes, sir. They wuz."

"Were there both *Gaspee* and *Beaver* seamen around you at any time?"

"Yes, sir. That seaman what come about, 'im who tol' the cap'n 'e knowed me from the *Gaspee*… I didn't know what to do. They put me in irons… an' after thet, Cap'n Linzee had the seaman swear on the Bible thet I was one o' them raiders, an' 'e said 'e would 'ang me from the yard arm…."

Commissioner Oliver cautioned, "What you say is for the record, Mister Briggs. Think carefully what you are about to say, and tell this court exactly what Captain Linzee said you."

Briggs paused, searching for details. "'E said… I could tell 'e meant 'is words, sir. 'E said, 'Lad, you see this man done declared you wuz there, an' if you don't tell who wuz there with you, I will hang you at the yard arm, immediately. And if you do, you shall not be hurt.' That's what 'e said, sir."

"And Captain Linzee did not hurt you. Is that correct?"

"Yes, sir. I was mightily afeared, though. Mightily afeared. 'E said 'e would 'ang me right there, an' I knowed he could do it."

"Yet, Captain Linzee kept you in irons. Is that correct?"

"Yes, sir."

"Governor Wanton, I have no further questions."

"Anyone?" the Governor asked, getting no response. He was pleased with the direction the investigation had taken and said, "Mister Briggs, I think you have done a fine thing in appearing before this court. A statement will be prepared for your agreement… Do you know what that is, Mister Briggs?"

"Yes, sir, I does. Jus' like with the Admiral."

"Good. The Secretary will read every word of your statement that has transpired here for you to place your mark as the solemn truth, so help you God. Are you prepared to do that?"

"Yes, sir."

"With no further questions, that will be all, Mister Briggs."

The secretary answered a knock at the chamber door and placed a letter before the Governor. "A letter from the Admiral, sir. Arrived about noon."

Governor Wanton opened the letter, read it and passed it to the other Commissioners for entering into the court's journal.

"The Admiral has arrived in Newport," he said, "by overland during the night previous, and he includes the statement of seaman Patrick Earle dated sixteen July 1772 along with a list of names of people to be summoned."

This unexpected turn troubled the Governor, and he gaveled the 9th session of the Commission closed, saying, "God save the King."

Chapter 18

Because the following day, Friday the 15th, was bitterly cold with a foul wind, the commissioners chose not to convene. With differing minds on many of the issues, they spent the day reviewing the material before them to pursue their own lines of reasoning, while trying their best to stay warm. Governor Wanton concluded that Judges Horsmanden and Auchmuty showed Tory leanings while Judges Smythe and Oliver were, as yet, not of any clear leaning. The Governor was certain that Briggs' testimony was fabricated, and, with the deposition of Patrick Earle in hand, containing no new information, he talked his way though several avenues of inquiry in preparation for further witnesses in coming days.

Mid-afternoon, he buttoned his overcoat and brought his hat firmly down on his head for the short walk from the Colony House to the White Horse Tavern. Few patrons braved the swirling winter storm to partake of Molly's fare, giving the Governor a table by the main downstairs fireplace to himself. Hearth pots simmering with the day's meal gave the room inviting aromas.

"Damn cold, it is, Guv'ner," Thomas said while placing a lid back on a iron pot. "Take yer coat an' 'at?"

"No, thank you. I'll lay them aside. What is to be our supper today, Thomas? By the way, young man, the Admiral is now in residence here, onboard the *Lizard*. Shall we send you to entertain him with your recitations?"

"Oh, no! Not me, sir. I stays clear of 'em what wear the King's uniforms."

"A wise thing. See that you do just that. So, what is for our supper this evening?"

"Clam pie's the main, baked right on the hearth 'ere." With

a long wooden spoon he tapped a large iron pot hanging over the flames. "Got salt fish chowder an' Devil's root an' love apples 'ere. To-ma-toes, they call them apples down Charlestown way. Got me first taste when Cap'n Maudsley put the *Sea Nymph* in there, back several year ago. Right good. T'ain't a bit poison like some folks say."

The Governor laughed. "Yours is an encouraging image. We shall call it tomato stew of fish and potatoes and not mention poison, shall we?"

Thomas grinned. "Reckon that'll work jes' the same." He inhaled deeply the inviting fragrances from Molly's oven in the kitchen. "Got breads, too. Comin' up quick. An' Molly's cornbread puddin' fer afters."

"That will do fine, to be sure. A spot of tea with cream to begin."

"Got a real treat, sir. I like it better'n tea."

"A treat? How so?"

"Molly's been samplin' that broma, some call it, others...."

"Broma? I am not aware of such. A drink you say?"

"All the rage up Boston way."

"Really. What is broma?"

"Don't rightly know. Comes from down South America, way back in them deep forests where strange things grow. Makes a little nut what, when dried and ground up real fine an' mixed with a drop or two o' vanilla an' sugar, makes real fine tastin', 'specially on cold days like today. I like mine with cream. Try one fer yerself?"

"I think I shall, a new adventure. Broma, you say?"

"Molly says people down that way call it the food o' the gods, made from them little beans called broma, some call them nuts cocoa beans."

"Well, I shall try it solely upon your recommendation."

Thomas left and returned with a mug of steaming broma. With the Governor's first taste, he exclaimed, "My, this is tasty. Tasty indeed. Will Molly be offering this brew regularly?"

"Don't know 'bout that. Depends, I reckon, on gettin' them beans. Molly done told Mr. Drury to keep her supplied, sayin' to every Cap'n what'll be sailin' come spring to bring her a whole sack full. Calls it hot cocoa, she does, all mixed together like this."

The Governor took another sip. "Well, young man. You have certainly given my day a turn for the better. Hot cocoa. I shall remember that."

"Beggin' yer pardon, sir. I'll be gettin' yer plate an' servin' up hearthside. Soup to begin? Made the soup meself."

"My, my. You are full of surprises, aren't you? Soup to begin and hearthside, too. That should keep body and soul together another day."

Thomas grinned and hurried off to his duties.

Once served, the Governor sat thinking about Patrick Earle's deposition while savoring his meal slowly when a tall man approached his table. "Guv'na. Good to see yew out sech a day as this, sir."

"Ah, Captain Vaughn. I trust that gathering *Gaspee* debris has long been completed?"

"Aye, 'tis. Yet, I been troubled since, sir, 'bout that fellow they got witnessin' against Mister Brown, an' I come to talk of 'im."

"Please, do sit down, Daniel. What do you know of the affair?"

"Well, sir, I collected the scrap from the wreck an' took as much of it as I could gather to Captain Linzee on the *Beaver*. You know that."

"Yes, I am well aware of your contributions, heartily thanking you for your efforts."

"Well, sir, I spoke with your Deputy in Providence an' come to repeat the same to yew, at his request. It were about two weeks or more after the schooner was burnt, I was sailing my sloop to Newport when I saw a small boat tied to the *Beaver* at anchor just above Prudence Island, there where Cap'n Linzee could watch the sailin' from Bristol, Providence an' Warwick to Newport. 'Somebody gone on that ship', I said to meself. Next day or so, I was alongside the *Beaver* to haul out some sugar fer Linzee, and goin' aboard that schooner, I noticed a mulatto lad in irons under the foc'sul. I spoke to the lad about bein' one of them rogues what burned the *Gaspee*, an' 'e said 'e didn't know a thing about that ship. I ask 'im what 'e come to the *Beaver* fer, an' 'e said 'e was determined to run off from 'is master what treated 'im badly. When they was goin' to whip that lad at the mast, that was when 'e declared 'e knew who burnt the vessel. Cap'n Linzee held the whip an' offered the threat of 'angin' the lad from the yardarm if'n he didn't tell what 'e knew, then naming Simeon Potter an' John Brown an' some more, but I don't remember their names. I was on the *Beaver* at that time an' saw what 'appened."

"Daniel, you possess important facts in the matter. I shall have to summon you to appear before the commission to repeat under oath what you have just told me."

"Thet's pahtly what I come 'ere to do, Guv'na. I've business in Newport fer the next few days, if we don't freeze first. Monday'll be a good day fer makin' sech."

"Hopefully, Monday's weather will be much improved. Whatever the case, we will convene the court. Should you have time now, would you care to join me for supper? Afterwards, we will walk over to the Colony House where I shall write your summons for the record of our proceedings."

"No, thank you, sir. Got to get along to Brinley's fer some small stuff, dice an' such with Benjamin an' some o' the lads. 'Bout all the worth of a day like this. Yew join in our frivolities, sir?"

"No, thank you. I shall have to pass for time to spend on details yet to be done in my work. Tell me, though. Have you sampled Molly's broma?" He held up his mug.

"No, can't say as I've heard o' sech."

"Well, if you get the chance, you should. Ask her dusty, Thomas. He knows about it. This is quite tasty, indeed."

"Heard 'im talkin' of it, jes' now. I'll remember thet, come suppertime tomorrow."

Two days later, the eleventh session of the commission convened with Daniel Vaughn's deposition the major event. Deputy Governor Sessions' letter to the Governor arrived, telling of Vaughn's statement to him and giving his assessment of Aaron Briggs' testimony as containing no truth whatever. Each of the commissioners reviewed the letter to be reminded that the Deupty Governor had taken statements from *Gaspee* crewmen the morning following the raid and that each man confirmed that the deep darkness of the night and lack of lights on either the schooner or the attacking longboats made identifying anyone by sight most uncertain. The crew's statements, agreed among themselves at that time, stating that some of the attackers were either negros or were blackened. With such recollections of the time firmly in mind, Sessions was convinced that any visual identification was in doubt.

Also considered was the Admiral's letter informing the commission that he planned to return to Boston within a few days. The commissioner's response was two-fold; the presence of Lieutenant Dudingston before them was required, that he should return from England, as was the presence of the Admiral for receiving those for further prosecution. Otherwise, the needs of the commissioners were such that they would adjourn until May 26th.

The next day, letters arrived from several people whose names had been supplied earlier by the Admiral, each giving their statements in response to summons for being unable, for various reasons, to attend, although each offered his sworn statement of knowing nothing of the affair other than hearsay or of a peripheral nature. With no new information, and with adjourning to return home on their minds, the commissioners drafted a letter to the Earl of Dartmouth summarizing their findings.

"...Taking all these matters into consideration, and the

extreme rigor of the season, which renders it almost impossible to procure witnesses as we could obtain... in the business we are upon; but find it impossible at present to make a report, not having all the evidence we have reason to expect..."(2)

Governor Wanton made his sworn statement summarizing the Gaspee affair as he knew it and the lack of cooperation from Lieutenant Dudingston, concluding from the depositions of those who lived with Briggs that, "...Arron was a runaway, and could not, for the reasons given in their depositions, have any knowledge of that transaction..."(2)

On the 22nd of January, the commission adjourned, to reconvene May 26th. Judge Horsmanden was not pleased with what he had found in Rhode Island. Once back in New York he penned a long letter to Lord Dartmouth stating various sentiments.

"20th February, 1773
"...On my arrival at that place, on the 31st of December, I was surprised to find that the main object of our errand was become public, which, in prudence was to be kept secret; nevertheless, Your Lordship's letter to Governor Wanton, was published in the Boston weekly paper, and spread industriously over all of New England.

"However amazing to us, upon inquiry, it came out, that the Governor had communicated it to his Assembly, who had got it printed; upon expostulating with the Governor upon it, he said, he by law was obliged to communicate all dispatches from the ministry to his corporation, and sworn so to do...

"My Lord, as to the government (if it deserves that name), it is a downright democracy; the Governor is a mere nominal one, and therefore a cipher, without power or authority; entirely controlled by the populace, elected annually, as all other magistrates and officers whatsoever.

"To show that the Governor has not the least power or authority, he could not command the sheriff or constable to attend us; he prevailed with them, indeed; but in expectation of being paid their daily wages by the commissioners, so that they were hired for this service, at our expense... the commissioners found it necessary to advance their own money; also for the very firewood expended for our accommodation in the council chamber...

"My Lord, as to the negro evidence, which seems to be the foundation of this inquiry, it is much to be suspected...

"My Lord, the commissioners did not enter upon counter evidence, though, I myself, was inclined to do it, as we proceeded;

and bring the witnesses face to face...

"I was told by a gentleman of law there, he had known a land cause of considerable value that had judgment reversed different ways seven or eight time; property being thus rendered wholly insecure, no wonder that persons of property and best sense and most sincerity, among them, have long wished for a change of government, and to be under His Majesty's more immediate protection.

"Though by their charter, they are inhibited from passing laws contrary to those of England, but to be near as may be, agreeable to them, yet they seem to have paid little regard to that injunction...

"Under these circumstances, Your Lordship will not wonder that they are in a state of anarchy; and I assure Your Lordship, that their sister colony Connecticut, is in the same condition in all respects; justice has long since fled that country...

"My Lord, these colonies united, what at times are so alike in features, temper and disposition, that it were a pity they should remain separate... I am fully persuaded, that the better sort of them have long groaned under their motley administrations, and wish for a deliverance; to be taken more immediately under the protection of the crown. These two, consolidated, might become a respectable royal government...   Dan. Horsmanden"(2)

The Judge sent his letter secretly to Whitehall. A month later, still in the grip of the bitter winter, Governor Wanton was deeply troubled by his suspicions of the Judge, whose Royal leanings were apparent. Who else among the Commissioners might side with the Judge caused much concern as to how the *Gaspee* affair could be manipulated to the gain of those seeking benefit from having Rhode Island dissolved. His thoughts included those long-standing arguments that, because of the colony's small size and natural division along the Narragansett River, dissolving Rhode Island's charter could split the colony to become new counties of Massachusetts and Connecticut. He shook his head in despair at the prospects that the Bay's excellent harbor and long coastline offered the King's navy a well constructed port to enforce such a division, not just vessels in the revenue service but ships of the line bringing dragoons, a step toward martial law and the tightening of the King's grip on the colonies, the end of free Newport. He increasingly imagined the end of the great, century-long political experiment begun by Roger Williams and followers, the failure of democracy where government by the people for the people with elected representatives is constrained to assembly law. A sense of desperation settled over him as he placed another stick of wood on the fire, its sparks rising up the chimney.

"What have we done, Rhode Island?" he asked the sparks, each one a glowing ember on its own flight.

In the quiet moment that followed, he rested, only to be interrupted when the doors burst open and his excited secretary blurted, "Governor, sir! An immediate dispatch from Virginia."

"From Virginia?" Governor Wanton puzzled.

"Very much so, sir. Accompanied by a man of much insistence that it be placed in your hands without delay."

"Really? What on earth would be of such importance to Virginia?"

The Governor broke the wax seal and opened the parchment. He placed a set of Mister Franklin's lens on his nose, and the writing leaped into his consciousness as he read aloud.

"12 March, 1773
"House of Burgesses, Colony of Virginia
"A resolution.
"His Majesty's faithful subjects have been much disturbed by various rumors and reports of proceedings, tending to deprive them of their ancient, legal and constitutional rights...

"... a committee of correspondence and inquiry is instructed to obtain the most early and authentic intelligence of all such acts, and resolutions of the British Parliament, or proceedings of the administration, as may relate to, or affect the British colonies in America; and to keep and maintain a correspondence with our sister colony, respecting these important considerations; and the result of such their proceedings from time to time, to lay before the House."(2)

The committee was instructed, "...to inform themselves particularly of the principles and authority on which was constituted a court of inquiry, said to have been lately held in Rhode Island, with power to transport persons accused of offences committed in America, to places beyond the sea, to be tried."

The document was signed, "Thomas Jefferson, Patrick Henry, Peyton Randolph, Richard Henry Lee..."(2)

Governor Wanton was stunned, unable to more than breathe.

"Mister Randolph, the carrier, to see you sir."
"Mister Randolph, signer of this document... here?"
"Yes, sir, awaiting your pleasure, sir."
"My! Please do see him in."
The thin secretary stood erect, his stockinged legs quivering.

"May I ask what this means, sir?"

"I am not at all certain, but, I assure you, this is most welcome."

The secretary breathed a sigh of relief and hurriedly stepped out, then saw Mister Randolph in, closing the doors behind him.

"Mister Randolph," the Governor said welcomingly, extending his hand. "Welcome to Rhode Island. Yours has been a most arduous venture this time of year, I suspect. "

"A pleasure to meet you, Governor," Mister Randolph said cooly, bowing to avoid shaking hands. "I have come overland on a matter seen in Virginia as extremely urgent."

"Yes, I have just read this resolution, and I find it most interesting. I must inform you, however, that I am required to relay all proceedings of a legislative nature to our General Assembly. You must see our Speaker, Mister Metcalf Bowler."

Mister Randolph, cautious of the Governor whose splendid display of powdered wig, ruffles and long coat spoke British, not American, kept his distance. "It is our intent, sir, to have a corresponding committee among your burgesses to maintain contact between our colonies."

"So I read, a most intriguing idea, apparently already in place to have brought you here."

Their brief conversation centered on the whereabouts of Mister Bowler, with the Governor continuing his welcome. "You must be exhausted, Mr. Randolph. May I extend our hospitality with an invitation to dine? We have a selection of quite good inns for the night as well."

"I have found my way to the White Horse Tavern and supped well, sir," Randolph said, suspicious of the Governor's Tory leanings. "There I learned of your Colony House."

The Governor smiled. "As you wish, sir. Now, you must go in haste to meet with Mister Bowler."

Upon departure of his visitor, Governor Wanton sat down slowly, with a new perspective. "What have we done, indeed, Rhode Island?" he mused to himself. "A common cause with Virginia... Hmmm. Perhaps among all the colonies...."

Due to the length of time taken to traverse the Atlantic both ways, the rise of foment in the Colonies was slow to reach England. During April, dispatches from Rhode Island arrived at Whitehall, and Lord Dartmouth penned his responses to the various letters received. In his response to Governor Wanton, chastising him for allowing his secret and confidential correspondence to become public, he concluded, "I sincerely hope that it will appear by the report of the commissioners for inquiring into the affair of the *Gaspee* schooner, that no part of the corporation of the colony of Rhode Island has failed in obedience due to the laws and authority of this kingdom...."(2)

When reading Lord Dartmouth's letter, Governor Wanton's feelings of despair returned. The threat was clear, and he feared that the *Gaspee* raiders had set a course of events that he could not contain. On each of his daily walks, he searched the Bay for newly arrived warships, and each day that none more than the usual were in the harbor brought relief. Fear that the next dispatch from the Crown would bring notice of martial law imposed on Rhode Island caused him to hardly notice spring, a sudden bursting of flowers and warmth that he usually enjoyed. Each day, he stopped by the ruins of Malbone Hall as a reminder of what the path of military government would surely bring. How to prevent such a thing was everpresent on his mind.

The following month, May, the Governor met with the Assembly. Virginia's Resolution had circulated widely with much discussion, and, in response, the Assembly passed a Resolution appointing seven members to Rhode Island's Committee of Correspondence. At the Assembly's closing, a Resolution lay before the Speaker who was charged with writing to all the colonies in America informing them of the proceedings of the Assembly... "relating to the preservation of the rights of the colony."(2)

During one proceeding when the Assembly demanded the Governor's commission of office, he handed it to the Speaker with a feeling of being ostracized by his own friends and neighbors who did not realize his efforts. A sense that control was slipping from his fingers consumed him, and he wanted to speak of steering the findings of the Court but could not until after it closed its work, and only then could he speak unofficially for fear of inciting the King to military action. As one of the judges of the Commission, with findings yet to be announced, everyone seemed suspicious of him.

During the following weeks, the Governor saw the *Gaspee* affair grow far beyond the act of burning a revenue schooner of the Crown to become more than talk of bravado among taverners; it was the subject of governing assemblies throughout the colonies, as far north as Nova Scotia as shown by the response from its council who responded to Rhode Island's letter from its Committee of Correspondence.

By late spring 1773, the Governor feared that division between Tory and Patriot were near to rebellion. Everywhere he went, open debate in the streets mirrored those at the highest levels in colonial assemblies, and he grew increasingly concerned that loyalists recognized neither the anger nor the determination of their fellow colonists. Citizens, not yet Patriot or Tory, increasingly found themselves forced into division, compelled by arguments about rights, liberties, and responsibilities of government, and some freely and openly took the patriotic side with much disdain for the opposite view. The raid on the *Gaspee* and resulting King's Proclamation had shaped political orientation throughout New England and beyond, and he kept returning to the idea of other colonies rallying to the aid of Rhode Island, if only in temperament, and realized that, for the first time, the colonies had a common cause.

Chapter 19

Bitter winter days passed through the hungry months of February and March into a late spring that brought thawing to the upper reaches of the frozen Bay. Fishermen were finally back to their crafts of the sea, much to the delight of those who relished a change from meals of salt fish prepared every way imaginable, and plots of ground all around the Bay were newly tilled for the year's gardens. After the day's cooking was on, especially during sun-warmed afternoons, Thomas and Benjamin worked the garden of the Tavern's back lot beyond the wood pile to put in new patches of Devil's root, love apples, stringer beans, and vegetables of many types, with seeds saved from the previous year's growth. Spicings went into patches along the walkways around the Tavern, making their picking quicker when needed for Molly's recipes. After they finished pruning the fruit trees one day, they stopped to rest. Talk of apple dumplings and pies to come made their mouths water.

The warmth of the late morning sun gave Benjamin pause for turning to great concerns gnawing at him. "The Commission was good for business back in the winter," he said to no one in particular. "Reckon its reconvenin' will do so once again."

"What's yer supposin's of their concludin'?" Thomas asked.

"Don't know for certain. Seems like they weren't able to proceed without the Admiral. Reckon he'll be arrivin' any day now. Then they'll get back to it."

"Comin' up on a year since, none quartered so far," Thomas quipped with a grin.

"Seems like the Admiral is the linchpin in fetchin' people to testify. Beset with the itch to 'ang somebody, 'e is... the talk what's goin' on. That man would 'ave nothin' better for 'is delight than 'angin' the whole of the colony."

Thomas smiled. "Been a year, mostly. No 'angin's...."

Benjamin turned with a jerk. "Yer mind ain't seein' right, Thomas! It were fifty years past, Black '23 it was, when Newport's gallows along Long Wharf hung with the dead, twenty-six. People still talk about that, some rememberin', some sayin' yer own great-granddaddy shoulda been with 'em, others glad 'e weren't, God rest 'is soul. Many families gave up one of their own among 'em 'anging from them gallows, and if it comes to that again, I 'ave great fear that the curse of the damned will descend on Newport, what with already bein' called pirates from all sides. And we'll most likely 'ave dragoons tromping our streets, too, an' in our 'omes, with us supportin' their needs from our own 'ands. I fear our descendin' into a great quagmire of troubles with the Crown."

"Nothin' so far," Thomas quipped again as he broke another clod of dirt with his hoe. "An' summer's comin' on, near a year past now. Seems like the schooner an' its crew got jes' what was comin' to 'em."

Benjamin pursed his lips and shook his head. "Yer mind just ain't seein' what's to come, Thomas. Once them commissioners issue their writs accusin', there'll be hell to pay fer takin' on the Crown in that stupid, stupid ransackin', an' the whole colony will pay with its blood. Word a'floatin' says nigh on to three hunderd took that ship. Once they starts tellin' who else was involved... Lord a'mighty, the troubles we are in for."

Remembering repeated warnings, Thomas bit his tongue to keep from blurting out what he shouldn't. Just then, a familiar voice calling from beyond the wood pile, "Ahoy! Yew there!" relieved the moment.

Thomas brightened. "Cap'n Brinley!" he yelled and waved. "Top o' the marnin' to ya."

"Aye, lad," Brinley yelled back. "Benjamin, be 'avin' a goodly supply o' littlenecks on the morrow's marnin'. Got enough 'ere fer a stewpot. Deliver to yer lady, shall I?"

"Be needin' sech, captain," Benjamin yelled back. "Molly'll take 'em there at the side door."

Thomas watched Brinley and Molly conduct their business across the door sill and spoke his thoughts, "Brinley said that you was 'is best lad, back when growin' up."

"Said that, did 'e?"

"Aye. Thinks 'ighly of you, 'e does."

"Said that, too, did 'e?"

"Aye. Got no family, jes' that 'ouse on the cove. Recollects right much. Got the gumpers for it, I suppose."

"Said that, did 'e?"

"Did I ever tell of the time me an' Brinley wuz on the *Sea*

Nymph...."

"Told that."

"Well, 'e's a right good seaman, a 'onest tanky, too, if you ask me."

"Didn't ask."

"Wuz you an' Brinley, best lads once?"

Benjamin stopped his hoeing and rested on its long handle, thinking back. "Always wondered about 'is travels, all them far away places what I'll never see. Me own father shackled me to the tavern when I wuz jest a lad, dyin' with me only of twenty years, never been nowhere, never done anythin', never seen... Brother Jonathan become me taskmaster then, workin' for our mum, we wuz. Keepin' the tavern." He sighed deeply. "Never a far isle will I see." Then, realizing what he had said, he rushed to reconsider. "Now... don't you say a word 'bout me musin's to Molly, you 'ear?!"

"Aye," Thomas agreed. "Lately been learnin' a lot about what people don't want others to know."

"Well, you jest keep it to yerself. An' keep yer travels to yerself, too. Gives me the yearnin's, what I don't need, what with cookin' an' servin' an' cleanin' after, an' gardenin'," he gestured about them. "No time fer wanderings. Got fahmin' to do."

"Brinley's a good 'and at recitation, too. Did you ever 'ear the one what 'e calls the 'Sailor's Lament"?"

"Sailor's Lament?" Benjamin questioned. "What with all the sailin' to far off wonders, what 'ave sailors got to lament?"

"Molly."

Benjamin wheeled about to Thomas with a start, then reconsidered. "I reckon we wuz best lads. Then we growed up; 'e got the life of adventures, I got the tavern. Then, Molly come along, once 'er pining after Brinley was spent." He breathed the cool air deeply. "Granny Mary's Chronicles is about all the adventures I'll ever see, them what she set to word 'bout her brother, yer own great-granddaddy, his piratin' tales, an' this tavern." Looking at the massively beamed two-story structure, he thought out loud, "Reckon Brinley considers hisself connected to it, what with it bein' his great-grandaddy's place before Mayes the elder bought it for a public house long time ago."

"What!?" Thomas blurted. "This was Brinley's place?"

"Fer certain. Sold, it were, by Francis Brinley... great-grandpappy, I reckon."

"Well, I'll be," Thomas exclaimed. "Brinley told of growin' up on Marlborough Street, neighbor, I s'pose, to Molly. An' all this time 'e never mentioned the White Horse once bein' in 'is family."

"Weren't a tavern then," Benjamin said. "It were the Brinley 'ome, strong built, fine timbers suitable for expandin', maybe.... I been thinkin' 'bout addin' on a gambrel roof so's to 'ave more room. Anyway... fer Brinley, don't make no difference, now. Bought by yer piratin' forebear's daddy and turned into a public house what the ol' pirate, hisself, kept to his dyin' day. You got a lot of learnin' to do about who's connected to what, if that be yer interest."

"Didn't know, that's all. When yew gonna build?"

"Got garden to put in... got paintin' to do... got cookin' to do.... No end in sight, daylight to dark. Weren't fer Molly... an' yew, yew little runt, don't know what I'd do to get it all done without yew.... Reckon I ought to say it, Thomas... yew been good 'elp, an' I 'ope yew'll be around awhile, Aunt Nettie permittin'."

Thomas smiled, his mind on other things. "Did you ever read *The Adventures of Robinson Crusoe*?" he asked.

"Aye. What's that got to do with Molly or Brinley or anythin'?"

"I read that book over an' over, bought it down in the Spanish Main, and I come to know 'ow a man what got shipwrecked by 'isself on a island got along. Paradise it were, with all 'e needed to live a fine life, but 'e wanted more than anything to be back with people, right?"

"That be the story."

"His were a lonesome paradise, it were. So, after 'e got rescued, 'e gave up all that was paradise...."

"Ha!" Benjamin interrupted. "An' you think I sees that Brinley's got the paradise o' wonders, but don't know it, an' 'e woulda give it up for Molly, while you thinks 'e sees I got the paradise of Molly and the Tavern, an' don't know it fer yearnin' fer wonders, do ye?"

Thomas smiled.

"Rubbish!" Benjamin said. "Life ain't like story books. Life's about what's 'avin' to be done day after day. Ain't no wonders, 'cept fer them what leaves on travels... them what do got tales to tell, wonders for other people what don't leave...." His voice trailed off. "Well," he sighed. "'Avin' tales to tell is a measure of a man's life, I reckon. Don't 'ave none, 'ave I. You got tales, you little turd, sailin' down in them islands... makes me right mad that you got 'em an' I don't. Next thing, you'll be tellin' about burnin' that damned *Gaspee*. I 'eard you recitin' about that ship, Cap'n Swan's verse. Where'd you get that, anyway?"

"Bristol, at the Boar's Head."

"The Boar's Head? Ain't a more desperate hole in the colony than that place, what with them Sons o' Liberty...." Benjamin stood erect slowly and looked at Thomas. "What you doin' in the Boar's Head?"

"Brinley, sailin' the *Molly B*."

"Brinley? 'E been learnin' you the Bay's doin's 'as 'e? Best watch yer step, lad." Benjamin didn't notice Thomas' smile. "Better stop this yappin' an' turn this garden or Molly'll 'ave both our 'ides."

At that moment, Governor Wanton, sixty-eight years old and spry, and Dr. Mawney, less than a quarter of the Governor's age, were on the Governor's morning walk, his daily constitutional to help keep his vigor up and his weight down. As they passed the ruins of Malbone Hall at Miantonomi Hill, the Governor stopped. "John, what do you see here?"

"Burnt out ruins... once fine gardens gone to weed."

The Govenor sighed. "Yes, to be sure, a waste of lavish wealth lying in ash and ruin. Hearsay tells that the princely sum of twenty thousand pounds was spent building this estate, a most impressive stone structure thought permanent. I recall it ever so well with great admiration and yearning, I might add. I am quite certain that it was the finest estate in all of Rhode Island."

"Finest in all the colonies, so I hear," Doctor Mawney added.

The governor shook his head slowly. "Built on the trade of souls... a trade that our Minister Hopkins fiercely rails against from the pulpit while ships filled with them lay at anchor in the Bay. Reduced to ashes, now abandoned ruins, blackened by fire. What irony."

"Irony, sir?"

"Yes, I see irony in the course of things correcting for balance. The Captain amassed great wealth slaving in Virginia, then spent lavishly here, a grandee who lived in grandeur trading the lives of other human beings, ultimately to be reduced to this. Ruins... reduced by fire.... Ironic, I think."

Dr. Mawney thought a moment. "I recall the smoldering ruins. Let me see... I was sixteen at the time. Some of the lads and I sailed with the elder Captain Tillinghast from Providence, having previously marveled at the castle, just to see the ruins the day after. Sad to have so much reduced so thoroughly, but the Malbone townhouse on Thames Street isn't such a paltry dwelling."

"Quite so... as are the Malbone holdings throughout Newport... and our colony. The Malbone penchant for gathering wealth seems to be the family's touch." Governor Wanton shook his head slowly. "I recall so vividly Captain Malbone reconvening the dinner in another location saying, 'If I have lost my house, that is no reason why we should lose our dinners.'(1) That was a most remarkable thing to say as flames, beginning from the kitchen chimney, there," he pointed, "consumed the place from the roof down. After salvaging what could be kept from the onslaught of flames, all of us quietly retired to our impromptu dinners within the light of the flames. That great fire devoured the mansion as a hungry beast while we quietly consumed a fine meal prepared in its kitchens, each wondering if Malbone sparks were setting our wooden town alight."

"Some sight to see, I imagine," Dr. Mawney mused.

"Were it not for the Captain's servants quickly salvaging goods from inside, the entire structure and all its holdings would have gone with the flames. Further irony appears to me, John, to have followed with ships of the Captain lost at sea subsequently, a run of bad luck, I suppose, particularly when thinking of all the souls lost with them. The Captain became sufficiently disillusioned that he left Newport for family holdings in Connecticut, a great loss to Newport. What I see in those events is the current unfolding; just as this family's holdings were reduced by fire amid other turns for the worse, we Rhode Islanders have taken to fire when it suits us, first the *Liberty*, then the *Gaspee*, the latter a most delicate matter that we must tread ever so lightly. I fear that, just as fire upon these Tory holdings reduced Godfrey from grandee to a servant of the land, we, too, are on the precipice of change, forced by fire, that may very well drag us down in the flames of war."

"War, sir?"

"I fear that this *Gaspee* affair could well come to it, certainly if Lord Dartmouth gets his way. A second insult to the Crown, of the same fashion, would achieve that end, to his delight. I have, however, managed to steer a course that my fellow Commissioners are, as yet, not prone to follow. As mentioned in past conversations, to be relayed to our friends northward, Lord Dartmouth is convinced that he has Rhode Islanders in his grasp this time, yet proceedings of law have pointed to no one, so far. We must stay this course with no further outbursts of a riotous nature."

"I understand, sir. And I shall convey your sentiments as you wish. About the Malbone family, tell me, Governor: I have long wondered if Francis and Godfrey were brothers?"

"Oh no. Not brothers at all. Most likely, due to your youth, you have no recollection of old Peter Malbone the younger. He fathered Godfrey the elder, taking his wife's maiden name for the child's given name. The first of Godfrey the elder's sons died as an infant, and the name was bestowed upon the next child, also male. The elder produced our Godfrey of these ruins, the third, I believe. As I recall, the father of Peter the younger was Peter the elder whose second marriage produced, in some generations, Francis the elder, our famed merchant of horses and rum, and his wide ranging family, siblings and offspring. He has, I might add, done Newport the great service of selling our various furnitures throughout the colonies... at handsome profits, particularly, to the Townsend family of fine craftsmen ... and our horses to the islands, much to the profit of our good friends, the Browns in Providence...."

Recalling the existence of the captain's subterranean tunnels from the basement of his Thames Street mansion under his wharf, a means of moving goods to bypass British customs, the Governor mused further, "He is a fine merchant, indeed, and quite resourceful. I might add that his son, young Francis, whom you must know, gives all appearances of continuing the family's fortunes."

"So, Peter the elder was... what to them, Godfrey and Francis?"

"Their common great-grandfather from different maternal lines, I believe," the Governor said, then offered, "Several generations, that. All of them of American soil."

The two men took up their walk. "And your family, sir. Wanton. The same, I presume?"

"Oh, yes. Yes, indeed. Long since Rhode Islanders through and through. I was born here in Newport, and here I shall die."

"If I may, sir... Our colony has no finer or a more upstanding family than yours, sir, to be proud, what with past Governors and Deputy Governors. I find it fascinating to think how all of our families have become affiliated, each of this land and sea, yet I wonder how the colonies are to survive... the flames of rebellion, sir...."

"Rebellion!" Governor Wanton snorted. "Rebellion is the last thing we need, if that. In my fifty years of adult life, I have seen what mankind needs, commerce amid civility. Take that lesson to heart, I assure you, John. Rebellion can easily lead to war that will draw resources, manpower and time from building better lives through advancing commerce and prosperity, fragile things that survive only with proper attention. You are, perhaps, too young to know of the firm, Collins, Flagg and Engs?"

"Not that I recall, sir."

"Understandable. That firm, our competitors, Joseph and William Wanton, Merchants, my brother and I furthering our father's lifelong enterprise, was unable to survive the rigors of the French and Indian War and became insolvent some eight years ago, 1765, I believe. With the tightening of enforcement of the Crown's Maritime Laws subsequent to that war, to pay the King's war debts, no doubt, each of those families was set upon difficult times, having previously been tirelessly devoted to Newport in many civic ways. Henry Collins lost his entire holdings. No, I assure you; rebellion is disruption of the fabric of our lives, lives that are woven daily from peaceful exchange of goods. Newport... our entire colony... has enjoyed relative peace doing so since then, until the arrival of that infernal Dudingston. If change is needed, let it be done through means available to us, the courts, not delivered by heavy handed policing. Perhaps slow and irksome, but when handled properly we can achieve our goals without rebellion. I know of the talk, certainly, and I extend much thanks to you for relaying our communications privately to our Providence friends... please do extend my congratulations for their efforts in keeping the inflammatory rhetoric at bay. We have done well, so far, and we should continue along the same path. A year has all but passed without a single arrest warrant... I cannot stress the value in that, given Lord Dartmouth's zeal to have a host of Rhode Islanders dangle from his gallows. We must play these hands we are dealt very carefully, without rebellion. I say again, we have done well so far."

"I do not mean to dispute you, sir, however, I sense that the *Gaspee* affair has grown to become its own entity far beyond the work of the Commission. Like the *Liberty* before it with no convictions, burning the *Gaspee* without convictions has fueled much anger that we colonials can fight the injustices of the Crown."

"Good Lord!" Governor Wanton snapped. "We are fighting this thing in a single courtroom, and there it must stay. The flames of rebellion are as those that consumed Malbone Hall... and the *Gaspee*, unstoppable once set! We must not loosen our hold on the reins of managing this affair such that no one comes to conviction. We are near to achieving that goal within the transactions of law. You must relay to our friends that success is within our grasp. We need not resort to violence, which will, most certainly, be conducted on our soil to our great loss."

"I suspect, sir, that your thoughts are in kind with those of our friends. However, from both within and without our colony, flames of rebellion are fanned by talk in taverns and ale houses where I hear and see much contempt for the King aired by patrons and travelers alike. Much correspondence is conveyed, privately, from Boston to Virginia, sir."

Governor Wanton sighed deeply. "I can only hope that firebrands among us do not become the instigators of bedlam." He shook his head despairingly and recited. "'No man is so insane as to prefer war to peace. In peacetime, children bury their fathers; in wartime, fathers bury their children.' The great Greek historian, Herodotus, wrote those lines well over two thousand years before us, and such insight still applies today, as always. I have long kept these two lines foremost in mind as my guide... particularly useful in times such as these. Never before in my life have I seen them more important to follow. Take this ancient insight to heart, John, and relay its sentiments to our friends. We must steer a careful course; we must avoid rebellion if we are to avoid invasion."

Chapter 20

Early June brought longer days of sunlight and warm refreshing breezes. The Commissioners had reconvened some days earlier, and Governor Wanton hosted them to a working dinner in his home on Thames Street. With after-dinner brandies in hand, they sat by the large fireplace in the Governor's sitting room discussing their investigations, particularly the testimony of Aaron Briggs and Patrick Earle.

"I remain troubled by the timing of Briggs' statement," Governor Wanton said. "He claims that he went directly home to Prudence Island and re-entered his master's residence before dawn, a clever act of stealth to be sure for having waked no one. Then, upon the new day, he set to rounding up the cows for the morning milking, a matter that his master and other servants affirm in their affidavits, stating that nothing unusual was present in the servant's behavior. And no mention whatever has been made of the man having two dollars, a rather large some of money for someone in his position, don't you think?"

"Quite so," remarked a commissioner in the background.

"Yet Patrick Earle confirmed that he saw Briggs on the *Beaver*, chained in the galley, some time after the servant's capture. Captain Vaughan, whom I know to be a most reliable citizen... a man who pursues his duties to the Crown, I might add, has stated under oath before us that he saw Briggs chained under the foc'sul of the *Beaver*, a different location. That gives me pause to wonder; within the ship and on its deck? Presumably, Briggs, in chains, could have been moved about the ship, but no mention of such has been made at all. Then, when speaking to Briggs, Captain Vaughan swears that he received the confession that the captive knew nothing of the raid, while, under threat of lashings, Briggs confessed to know of it, subsequently identified by Earle as a member of the raiding party. The sequence of events remains confused to me, and I ask myself, what possible gain does Captain Vaughan have by identifying himself in the affair? None that I can determine. And we should not overlook the last entry in Captain Vaughan's deposition, that Briggs was looked upon by those who know him best as much disposed to lying. With such a recognized nature, untangling the truth from untruth is quite formidable."

Commissioner Oliver added his thoughts saying, "I remain troubled as well. If Mister Briggs went directly to the *Beaver* from Prudence Island sometime after the *Gaspee* was burnt, he may well have brought with him first-hand knowledge of the affair, if he was involved. If he was not, such knowledge would be no more than hearsay. Yet his master confirms that the boy was properly at home as late as nine o'clock the evening the ship was seized, when sent off to bed with the other servants and with no hint of unusual behavior either then or the next morning, indicating that Briggs could not have been involved. The time lapse between the raid and Briggs approaching the *Beaver* is such that visitors to his master's home, bringing news of the raid that was, apparently, on everyone's lips, could easily have provided the information that Briggs later confessed to know. Someone is lying. Briggs? Earle? Vaughan? If Briggs was actually attempting to break with his indenture by approaching the *Beaver*, then being shackled in the galley or the foc'sul, he could well have assimilated the knowledge from the talk around him and used it in hopes of avoiding harm, as stated by Captain Linzee whose threats were, quite clearly, illegal and forced a confession under duress. Perhaps Briggs acted toward escaping his indenture, perhaps with the goal of a reward as well. The British seamen may not be lying; they may simply have identified someone as a raider who was not, one who had at least two subsequent opportunities to learn a few names said to be among the raiders. Most confusing."

Governor Wanton could not keep a wry smile from his lips and sipped his cognac to hide his grin. Confusion was precisely what he hoped would result.

Commissioner Smyth agreed. "Gentlemen, I confess that sufficient confusion surrounds this case to confound any attempt to resolve the matter with certainty. The matter is of a year since, with much discussion throughout the colony spreading as gossip, infinitely compounding the problem. Consequently, I wonder which memories are trustworthy, if any, and conclude that all are questionable. Do we have actual recollections in hand, or do we have concoctions? Mr. Earle may be quite wrong about first seeing Briggs as oarsman on their launch, having been a deeply dark night as all the *Gaspee* seamen assert, with only a red and white headwrap as identification, the same sort of thing that Mister Briggs continues to wear, as do many seafarers about this colony. With his master and father-in-law, along with two additional servants testifying without fault that the skiff Briggs professed to have used the night of the raid was not usable until some days later leaves many questions. Appearances are, indeed, that lies abound."

"Hear, hear," Commissioner Horsmanden remarked disgustedly.

Governer Wanton turned to the fire, away from the commissioners, and sipped his cognac again. As the flames flickered on his face, he was pleased, although Horsmanden's position remained worrisome to him. He continued, "Gentlemen, we have followed each lead provided to us by the Admiral, among all others that have come to our attention. In total, the affidavits in hand provide a broad sweep of the affair.

"I now wish to recall for your benefit that Lieutenant Dudingston's own behavior precipitated much contempt for him that, apparently, contributed significantly to the fate of his ship and crew, as provided in my own deposition presented to this commission during our first convening. Please recall that I am on record as citing the occasion when Officer Dundas appeared before me with his Captain's commission and other papers in hand, Mister Dudingston having already set the colony alight with his several transgressions, apparently afraid of coming ashore himself for fear of being arrested. One transgression was, at that time, in the Court of the Admiralty of this colony.

"Upon meeting with Mister Dundas, I took the opportunity to remind him, for his captain's benefit, that Mister Dudingston had violated an Act of Parliament made and passed in the eighth year of his Majesty's reign, that proceedings of law are to be conducted within the colony, not in Boston as was demonstrated in Mister Dudingston's seizure of a sizable cargo belonging to Rufus Greene the younger, a family of merchants I have long known to be most upright. Mister Greene subsequently filed his complaint with the Court of the Admiralty.

"Furthermore, a short time after meeting with Mister Dundas, another of Mister Dudingston's transgressions came before me. *Gaspee* crewmen trespassed upon the land of one Faulkner of Gould Island, cutting some thirty or more trees on his property and taking the timber while leaving the waste. To avoid proceedings of a suit, Mister Dudingston paid Faulkner fifteen dollars, to the man's satisfaction, to prevent a court proceeding. This action, gentlemen, confirms that Mister Dudingston knew his actions to be contrary to the laws of this colony, ignoring both the latter and his Majesty's law as cited to Mister Dundas, the result giving our citizenry great cause for outrage."

Commissioner Horsmanden interjected. "Governor! Sir, we are not convened here to discuss the report with which the Crown conducts business within this colony. And neither are we to pass judgment regarding who may or may not have insulted the legalities as you know them. Our responsibility is to repair the perpetrators of this action to Lord Dartmouth!"

Governor Wanton restrained his delight. "Quite correct, Judge Horsmanden. Clearly, sir, you have the crux of the matter in hand. Have you a perpetrator identified for our Commission to proceed upon, sir? You have that authority."

The Judge snorted, "They are out there! Out there among your Rhode Islanders, sir, hundreds of them, if testimony so far is to be believed. How is it possible that not one of them is known to us indisputably? How is it possible, at this late date more than a year past, that we have nothing more than a servant's testimony, it giving all appearances of being contrived, to which those named by him have remained clear of warrants! If Briggs was not a participant, those named must be the subjects of innumerable conversations among your citizens to have reached his ears. If those named are so much the talk of the colony, how is it that we have not a thread leading to a single one of them to act upon? Is it possible, sir, that your entire colony has coalesced around the motive of not identifying the perpetrators among them, criminals one and all?"

"Well said, Judge," Governor Wanton confirmed. "I believe that your deep experience with law has brought you to ask important questions. As to the perpetrators, we have only the testimonies in hand to act upon, to do so strictly in accordance with the King's Proclamation with his Royal Instructions for guidance, which we have done. Within the body of evidence before us, please do not overlook the statement of the twelfth of June of the year past from my Deputy, Mr. Sessions and sworn in my presence. This statement, signed by John and Nicholas Brown, the very men whose names have been bantered about as the leaders of the raid, among several other men of impeccable stature, was an appeal to me for quick action. Also included was the judgment of our Chief Justice Stephen Hopkins that without being sworn into his office, Mister Dudingston was guilty of trespass, if not piracy for his actions...."

"Governor! If you please," Judge Horsmanden scolded. "We are not here to act upon colonial law. Our charter is a King's Commission. Our charter clearly states our proceedings as THE law. All others being mere constructs for local organization!"

"Quite so, Judge. Yet, in your great experience, would you agree that the conduct of law is the same, regardless of the origin of a body of law? Aren't practitioners to act in accordance with law as written? In the case of this commission, the prevailing body of law is the King's Proclamation that charters us to gather the truth and bring the perpetrators to justice, toward which these proceedings have been conducted. Yet, we have no evidence on which to serve warrants, only hearsay."

"Hmmpf!" Judge Horsmanden snorted. "Yes, of course, of course. Due process of law, of course. This case has no process because we have no compelling evidence to collar anyone. Yet, the deed was done!"

"Well said, sir. I am equally at a loss to account for the lack of those coming forth with information and presume that you have, once again, correctly judged the temperament of this colony to have become so pervasive against Mister Dudingston that those who know the facts regarding the *Gaspee* to have resolved that the Lieutenant received what was deserved."

"And you speak of law, sir!?" Horsmanden roared. "Citizens taking law into their own hands!? Then cover themselves with a conspiracy of silence that pervades the land! Anarchy, sir. That is what you preside over, anarchy, from all appearances, rampant throughout this colony!"

Governor Wanton recognized that he must choose his response carefully. "I was offering mere speculation, sir, an attempt to provide a logical answer to your question regarding the temper of our colony. I agree that some dozens, if not hundreds, of people attacked and burned the *Gaspee*. Who they were eludes me as well, having issued, as you know, my own Proclamation with reward offered prior to the King doing so with much more reward. Both, apparently, arriving at the same result." Remembering Thomas' recitation, he went on, "Some say Narragansett Indians...."

"Poppycock!" Commissioner Horsmanden blared. "Indians, sir! Absurd! These were Englishmen of dress and language without doubt! Men of quality, I am certain! Indians do not wear ruffled blouses and waistcoats, sir!"

"Merely another speculation, judge, to let you know that talk among citizens also shows ignorance of who the raiders were. The fact that the events occurred and that they were carried out under circumstances that we continue to find confusing lends the matter to much speculation throughout this colony."

Governor Wanton shifted this line from further discussion, with the concept of 'conspiracy of silence' ringing in his thoughts, and asked, "What do you make of the Admiral removing himself from the matter by an official appointment of a lesser officer, with agreement from the Lords Commissioners of the Admiralty, presumably Lord Dartmouth as well?"

Judge Horsmanden grunted his displeasure. "I read the letter of the Royal Instructions to mean that the Admiral is to receive all assigned by warrant to transport to England. Given that reading, our High Commission is unable to fulfill the letter of the King's Proclamation, yet we are oblidged to proceed with the able attendance of the duly assigned officer of the Crown acting on the Admiral's command. In my view, we should proceed with the presence of Captain Keeler, as noted in your letter to him of the second of June."

"Hear, hear," confirmed the other Commissioners.

"We all agree," Governor Wanton confirmed, having set the stage for the balance of the Commission's work. "And of today's Deposition from William Dickinson entered into testimony...."

Judge Auchmuty spoke up, almost derailing the course the Governor had set. "Can such a condition persist in the presence of a High Commission?"

"Sir?" the Governor asked.

"I perceive that time has helped cloud the facts. The weather has conspired against further revelations, and Dudingston's attacker has received no mention whatsoever. He must be a man who knows muskets well enough to land a wound from the unfirm footing of a boat upon the bay, a wound whose intent would have been fatal but for a surgeon or two in the party. Was the musketeer's intent to slay the subject of his ire? If so, how would the shooter have known, in the darkness, that his target was the Captain rather than a crewman? The surgeon's intent was the opposite; he would clearly have known what was expected of him.

"I also note that, regarding Mister Dickinson's testimony, several shots were fired between the crew and assailants, yet, so far as is known, only the Captain was wounded, despite Briggs' statement of someone wounded in the thigh, no such person having been pointed out. Were it not for Dudingston' own testimony of standing on the freeboard facing outward from the ship, I might conclude that one of his own men shot him. Such not being the case, the shot must have come from the assailants, among whom none were injured that we know about.

"Given these facts, one could conjure a conspiracy among the raiders and crew to attack Mister Dudingston! Such a conspiracy, however, does not seem to be afoot. In any case, after the shot, the shooter could easily have faded into obscurity and has done so. The surgeon, however, must be among a select few of such training, in age estimated to be early twenties. This commission has requested the presence of Mister Dudingston; why do we not also gather the colony's surgeons and see who fits the description, and pare down the number from there, and subject those who remain to the scrutiny of Mister Dudingston?"

Governor Wanton was horrified but forced himself to contain his emotions. Everything he had so carefully laid out was swept up into the kind of investigation that he knew must be avoided, face-to-face testimony. To give himself time to think, he mused, "Hmm. Yes, indeed. Mister Dickinson clearly stated that the crew fired upon the assailants and was, in return, fired upon, his captain being wounded at that point. Mister Dickinson has testified that, once in the cabin with his Captain's wounds being dressed, the ship's papers were demanded of him, so agreed by his Captain. The raiders put them in their pockets, then later, upon abandoning the ship, put him ashore with other crewmen some two miles from the *Gaspee*. Dickinson has testified that he was left alone on that shore for an hour or more until the light of day, and told of seeing three boats cast off from the burning ship, one heading for Pawtuxet and two other boats rowed toward Providence. He mentioned several negros among the assailants.... I wonder, gentlemen. Could either of you make out the difference in blackened skin and a negro from two miles, in the faint light of dawn?"

"Hardly," confirmed Judge Smythe. "At my age, I have difficulty seeing my dinner."

Chuckles lightened the gathering, bringing relief to the Governor. He had successfully deflected Judge Auchmuty's thoughts.

Commissioner Oliver knitted his brow. "One moment, if you please. Among his depositions over time, Mister Dickinson has stated that he was among the party in a second boat not containing Mister Dudingston. Being wounded, Dudingston has said that he was carried from the boat to a house in Pawtuxet, while, unknown to him, the crew was confined to the cellar of a different house, all this having transpired in darkness, according to Mister Dudingston. Mister Dickinson, as you relate, claims to have been left out of these transactions and to have remained on the shore two miles, by his own estimate, from the wreck for more than an hour, witnessing the last of the raiders leaving the burning ship in daylight. Daylight or darkness; which was it? And all others captive but himself? I find leaving him on the beach quite curious, that the raiders would have left him and no others on the beach."

Governor Wanton was pleased with the shift in the direction of inquiry, and, pouring another round of his fine cognac into each of the commissioner's crystal snifters, he carefully steered further conversation away from witnesses testifying in the presence of other witnesses.

Chapter 21

When the Commission reconvened, with Judge Oliver soon to depart, Governor Wanton was relieved to have only three principals to manage, Judge Horsmanden appearing to be the last to arrive at agreement. With Judge Oliver's consent to compose their findings with his name absent, the work of the Commission was almost complete, and Governor Wanton's ambition as well, almost settled. Having the results of calling upon the judges of Rhode Island's high court to review the case and provide its opinion, the Commission's inquiry into the *Gaspee* affair was about to be laid to rest with no warrants served. When reading the colonial Court's report, Governor Wanton smiled, his only reward.

Chief Justice Stephen Hopkins and his three assistant judges signed their names to their statement of having reviewed the evidence.

"June 11th, 1773

"Upon the whole, we are all of opinion that, the several matters and things contained in said depositions, do not include a probable suspicion, that the persons mentioned therein, or either of them, are guilty of the crime aforesaid...."(2)

The Governor saw his plan nearing completion until ten days later. During summary, Judge Smythe proposed to the Commission that, "...on Saturday last, documents came into my possession regarding great irregularity, violence and disorder culminating in an attack by the gunner of Fort George firing upon an armed schooner of the Crown, the *St. John*, just beyond Newport's Harbor, signed by two magistrates, dated July, 1764. I desire the enclosed documents, may be included in the journal of

195

this commission... I believe that action to have bearing upon our work as a leading cause to the destruction of the *Gaspee,* and I request that the Commission consider, in the interest of thoroughness toward completing our charter, that this matter be fully investigated for the record."(2)

Judge Horsmanden banged his fist on the table before him. "Yes! Yes, indeed! I wholeheartedly agree, sir. Such anarchy need be explored!"

Governor Wanton was stunned but held his breath, silently counting to ten before answering. He wondered what the colony of New Jersey stood to gain with condemnation of Rhode Island and recognized that broadening the Commission's investigations into past civil actions in Newport and the Bay served only to focus the temper of his colony as opposed to the Crown. He also recognized that the information received by Judge Smythe came from Tories, who, if permitted, could change the course he had successfully steered to this point. Having Judge Horsmanden firmly supporting the proposal meant that the Governor must carefully tread the next few moments. Now so close, he could not allow the court to upset his path, but he was unsure of how to proceed. Speaking cautiously, his suggestion seemed compliant saying, "My son was Deputy Governor at that time... and the gunner, Captain Vaughan, who has testified before us, is still in residence near this town. Each of them could be called upon. However, I wonder of the value to our efforts of such indirect material. However, gentlemen, since it is late in the day at this time, shall we consider the request overnight?"

Judge Horsmanden grumbled his displeasure, but weighted by the other Commissioners siding with the thought of a warm supper, he relented. All agreed and adjourned for the day to take up the matter again the next day. With a sense of relief, although temporary, the Governor came near to suggesting that they dine at the White Horse Tavern, continuing its long history of hosting official functions for dinner, but reconsidered when thinking of the possibility of some outburst or recitation upsetting the delicate balance that he had constructed. He recognized the alternative for the evening was, surely, that each of the judges would be hosted by those of loyal leanings who would exhort action in their favor. Thinking of the prospects of having to wade through such matters required a reassuring breath. The Governor suspected that their gathering the following morning would, most likely, require more manipulations to stay his course.

Once the other Commissioners had made their way out of Colony House, the quiet of the evening surrounded the Governor who sat alone in the red glow of the sun and long shadows of its waning light falling through the tall windows of his office. He thought through the various impacts of Judge Smythe's request, then arrived at the conclusion that the affair of the *St. John* was already well known and fully documented in records to the Lords Commissioners. He breathed a sigh of relief, resolved that including such information would have no impact on their conclusions, soon to be put to pen and relayed to Lord Dartmouth at Whitehall and the Royal court. In a quiet moment he rested, recognizing that he was at a crossroad, and, for the first time, he felt a degree of relief that his plan was nearing completion.

The next day, Judge Smythe stressed his opinion that a full inquiry into the *St. John* should be included in their findings in the interest of thorough investigations saying, "I believe the temper of this colony to be expressed in the sequence of events beginning with the *St. John*, then the *Liberty*, riots against one Royal Act after another and so on leading to the *Gaspee*...."(2)

"Hear! Hear!" Judge Horsmanden railed, seizing the opportunity to further push Rhode Island toward dissolution. Reflecting upon his earlier secret outlining of that scheme to Lord Dartmouth and thinking that division along the Narragansett River was a most convenient boundary, a sly grin crept across his face.

"Sirs," Governor Wanton replied. "I offer no rebuttal. With my son having been Deputy Governor at that time, and being thoroughly familiar with the incident, including the fact that full disclosure has already been made to His Majesty, little benefit exists for inclusion or exclusion. Upon the consensus of the judges, this material will be included herewith as addenda to the body of our report."

Judge Horsmanden knitted his brow.

"As for opening the matter to full investigation, given that we are a year removed from the seizure of the *Gaspee,* and having endured the matter at our own time and expense, I forecast that investigating the circumstances of the *St. John* to require at least the same effort, perhaps more. Shall we request of Lord Dartmouth an extension of our inquiry to fully prepare findings in that matter?"

The Commissioners sat in silence as Judge Horsmanden's frown showed his consternation, already some two hundred pounds out of pocket with no hint of recovery from the Crown. With no further comment, the Commission closed its proceedings and compiled its final report.

"June 22, 1773

"My Lord: So much time being necessarily spent in the business of His Majesty's royal commission, renders our return to our several colonies highly expedient, and having executed the same to the utmost of our abilities, we beg leave to enclose to Your Lordship, a report... No particular mode having yet been pointed out to us, for defraying these expenses by government, we have discharged the same..., we have used the utmost assiduity, and made the strongest possible efforts to the thorough accomplishment of the end and design of the commission...."(2)

Their report began,

"To the King's Most Excellent Majesty.

"May it please Your Majesty: In obedience to your royal commission and instructions... for the purpose of inquiring in, and reporting to Your Majesty, all the circumstances relative to the attacking, plundering and burning of the schooner *Gaspee*, wounding Lieutenant Dudingston, and all other matters in the same commission and instructions contained...

"...the place where the *Gaspee* was destroyed, is, at least, twenty-three miles from Newport, and the accident of her running aground but a few hours before the attack, takes away all possibility of the inhabitants of the town being instrumental in, or privy to, the destruction of her...

"After our utmost efforts, we are not able to discover any evidence...

"Upon the whole, we are all of opinion, that the several matters and things contained in said depositions, do not induce a probable suspicion, that the persons mentioned therein or either or any of them, are guilty of the crime, aforesaid...

"...there being no probability of our procuring any further light on the subject, determines our inquiry."

"All which is submitted to Your Majesty's royal wisdom."

J. Wanton   Fred. Smythe
Dan. Horsmanden   Robet. Auchmuty
Commissioners

"To His Majesty,
"Newport, Rhode Island, June 22, 1773."(2)

When Governor Wanton signed the document, satisfied that no warrants had been issued, followed by signatures of the other Commissioners, he felt a great weight lifted from him.

The copy sent to Rhode Island's Assembly, then copied and sent throughout New England, received wide attention. Until responses arrived from England, a matter of some months hence, Governor Wanton laid the *Gaspee* affair to rest, pleased with his efforts, although with some trepidation regarding Lord Dartmouth's response. Prospects of what was to come loomed large in his thoughts, but, for the moment, he was relieved that none of his subjects had been identified.

Each of the judges departed in his own way, but, having to wait for favorable wind and weather before sailing to New York, Judge Horsmanden remained in Newport for some time. The Commissioners reporting no findings rapidly spread throughout the town and brought a number of comments of disbelief from those of loyal leanings. How he was greeted on the streets reversed; previously cordial regards from those whom he knew to be loyal to the Crown became cool. Greetings from other people were of a lighter air than during the Commission.

While waiting for passage to New York, the Judge gave some time to short walks around Newport, costing nothing. Ever grumbling about accumulating expenses for everything, he was not of the temperament to enjoy Newport's famed summertime climate. Each day culminated with supper at the Pitt's Head Tavern or the White Horse Tavern, sitting alone in a somber atmosphere in either establishment until one evening when an officer of the Navy approached him.

"Judge Horsmanden, I believe?" he asked.

"Yes," the Judge said dryly.

"May I join you? I have information that may be of interest to you."

"Be my guest."

The officer seated himself as the Tavern became strangely quiet. "I am of the *Beaver*, sir," he said. "Although not called before your Commission...."

A month later, Judge Horsmanden penned a letter to Lord Dartmouth.

"New York, 23d July, 1773

"My Lord: ...For waiting some days at Newport, for a passage, wind and weather, I was accidentally informed of a piece of evidence, which, had it come to light sooner, would most probably have cut our business shorter.

"An officer of a man-of-war, stationed at Newport, to whom the negro Aaron was turned over, informed me that upon his examining the fellow one day, before his master, and his two negroes who came on board, and interrogating face to face, the fellow prevaricated much; but still persisted in the main of his story, notwithstanding confronted by the master, and his two negroes, who declare that he slept with them all that night, on which the *Gaspee* was destroyed.

"The master and his negroes being dismissed, the officer, upon what he had heard, from the master and his negroes, and had observed from the conduct of Aaron, upon the occasion, concluded he was an imposter, and charged him home, as such, and told him he was convinced he was no more concerned in that affair than he himself was; and conjured him to tell the truth; and at length, he confessed it was all a fiction, which he was constrained to, for saving himself from the punishment threatened him on board the other man-of-war, as they had charged him so positively with being one concerned; and therefore thought he must confess himself guilty, and name some principal people as accessories....

"And thus, My Lord, this forced confession of the negro Aaron has been held up by the marine, as a hopeful and sure clue to unravel this mystery of inquiry...."(2)

Chapter 22

July brought long days of sunlight and warm breezes across Newport. The town and Bay had weathered both a frigid winter and the potentially ruinous prospects of the King's Commission. Relieved of that burden with no warrants issued, Governor Wanton stepped lively along his morning constitutional. On returning from passing the ruins of Malbone Hall once again, he walked the length of Thames Street taking particular note of its boisterous commerce. Between Bowen's Wharf and Champlain's Wharf, he had to dodge several carts of ship's goods moving onto Thames Street and was delighted to exchange morning pleasantries with almost everyone he met, each similarly lifted of the great weight of concern about the future of their colony. The odors of seafaring laced the air that seemed unusually light, and, just as he approached the offices of William and Joseph Wanton, Merchants, his brother emerged.

"Hail, brother," William said cheerfully. "A fine morning, this."

"'Tis true. A fine morning indeed."

"Joseph, just wondering; have you thought about the proposal of our Friends?"

"No, not as yet. No time with the Commission at hand. I presume, though, that another great change is upon us. Convictions do run strongly among our solemn kin."

"Indeed!" his brother confirmed. "For my convictions, I do not believe it is the right thing to do. However, all appearances tell me that papers are being drafted as we speak. Yourself?"

"Hmmm. Although unresolved in my mind at this moment, I do believe we Rhode Islanders are continually in the forefront of radical changes, as is this thing, once again, much to the displeasure of the loyalists."

William was startled. "What!? Did I hear you take side just then?"

"A mere recognition of the factions all about us, Brother. You need not read more into my statements. As Governor... and you know well the vices and virtues of governing of which our family has such a great legacy... I am elected, as are all of our Governors, to represent the whole of the colony, not just a faction."

"Ever the politician, Joseph. We all know very well why you are elected year after year, Stephen Hopkins and his Providence weight behind you. Yet, I perceive that this Commission you have just concluded is likely to pass unnoticed for its importance. Strong and weak voices talk of it, yet none seem to recognize the handling of such an important burden, it coming to naught."

Governor Wanton sighed. "I am afraid that you are quite correct and observant as always. The year past has been most trying, to what gain for me personally? I...."

"Brother, you sell yourself short. You are the talk of Newport?"

"The talk of Newport! Surely you jest, William."

"Not at all."

"Really? To what talk do you refer? Loyalists who condemn me for lack of warrants and Patriots who cheer me for the same feat?"

"Indeed."

"Now William, our proceedings, I say to you as I say to everyone, were conducted by learned men of stature who carefully sifted the evidence to conclude that insufficient facts exist to arrest anyone. Ours was a fair and impartial jury whose opinion was supported by our Chief Justice and past Governor, Mister Hopkins, and his High Court, I might add."

William smiled. "To be sure; just as you say, Joseph. However, note that your role, however important to the outcome, will remain unknown until your position becomes known."

"We have discussed this matter many times, William, and I repeat myself to say that as an elected official of this Colony, my duty is to the Colony and all citizens to be fair and impartial."

"And new citizens about to be freed?"

"Of course. I can only suppose that our Friends find it in their souls to release their servants from bondage out of respect for mankind, whatever color of skin that mankind should have. You and I are freemen near to the same age, each having seen much in the business of trade during our lives, so I admonish you to look about our streets, our churches, our taverns, our homes here in Newport, and what do you see? The effects of commerce conducted civily, livelihoods pursued with confidence of protection by laws conducted among peers, tolerance for differing faiths. We are the benefactors of prosperity from commerce, prosperity that we have molded ourselves, such as you and I have pursued here in this establishment, among tradesmen throughout our colony, each a good example, as was our father before us."

"Yes, yes. All well and good, to be sure. You need not lecture me, Brother."

"Oh! Yes. Quite right. My apologies, William. I am a bit scatterbrained this morning, having achieved a most arduous goal that has left me rather adrift upon each day since."

"That achievement, Brother, is the very topic on the lips of those who speak highly of you for conducting that Commission, said to be unlawful with its unusual powers, I might add, toward no findings when you know...."

"Now Brother! The Commission has done its duty and the Lords Commissioners properly notified. Lest feathers continue to be ruffled over matters resolved by law, let us now enjoy the day and our way of life."

William smiled and touched his hat. "A fine good day to you, Brother," and stepped out onto Thames Street just as a group of rag-tag boys ran by playfully acting out their renditions of taking the *Gaspee* and wounding Lieutenant Dudingston. One boy yelled, "BANG!", and another fell to the cobblestones in a fetal position, moaning "Don't shoot me again, Mister Brown. Don't shoot me again!"

William looked back at the Governor and winked.

As the boys ran off cavorting noisily, the Governor smiled. While walking further along, more greetings were exchanged on his way toward Queen's Hive when his son, William, appointed by the Governor to the post of Naval Officer of customs records, was just leaving the building.

"Good morning, Father. A fine day to you."

"And to you, William. I just had the pleasure of conversing with your namesake."

"Uncle William? That old fart. I presume that he is still opposed to my joining the firm until achieving my letters?"

"To be sure. And, quite good advice, I might add."

"Father, you know well that I have no interest in classrooms when all the world lies before me here. Can you not bear upon him that fact? I am now twenty-five years experienced, no longer a youth."

"I'm afraid that his is the duty of our family business while I am tied to governing, this year past especially. He is the principal whom you must impress, but I shall put in a good word for you. Until then, your duties here are quite worthy."

"Signing on sailors to oaths? Maintaining bills of lading and inventory records? Surely, you do not believe that, Father. Little challenge exists in handling such documents day-in, day-out...."

"But a necessary function, and a quite valuable one that keeps your fingers on the pulse of shipping and your hand in the politics of our colony."

Just then, Thomas ran by. "Top o' the marnin', guv'na," he said hurriedly, then continued yelling the day's fare at the White Horse Tavern as he went.

"The Assembly is your avenue, as we have often discussed. You are well known and experienced now, a valuable combination to serve your citizens once again."

"I suppose... yet each year drags on, and I see little progress. Oh! By-the-way. The *St. John*. What is to become of that incident regarding the *Gaspee*?"

"An excellent case in point, William. Your brother's records of the *St. John* affair as Deputy Governor were of such clarity that they were included as addenda without further discussion. A most valuable contribution, I might add."

William thought a moment. "I see... Of such clarity to have no effect on the outcome?"

"Your observations are, once again, accurate."

"Well... congratulations on completing your Kingly duties to our advantage, Father. I must be off, a letter to post from Mother to Aunt Ruth wishing her a speedy recovery."

Walking further, the Governor turned up Marlborough Street to look over construction of the new jail, finding progress toward completing the robust structure to be to his expectations. Passing the White Horse Tavern and on to the Colony House, he hesitated before taking the steps up into the brick structure, standing for a moment looking westward down the Square, across its long expanse to Queen's Hive and Long Wharf out into the Bay with its abundance of white sails billowed in the sunlight.

Since the building's construction some decades past, he had remained impressed with the Colony House, as fine a public building as existed anywhere in the colonies, and his office for the past five years. Preoccupied with images of flames engulfing the *Gaspee*, his mind leaped to the crowd that gathered on the Square in late summer eight years past for announcing the latest Maritime Law from the second floor balcony above the steps, then turned riotous when the Stamp Act was read. Effigies of the Tory leaders, the hated Newport Junta, were burned there by fellow citizens on a rampage. He recalled once again the flames that engulfed the figure of tax collector Martin Howard, Jr. held above the crowd, hanging from a flimsy cross of wood with a rope around its neck.

Memories raced through his mind as he recalled the high emotions that rose in him as he read Howard's "A Letter from a Gentleman in Halifax to his Friend in Rhode Island," an insulting rebuke of his long time friend and supporter, Justice Stephen Hopkins who wrote "The Rights of Colonies, Examined" that was regarded widely as most sensible. Howard's condemnation of citizens for not adhering to Royal and Parliamentary authority had no parallel of contempt in Newport, contempt that was furthered with the O.Z. Letters of Dr. Robert Moffatt published in the *Newport Mercury* during that time. The crowd had not forgotten and held an effigy of Moffatt to the flames of Howard and hailed its consumption, roundly condemned to Hell as well. The crowd then repeated its angry cheers when the figure of Stamp Master Augustus Johnston similarly went up in flames. The crowd then lurching from the Square toward the substantial Howard house at 17 Broad Street, angry, gathering contempt with each step.

The Governor's recall from those events eight years past burned so clearly in his memories brought a foreboding of events to come. Turning in his mind's eye to follow the crowd, its rage unleashed, he shuddered at the visions of the house pelted with stones that smashed through windows and doors, the mob then bolting into the house destroying its interior and furnishings. Angry that they did not find Howard, who had sneaked out the back and ran to the Bay taking refuge on one of the King's ships, never to return to Newport, the mob rolled on to Moffatt's house to deliver the same fate. In similar footsteps as Howard's, the hated doctor made his exit to the *HMS Cygnet*, also never to return.

On this quiet summer morning of gentle breezes, the Governor stood across the expanse of Broad Street looking at the Howard house as peaceful and inviting as any in Newport. Purchased at auction a month after the attack by his Uncle John, it had been repaired and showed no signs of how closely it came to being consumed in the flames of rebellion.

"A fine morning to you, Governor," a familiar voice broke into his recollections.

Governor Wanton had been so lost in his thoughts that he did not hear Polly's approach. He turned to her pleasant smile and consuming beauty, "Indeed, Polly. A fine day indeed. So nice to see you."

"Shall you partake of tea with us, sir? Mother would be most delighted to serve her scones. They are quite tasty, you know."

The Governor could not resist returning Polly's smile and bent to her hand with a kiss. "Unfortunately, my dear, I must decline for duty calls. However, I would be most delighted to see you across the street to your doorstep."

"Your invitation is most welcome, sir."

The Governor held her hand as they walked across the street, then up the steps to her door. Polly's delightful smile and sparkling eyes were his reward. "Most gallant of you, sir. Mother will be heartbroken to hear of your decline. You must include our fair street in you constitutional more often, sir."

"So I shall, my dear. Please give warmest regards to your mother, and do not fail to offer the same for your grumpy father. Oh! And please convey to John, for me, if you please, that Mary and I would be most delighted to have the presence of his family for dinner soon."

"My, you are such a gentleman, Governor. I shall speak with Mother and Father on the matter. I can be most convincing, I assure you, sir."

Governor Wanton bowed his approval and bade Polly a good day, then stepped lightly back to the Colony House.

Epilogue

Real People of the time:

Lieutenant William Dudingston was called before a court martial and absolved of all responsibility associated with the *Gaspee* incident. He later rose in rank to Rear Admiral in the Royal Navy.

Admiral Montagu was the senior military officer of British forces in America. He established his base of operations in Boston and enjoyed the social benefits of his rank. The raid on the *Gaspee* was seen as an attack upon a ship and crew under his command, thus an affront to his authority. His support of Dudingston's actions and his disregard for the established maritime laws of both Rhode Island and the Crown contributed to the indignation of the colonists who sought resolution of legal affairs in their own courts where exercising such proceedings had been long practiced in Rhode Island. He was replaced by Admiral Graves by the time of the American Revolution.

Abraham Whipple, whose French War maritime expertise was proven as a privateer, led to his selection as leader of the *Gaspee* raid. Afterward, he rose to become the most celebrated American sea captain of the Revolutionary War. In a three week span during 1779, Whipple and his ship *Providence* in a force with two other privateers captured eight British merchantman. As a bold privateer commander, he proved highly capable of supplying American forces from goods captured in the sea lanes.

John Brown was prominent among merchants in Providence Plantations and Rhode Island, his family being one of the original settlers of Rhode Island. He was instrumental in furthering Rhode Island College, laying the cornerstone of University Hall, the first building of what became Brown University in his honor. A week after the battles of Lexington Green and Concord Bridge in Massachusetts, April 18, 1775, two American flour ships owned by John Brown were seized by the British man-of-war *HMS Rose*. Brown was aboard one and was taken prisoner by Capt. James Wallace, then sent to Gen. Thomas Gage on suspicion of involvement in the *Gaspee* affair and subsequent evasion of British authority. Brown's brother, Moses, having been kept completely unaware of *Gaspee* involvement, was so convinced of his brother's innocense that he rode horseback to Boston, got through the British lines, conferred with Chief Justice Oliver (one of the King's Commissioners who investigated the *Gaspee* incident) and Admiral Graves (the new ranking commander of British forces in America replacing Admiral Montagu) so convincingly that John was released. They returned to Providence on the same horse to a hero's welcome.

Nathaniel Greene, of the prominent Greene family of merchants in and around Providence, rose to become a commander of America forces in the Revolutionary Army. He was Gen. Washington's most favored General in the field and is credited with routing British forces in the southern colonies, thus preventing the British from splitting the colonies for further subjugation. Lt. Dudingston, commander of the *Gaspee*, seized a Greene family ship and its cargo in March, 1772 and illegally disposed of both, an action that further heightened legal and political anger focusing on Dudingston's conduct that grew into open conflict between British officials and Rhode Island colonists.

Stephen Hopkins of Providence rose to become Governor of Rhode Island over a total of nine years and was Chief Justice of the colony during the time of the *Gaspee* incident. He was an ardent patriot, always dressed in American made attire, and wore his own hair rather than powdered wigs common among gentry at the time. He wrote the pamphlet entitled, "The Rights of Colonies, Examined" supporting the legal basis of independent government that brought the rebuttal from Thomas Howard, Jr, ardent Royalist, who wrote, "A Letter from a Gentleman in Halifax to his Friend in Rhode Island" that fueled riots ignited by the Stamp Act of 1765, resulting in Howard being run out of Newport. Hopkins remained committed to citizen rights throughout his life, and a decade after the *Gaspee* incident, as a representative of the colony of Rhode Island at the Continental Congress, he signed the Declaration of Independence.

Joseph Wanton was first elected Governor of Rhode Island in 1769 at age 64 and was re-elected annually until deposed in 1775 for failure to sign commissions for officers of an "Army of Observation" that the Rhode Island Assembly authorized to support colonial neighbors embroiled in hostilities with the British, doing so being an act of treason as seen by the Crown. Wanton's family, wealthy Quaker merchants and third generation Newporters, had long been deeply involved in Rhode Island politics; both his father and uncle were Governors before him, and his son, Joseph Wanton, Jr., an ardent loyalist, was Deputy Governor also before him. Wanton's election to the high office was due to a coalition between Newporters and those of Providence, the two highest population centers, led by Stephen Hopkins who had been Governor when Joseph, Jr. was his Deputy. With the factional split between Tory and Patriot that grew strongly following the *Gaspee* incident, then the outbreak of the Revolution in 1775, positions were demanded resulting in taking of sides. Although deposed as Governor and considered a Tory by many, Gov. Wanton's position is perhaps best demonstrated in how he handled the *Gaspee* affair as the lead Commissioner in pursuit of the King's Proclamation issued to apprehend his fellow citizens and send them to England to hang. The *Gaspee* incident was another in a succession of serious confrontations between colonists and the Crown, this one focusing the philosophical basis of governmental jurisdiction by pitting the King's authority as superior to colonial authority as had long been administered. Whether Tory or Patriot or careful politician who steered the narrow balance between the two positions has long been debated. However, many years later in the settlement of his estate after his death, a rebel oath was found, signed by Joseph Wanton in 1775, to preserve his liberty and property while he lived among British forces that had occupied Newport and ruled by martial law at the outbreak of the Revolution. During British occupation, Newport was partially destroyed, many of its wooden homes pulled down for firewood, and the town never recovered its former commercial status. Wanton properties survived the occupation.

Dr. John Mawney was a man of means, and although a trained physician, his inheritance assured a life of leisure within which he excelled in both the classics and as a libertine. Little is known of him until older when he and other *Gaspee* raiders were increasingly honored during July 4th celebrations and similar days of remembrance in the Providence, Warwick and Cranston areas. His account of participating in the raid when about 22 years old has long been a cornerstone document of the incident.

Joseph Bucklin, like Dr. Mawney, was celebrated for his heroic *Gaspee* raid actions throughout his later life well into the 1800s.

His account of the raid has also been a long-standing tribute to the young man, probably no more than 17 or 18 at the time, who fired the first shot of the American Revolution, a shot within a broader attack upon a British Naval vessel, the *HMS Gaspee*, that stirred the King of England and his magistrates to levy an overwhelming Proclamation on Rhode Island condemning all raiders for their acts of high treason. Later, Bucklin owned and operated a prominent Providence tavern and lived a long life.

Ephraim Bowen, teenage friend of Bucklin, supplied the musket, his father's, that Bucklin used to wound Lt. Dudingston. Bowen was the last survivor of the *Gaspee* raid, and during the final year of his life, at age 86 in 1839, he penned his recollections in detail, a document that has remained a central accounting of the event.

Ezek Hopkins of Providence, brother of Stephen Hopkins, rose to become the first Commander-in-Chief of the Continental Navy when officially formed on December 22, 1775. He was commissioned at the rank of Commodore and successfully commanded the U.S. Navy's first action, a raid that captured British munitions stored in Nassau, Bahamas in early March, 1776. His return to Rhode Island brought much needed gun powder to the Continental Army.

Aaron Briggs, the Crown's chief witness, disappeared from the historical record after close of investigations by the King's Commission.

As of 1826, the jubilee year of the founding of the United States, the four surviving members of the raid on the *Gaspee* were, as listed in Bartlett's 1861 book, Col. Ephraim Bowen, Capt. Benjamin Page, Col. John Mawney and Capt. Turpin Smith.

The names of other characters in this book, Americans Capt. Lindsey, Capt. Maudsley, Capt. Malbone, the Nichols family, the Mayes family, the Wanton family, Capt. Potter, Capt. Swan, Capt. Tillinghast, Capt. Vaughan, Dr. Sterling, Saul Ramsdale, Peter Crooch and others; Britishers King George, the Earl of Hillsborough, Lord Dartmouth, Lt. Dudingston, Lt. Ried, Lt. Hill, Lt. Linzee, Lt. Dundas, sailors Caple, Cheever, Earle, Johnson, Dickinson and others; along with the King's Commissioners, Daniel Horsmanden, Robert Auchmuty, Frederick Smythe, and Peter Oliver are drawn from the historical record.

The *Gaspee* incident of June 9-10, 1772 gathered wide attention throughout New England and beyond. The King's Proclamation giving its commissioners unprecedented powers so alarmed Samuel Adams and Joseph Warren of Boston, and the colony's Assembly, that the first official colonial "Committee of Correspondence" was formed on November 2nd of that year. The purpose of the Committee was to establish formal communications between colonial assemblies. Resolution of the King's Proclamation the following year, without convictions, became an inspiration throughout the colonies as proof that colonists could successfully challenge the authority of the King. The primary result of this incident was the bonding of previously independent colonial governments into a national identity based on similar concerns that established a "Committee of Correspondence" in each of the colonies, as directed by their assemblies. These committees expedited the flow of accurate and timely information concerning events of mutual interest; the first binding of the colonies with a "common cause."

About the Author

Alex Gabbard is a widely published author of fiction and non-fiction whose work has received international acclaim resulting in two books receiving Book of the Year awards in their field. His photography has received a similar award and has illustrated hundreds of magazine and newspaper features over the past quarter-century. Among many published features on topics of US and European travel, some available on the Internet, the author received the year 2000 IAMA Silver Metal Award for travel writing. Following that award, the International Society of Poets bestowed upon him the Poet of Merit Award for the year 2002. Among more than fifteen books, a previous work of historical fiction based on a true and tragic story, Blood of the Roses, was a Freedom Book of the Month selection. Return to Thunder Road and Checkmate are also currently available where books are sold, from Amazon.com, alexgabbard.com, and GPPress@att.net. Order author signed books from:

GPPress
P.O. Box 22261
Knoxville, TN 37933-0261

Order any quantitly and selection of books for only $4.00 S&H within USA. Allow minimum of three weeks for delivery after receipt of order with payment enclosed. Thanks

Other author signed books available from GPPress:

    Vintage & Historic Racing Cars
    Fast Chevys
    Ford Total Performance
    INDY's Wildest Decade
    NASCAR's Wild Years

    and the following:

Alex Gabbard

Non-fiction

ISBN: 0-9622608-3-5
240 pages with index
Trade Paperback
57 illustrations
$11.95

Read the real-life story of moonshining as a way of life in the southern Appalachians. This is the story of backwoods survival the way it had been taught for generations, handed down from father to son. Ride with the moonshiners as they tell their stories from corn mash to car loads of "mountain dew." Listen to the U.S. Treasury Agents who were sent to stop them. This is the way it was, told in these pages by the men who live it! A powerful saga of an age gone by when making whiskey grew from "nuthin' to do but hoe corn and make moonshine" to a massive effort to shut down the multi-million dollar trade with a manhunt that put most moonshiners out of business, and many behind bars.

"Your knowledge of American and Automobile History is incomplete until you've read Return to Thunder Road." - *Southern Wheels Magazine*

"A darn good book." 5-stars - Amazon.com

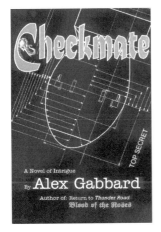

Fiction

ISBN: 0-9622608-9-4
294 pages
Trade Paperback
$15.95

Award winning author, Alex Gabbarad, thrusts you into lives of government secrecy, with assassins lurking about, a day-dreaming scientist, a frightened bomb builder, wantabe rock stars, an enterprising computer jock, a bungling secret agent, a failed concert pianist, Beethoven, da Vinci, and "The Babe," all wrapped in the sinister cloak of intrigue.

"Checkmate is tremendously imaginative, and it features some wonderfully off-beat characters and colorful dialogue... an awfully fun read."
  - *Red Wagon Entertainment*

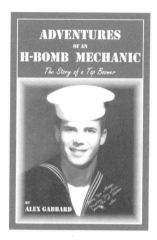

Adventures of an H-bomb Mechanic is the real-life story of a country boy whose transition from college into military life brought increasing involvement with advanced weaponry of the Cold War. This odyssey into the shadows of secrecy begins with the assassination of a President, then tells of becoming a Viet Nam era draftee who wore the uniform of a sailor rather than a soldier, then unfolds along paths that wind their way into cryptic, clandestine service as a Top Secret operative for a little known agency of the US Government. This account is from the hidden, obscure world of nuclear warheads and secret facilities, recollections of Cold War adventures that led from San Diego to Chicago to Albuquerque to Clarksville to Norfolk, then a Med cruise and many ports of call onboard the USS Forrestal, the story of a Top Boomer.

Non-fiction

ISBN: 0-9755358-1-1
Hardcover with jacket
260 pages
72 illustrations
$23.95

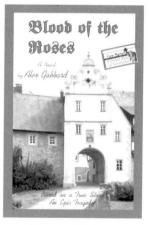

Freedom Book of the Month selection

"*Blood of the Roses* deserves to be widely read solely on the basis of its wonderful presentation of an inspiring story of freedom... The story of the White Rose and its principals, Hans and Sophie Scholl... Gabbard weaves a slow, inexorable magic... skill, that he can portray 'foredoomed' characters so convincingly...."
  - The Freedom Network

"Very highly recommended reading from cover to cover."   - The Mid-West Book Review

"...gave me nightmares..."   - Reviewer

Historical fiction

ISBN: 0-9622608-7-8
Casebound
  with dust jacket
248 pages, 3 illustrations
$22.95

Signed and numbered 1st editions, 1st printing available while they last.